PENGUIN BOOKS

UNTIL MORNING

Joyce Chua is the author of the young adult contemporary romance, *Lambs for Dinner* (Straits Times Press, 2013) and *Land of Sand and Song* (Penguin Random House SEA, 2021), the first of an Asian fantasy trilogy. She graduated from the National University of Singapore with a degree in English, and is now a finance editor by day and author by night. When not writing, she can be found on Instagram and TikTok at @joycechuawrites sharing her random poetry or fangirling over Asian dramas.

ADVANCE PRAISE FOR *UNTIL MORNING*

'Simply bewitching. I don't know what else I can say about Joyce's writing prowess except that I simply adore how magical it is. With *Until Morning*, Joyce transports you into a spellbinding world once again, and brings you on an enrapturing emotional journey with our leads that will capture your heart and soul.'

—Leslie W., author of *The Night of Legends*

'A mesmerising world that pulls you in at the first instance. Joyce Chua's writing left me teetering between the here and now and the dream world inhabited by Chris and Lexi. I couldn't stop reading. I couldn't stop dreaming.'

—Eva Wong Nava, author of *The House of Little Sisters*

'Joyce Chua knows magic realism like the back of her hand—she wields it with such purpose and flair, so much so that once you're in her world, you'll never want to leave.'

—Catherine Dellosa, author of the *Of Myths and Men* trilogy

'Gorgeously written and devastatingly romantic, Joyce Chua's prose is as vivid as a painting and magical as a dream. I devoured this novel in a single sitting.'

—Ann Liang, author of *If You Could See the Sun*

Until Morning

Joyce Chua

PENGUIN BOOKS
An imprint of Penguin Random House

PENGUIN BOOKS

USA | Canada | UK | Ireland | Australia
New Zealand | India | South Africa | China | Southeast Asia

Penguin Books is part of the Penguin Random House group of companies
whose addresses can be found at global.penguinrandomhouse.com

Published by Penguin Random House SEA Pte. Ltd
9, Changi South Street 3, Level 08-01,
Singapore 486361

Penguin Random House SEA

First published in Penguin Books by Penguin Random House SEA 2023

10 9 8 7 6 5 4 3 2 1

ISBN 9789815127775

Typeset in Garamond by MAP Systems, Bengaluru, India

www.penguin.sg

To the ones seeking the light in dark places

Dear Night,

I feel like the older we get, the more complicated our wishes become. We don't only want more, but we also want more impossible things. Or, maybe, we just begin to realize how hard it is to have even the simplest things.

When I was seven, I wished I could wear a different skin every day. Perhaps gold foil today, perhaps silk tomorrow. At the end of the day, I'd strip off the worn skin and become a brand-new person again the next day.

When I was eight, I wished I could be invisible.

When I was ten, I wished I could live in books—specifically, Alice in Wonderland, *where everything and nothing made sense, and every turn took you further away from where you started.*

When I was fifteen, I wished I could control people's moods. Keep them—and myself—wrapped in a cloud of bliss all day, protected from tears and fears and guilt.

When I was sixteen, I wished I could fly. Just drift off into the sky and watch the world go by at my feet.

Lately, I've been wishing to be that girl in your painting, the one sailing through the sky with her eyes closed and stars shimmering in her pockets. Sailing towards you.

Funny how my wishes seem so similar when I look at them now. They all point towards one thing: escape.

Wishfully yours,
Lexi

Chapter 1

Lexi

Ever since I found one of Night's paintings tucked away in an alley down the street where I lived, my dreams had felt like fairy tales. I dreamt of soft rain on empty gleaming streets, of vast starlit nights, and colours that swept me away on roaring waves.

Night's paintings didn't just tell stories; they *were* stories. And sometimes—like right now—I couldn't tell if I was living in them. They were truth and fiction, dream and reality, all at once.

Was I dreaming now? The line was blurry these days.

Overhead, the edges of the night sky were fuzzy, but something in the air shimmered and shone like powdered stars, something that made this dream both wild and comforting.

And then I spotted the birds. They were the biggest clue to where I was now.

In Night's painting, the birds were a riot of feathers and colours taking flight against the indigo sky—save for one on the ground. Unlike the others, it was pure white, stark against the dark street. The other birds circled gracefully above, their plumage almost iridescent against the sky.

I inched towards the white one, holding out my hand. Footsteps rang out in the silence, hurried and purposeful. Someone came to a stop before me. The white bird took off, startled, and joined its companions. They soared higher and higher and finally disappeared into the night, their colours swallowed by the dark.

'Are we the only ones here?'

The newcomer was a boy slightly older than me. I had never seen him in my life. Did we usually dream about people of whom we had no impression?

Dressed in a crisp white shirt—unbuttoned, with sleeves rolled up to the elbows—and dark-wash jeans, he looked too clean-pressed for this ramshackle part of this quiet town. He had what Eliza would call an 'extremely agreeable' face—chiselled but boyish, and his gaze intense but curious. Add full, curved lips to that and here was a boy Eliza would have gone wild with back in her day.

Wait, why was I looking at his lips?

'Do you know where we are?' He had been watching me with a curious look in his eyes, but now he glanced around, squinting into the distance at a signpost with no words, the dim silhouette of buildings behind us.

'I think so,' I said before I could stop myself.

His gaze slid back to me. 'You do?'

If I told him we were in Night's painting, he would think I was delusional. Then again, if this *were* a dream, it wouldn't matter what he thought of me.

'We're in Night's painting.' I tried to contain my excitement, but my voice shook with glee anyway. In a way, I was walking around in Night's mind. It was a familiar landscape, even though I had never met him in my life. I had stared long and hard enough at each painting of his I'd found, traced their edges, and memorized every detail.

'Night,' the boy repeated, raising a doubtful brow. 'You know him?'

'I've seen his paintings. He leaves them all over the city in the middle of the night. I've been meaning to catch him in action, but he's like a phantom. A wildly talented phantom.'

A corner of his lips rose, as though he was secretly laughing at me. 'What makes you think he's not some unemployed bum seeking attention?'

'Because,' I snapped, 'if he wanted attention, he wouldn't be so elusive.' I stared in the direction the birds had gone. 'I feel like I understand him through his art.'

He folded his arms and appraised me silently. I got the sense that he was still smirking at me underneath that poker face.

I narrowed my eyes at him. 'Who did you say you were again?'

'Chris.' He glanced around. 'Seriously, do you know where we are? I think I'm lost, and you're the only person I've met here so far. I just … appeared here all of a sudden.'

So had I. There was only one explanation that made sense. This lonely landscape belonged to Night's painting, and I belonged here now.

'I told you where we are,' I replied. 'Did you see those birds? Night painted them. I'm dreaming, and you're in my dream.'

He shook his head, letting out a sigh like I was a child he had no patience for. 'I need to get back. I have work to do.'

I shrugged. 'It's nice here. So quiet. So peaceful.'

'Okay, then.' He turned to leave.

I watched him go. His back seemed lonely—almost defeated—despite how tall he walked.

'Chris!' I called. My voice echoed across the space between us. He paused for a split second, as though debating whether to turn around. He did. 'Pretty rude of you to not even ask for my name.'

'What's your name?'

I smiled and caught up with him. 'Lexi.'

His lips rose a fraction. This time, it wasn't the mocking one he gave me before, but one that made his eyes shine a little brighter under the streetlight. Then his brows went back to furrow mode as he scanned our surroundings.

'How is it possible that there's no one around at all? What time is it?' He flicked his wrist and checked his watch, not waiting for my answer. He tapped his watch a couple of times, his frown deepening.

I snuck a peek at his watch. Time had apparently stopped at quarter past ten. 'Time wouldn't matter in a dream, would it?'

He tapped his watch again but didn't reply.

I pushed his hand down. 'Who cares what time it is? It's Night-time. And it's quiet, for a change.' I took a deep breath, filling up on the heady scent of freedom.

'It's unnatural,' he muttered.

'Well, I've got something natural for you,' I said. 'I'm hungry. Let's eat.'

'The sooner we find our way back, the sooner you can eat.' He paused and gave me an inquiring look. 'You're not in a hurry to get home.'

I turned away from his scrutiny. 'It's a nice night for a walk.'

'For you, maybe,' he said. 'But I have a meeting to prepare for tomorrow.'

'Lighten up, Chris.' The look he shot me made it obvious that I wasn't the first person to say that to him. 'Wait. You're preparing for a meeting? For work? You don't look that old.'

'I work at my dad's company during the holidays. Kingdom Heights—heard of it?'

'*Have* I?' I raised my brows. 'Big shoes to fill, then.'

Kingdom Heights was the largest property development company in Southeast Asia, responsible for most of the top holiday resorts, amusement parks, and waterfront developments in the region. Its latest project, according to Eliza, was the multiplex it intended to build right where our inn was. *Prime piece of land* were the words she had used, which made me think of a slab of beef sizzling on a pan. We were about to be devoured.

Chris shrugged and scanned our surroundings for an escape route.

I tugged on his arm. 'Come on, let's go grab a bite.'

He stared down at my hand on his arm. 'How about let's go home?'

'There's no public transport at this hour,' I pointed out, even though I had no idea what hour this was exactly. But the sky was black as ink—the night was so thick and deep we could almost swim in it.

'There's something called a taxi, though,' Chris said.

'Why the hurry? The meeting will take care of itself. Besides, are you really going to let such a lovely night go to waste?'

He stared up at the sky, thinking.

'Come on,' I wheedled. 'We could take a relaxing stroll, grab a bite, and then go our separate ways.'

He leaned down to peer at my face. 'Let me see—quiet, peaceful … I'm guessing all's not pretty at home?'

'Wow, Sherlock. Look at you, reading too much into things.' I turned to walk away.

'I'm right, aren't I?' He called after me. 'You're running away?'

'Prying, Chris,' I called over my shoulder. Most people would follow up with an apology—or more questions, depending on how well you understood boundaries—but when I turned back, Chris was still standing there, watching me leave.

'This,' I said, coming to a stop, 'is the part where you run up to me and apologize for asking too many intrusive questions. And offer to buy me supper as atonement,' I added as an afterthought.

He rolled his eyes but caught up with me anyway. 'I'll offer to pay for a cab and nothing else.'

'*If* you can find one around here. You should eat something. Maybe having some food in your system will make you less cranky.'

'I'm not—' he said, '—cranky.'

It was fun riling him up. It beat sitting on a deserted curb staring at a bird.

'I'm not sure why you're running away, and I don't need to know,' Chris said. 'But it's dangerous for you to be wandering around the streets at night.'

I sent him a crooked smile. 'You don't have to worry about me, Chris. This isn't my first time wandering around the streets at night. Besides, there's no one else around.'

He protested some more, but shrugged. 'Don't say I didn't warn you.' A pause. 'Whatever it is, things will look better in the morning.'

I wrinkled my nose. 'Platitudes, Chris? Very original.'

Chris shrugged again. 'It's the best I've got.'

'Then your best isn't good enough.' I meant it in jest, but something flashed in his eyes, like a subtle flinch.

'You sound like my dad,' he said.

I peered up at his face. 'I take it that's a bad thing?'

He shook his head, taking a step back. 'No. Not bad. I never said it's bad.'

'Your tone implies it is.'

'What are you now, the tone police? My dad is fine. *We* are fine.' But it seemed like he was trying to convince himself more than he was convincing me.

'Except that you're up in the middle of the night preparing for a meeting for him.'

He threw me a glare before walking away. 'Come on, let's find a cab and get out of here.'

I fell into step with him. As we rounded the corner, the scene shifted—in quite literally the blink of an eye. Gone was the lonely stretch of road and the faceless buildings in the distance dimly lit by lamp posts. Now, it was cobblestone pavements and pots of hydrangeas along the sidewalk and the darkened faces of shop-houses.

I came to a stop. 'Oh!'

Chris flinched a little. My voice sounded extra loud in the stillness.

'I know where we are!' I broke into a run, my feet taking off in the direction they knew best. I wasn't chasing just a dream, but a memory. Suddenly, I was eight again, on a trip to the old bakery.

'Where are you going?' Chris's footsteps pounded behind me.

I came to a stop in front of a bakery. *The* bakery. It looked like any other bakery, with a simple shop front and a chalkboard out on the pavement that listed out the day's specials, but the sight of it calmed something inside me. It was the only well-lit shop on the deserted street, even though there was no sign of anyone inside.

Chris came to a stop next to me. 'Are you *that* hungry?'

'This is my old neighbourhood. My parents moved here when I was eight. After the … never mind.'

He raised his brows but didn't push the topic.

'My mum would bring me to this bakery on Sunday mornings,' I said, 'since we were the early risers in the family. We came here so often that the lady who owns the shop would prepare the biggest, freshest baguette for us. Auntie Fong, her name was. But she died a couple of years back, I heard, and one of her sons took over.'

I could smell the bread now, inhale its comforting scent. Mum and I would split the baguette between ourselves as we strolled through town all morning.

A sigh from Chris pulled me out of my memory. 'Fine,' he said. 'We'll get something to eat. Then we'll find our way home.'

I shot him a grin as he held the door open for me. He stared at me the same way he had when we first met, as though he had seen me somewhere else before.

I ignored his strange look and stepped into the shop, taking in the racks of assorted artisan bread against the walls, the local corner with the *pandan* cakes, *kueh lapis*, and my favourite peanut cookies—and finally, the cake display. Perched on a table smack in the middle of the shop was a confectionary masterpiece of a fairy-tale garden, complete with a miniature fountain in the heart of a flowering hedge maze dotted with red and pink icing. There would be a different one on display every week; sometimes, Auntie Fong would ask me for suggestions, and she'd bring those ideas to life the following week.

'Anybody here?' Chris called, breaking my attention from the cake display.

I rolled my eyes. 'Are you expecting a reply from the bread? There's obviously no one here.'

'Doesn't it bother you that no one is around but the shop is open?'

'Not really.' I nodded at the tray stand. 'Grab me a tray, will you? We'll get a bit of everything. Best thing about no one being around? We don't have to pay.' I grinned.

His eyes widened. 'We can't do that.'

I laughed at his horrified expression, then reached past him for the plastic tongs and tray myself. 'Why not?'

'Because that's stealing. I'm not going to pull some Oliver Twist stunt with you. I've wasted enough time here; I'm going home.'

I shot him my best dry look, one I learnt from Eliza. 'Chris. Do you need help removing that stick from your butt? Because I can do that once I'm fed.'

'Think about it,' he said as I placed a blueberry scone on my tray. 'You're stealing from Auntie Fong's store. The one who made you baguettes on Sundays.'

'I love how you make everything sound so dramatic. It's only considered stealing if it belongs to someone. Do you see anyone around?'

'So you think the shop just opened itself and offered you free bread?'

He was starting to drive me up the wall. What good was being in a dream if I had to spend it with a boy—albeit a cute one—who was such a buzzkill?

'You can pay for it if you want to, okay? Now shut up. I need to think—baguette or focaccia?'

Chris glanced down at my tray, then up at me. 'You're going to polish off all that on your own?'

'The night is long. Plus, you're eating with me.'

He shook his head, giving up. 'Baguette,' he said. In his crisp white shirt and with his exquisite features, he looked decidedly out of place in the humble little bakery. Unlike the unassuming bakery, content in its humbleness, Chris seemed like he was spilling over with misplaced purpose.

I got both the baguette and focaccia, then headed to the counter for paper bags.

Chris reached into his pockets but came up with nothing. 'Where's my wallet?'

'Hey, don't look at me. I didn't take anything of yours.'

His gaze narrowed. 'I never go out without my wallet.'

'There's a first for everything. Looks like we'll have to be felons tonight.' I grinned.

'You are way too excited about this.'

'How often do we get away with stealing bread?' I reached over the counter and nudged his shoulder. 'Come on. Live a little. It's just bread.'

His brows furrowed. At last, he said, 'Just so we're clear, this was your idea.'

'Whatever.'

A grudging smile flickered past his face.

I dove under the counter for the paper bags. When I resurfaced, Chris was nowhere to be seen.

'Chris?' I called.

The shop was empty. I sank into the stool, clutching my useless stack of paper bags, sitting before a tray of bread and pastries meant for two. The fairy tale cake that seemed so magical a moment ago now looked sad, all dolled up with no one to appreciate it.

Sometimes, I didn't know if I was happier with or without company.

Chapter 2

Chris

'Chris. *Chris.* Wake up.' Hayley's voice rang in my ear, coupled with vigorous shaking. Finally, she punched me on the shoulder.

I jolted awake. Paper rustled under my arms. My sketches lay in a scattered pile before me, and my pencil had rolled off the table.

It took me a while to recall where I was. Not in the middle of a bakery or an empty street. Not with a strange, irreverent girl who loved bread. The setting was familiar this time—my desk at the back of Bobby's art studio, with its perennial smell of turpentine and canvas. It wasn't a big space. In fact, it needed some refurbishing, but Bobby was always too busy to give his home art studio a major overhaul.

So it had only been a dream, though it was unlike any I'd ever had. It clung to my skin like sea salt after a dip in the ocean. The lingering scent of bread, the soft glow of streetlights, Lexi's voice, and the spark in her eyes.

I glanced out the window. It was night, still, although my company wasn't Lexi, but my best friend Hayley—who was also Bobby's daughter—in her pyjamas.

'Hayley,' I mumbled, rubbing my eyes. 'What time is it?'

'Past your bedtime.' She plopped into a chair next to me and handed me a cup of tea. 'You look like crap.'

'And you're a real self-esteem booster. Why aren't you in bed?'

'Thought I'd check in on you, see if you've left.' She shook her head. 'What was that about?'

'What?'

'You were dead to the world.'

'That's usually the case when you're in deep sleep, Hayl.'

'Not like that,' she insisted. 'I practically had to manhandle you and pry your eyelids open.'

The thought of the pint-sized Hayley manhandling me made me chortle.

'Do you think it might be sleep apnoea?' Hayley asked, gripping my shoulder. 'Because I swear you stopped breathing for a moment there.'

'I'm sure punching me helps.'

'I'm serious, Chris. You should see a doctor, get that checked out.'

I made a noncommittal sound and started gathering my things.

'Aren't you going to roam tonight?' Hayley asked.

By roam, she meant find a good place around the city to hide my latest piece. I had done enough roaming for tonight, I wanted to say. But of course, that wouldn't make any sense to her. To her, I had come here straight after tying up every loose end at work and then fallen asleep at the desk—not wander along a deserted street and steal bread with a girl I didn't even know.

'It's not ready yet,' I said instead.

'Can I see it?'

'It's not ready yet,' I repeated.

'Just the sketch, then.' She reached past me for my sketchpad before I could snatch it away.

My latest sketch was the fourth in a series I started working on about a month ago. There wasn't any specific theme to it, just random images that came to mind. A girl kneeling on the ground watching a white bird; a man with birds tied to his wrists by strings, preparing to take flight; a hand on a doorknob, the door leading to a shop filled with golden light.

I thought about Lexi and her hand on the doorknob, about to enter the bakery. Lexi with her arms wrapped around her knees as she observed the white bird, a vibrant flock circling in the night sky above her.

It *had* to be a dream. I was dreaming of my paintings. Lexi was probably just someone I had seen before but didn't remember—a girl stored in my preconscious.

Yes, that had to be it.

'I wish I could draw like you,' Hayley said, observing my sketch. It was a common refrain of hers. She waved the sketchpad in my face. 'I would hate you if I didn't have a crush on you.' This was another common refrain of hers, even though she knew I saw her as nothing more than a younger sister.

I shook my head, plucking my sketchpad from her hand. This latest one was of a handprint on a grimy opaque window. 'It just takes practice.'

I hadn't thought of where I was going to place it yet. But the city had no shortage of places to hide a painting.

It started two years ago, just before my eighteenth birthday, when Mum had her first bipolar episode. I didn't have any formal training in painting, and mostly just doodled until Bobby found me sketching at the public football stadium one day and decided to let me use his art studio. He said that I seemed to lack fire, that I needed a way to speak. So he took me to his studio, handed me a brush and a box of colours, and told me to paint the first thing that came to mind, to hell with form and angles and texture.

The first time I picked up that paintbrush—felt its weight in my hand and closed my fingers around it—I was swept away by the hypnotizing lull of brush strokes on canvas. A sense of rightness settled into me the way it never had when I was looking over floor plans and marketing proposals with my dad. When I was painting, there was no need for words or reassuring smiles, no expectations to be met. All that mattered was spilling out the story on to paper.

Bobby had sat next to me, watching silently as I painted. It felt like time had been suspended, if only for a while. I forgot he was even there; it was just me and the picture in my mind.

The painting hadn't come out the way I expected it to, far from it. But I got closer and closer the more I painted.

Later, Bobby wanted to take me in as his student, but between school and work I just didn't have spare time for art classes. In return for letting me use his studio and supplies, I tutored Hayley on weekends, a deal Hayley was most enthusiastic about.

The only time I could paint was after hours when I was free of my textbooks and work emails. This deep in the night, I was alone with my brush and canvas and colours. Here, we spoke a language of our own. We *were* a world of our own.

But I couldn't hide in here for long, no matter how comfortable it was. I got up and started packing my things. 'Go back to bed, Hayley,' I said, glancing at my watch. Three-fifteen. There was still some time to prepare for the 9 a.m. meeting.

'Are you coming tomorrow?' Hayley asked.

'Tomorrow's Friday,' I reminded her. Friday evenings were reserved for one thing only.

'Oh, right. Say hi to your mum for me.' She would always say this, despite having never met my mum in all the time she'd known me. Still, I'd pass along her greeting every time.

After waving off a parting reminder from Hayley to see a doctor for my sleep condition, I left the studio and headed for my bicycle parked outside. I couldn't use Dad's car since he had sent it for repair after colliding into a lamp post on the way home. It was easier to roam around the city on a bicycle anyway—I could worm into tight corners to leave my paintings.

It was a night not unlike the one in my dream. The sky was clear, black as ink and speckled with stars, and the streets were pretty much empty, save for the occasional taxi. But there was a different kind of rhythm here. The silence felt fragile, unlike in my dream, where it sat around us like a thick, reassuring blanket.

I slung my messenger bag and took off, my mind already sketching out Lexi—from her dark, tousled hair to her wide, bright eyes. In my mind, she held a tray laden with scones and pastries and rolls. In my mind, I filled her with colours and light.

Then I remembered the way I had left her in the bakery—no warning, no apology. I had abandoned her in my dream, all because I had woken up prematurely.

No, I was being ridiculous. Lexi wasn't real, no matter how real she felt in the dream. She was just a girl from a *dream*. Why was I feeling guilty?

Sleep. That was what I needed. I was running low on sleep.

* * *

Dreams evaded me for the rest of the night as I slept, so I never got to find out if Lexi ended up going through with the bread-stealing on her own.

The next morning, Dad was neither in his room nor anywhere in the house when I looked for him. He had most likely spent the night at the office again. This latest project was one of Kingdom Heights' biggest endeavours—with its upscale shopping belt, art gallery, and amphitheatre—and we were only in the first phase of construction. Some existing shop-owners there weren't willing to relocate despite the generous deal Dad offered them, so he had assigned me the task of winning them over.

Hence today's meeting with the reluctant proprietors—or at least, those who were willing to give us the time of day. I could understand why they didn't want to sell, though. Long Street, with its labyrinth of shophouses refurbished into backpacker inns, cafés, and provision stores, had been around since the sixties. You couldn't just raze down that heritage or wipe its history clean with money, even if the new multiplex came with better amenities.

But in Dad's world, new was good. New meant a market to expand into. And nothing would stand in his way of transforming Long Street into the most comprehensive entertainment belt in the country. We had already secured the lease; all that was left to do was make the natives go willingly into the good night.

But the turnout today was dismal. Only five of the fifteen proprietors were present, and most of them didn't seem to be here to negotiate, but to fight for Long Street. This was my first time meeting most of them, and all I knew about them came from Dad.

At least there was Maude. The owner of the textile shop next to the Welcome Inn was one of the few shop-owners who weren't vehemently opposed to Kingdom's takeover of Long Street. She had let me hide a couple of my paintings in her shop before, instead of throwing them out when she discovered them.

Then, there was also Charlie, the owner of the Welcome Inn and by far the most vocal protestor against our refurbishment project. He wasn't the sole owner of the Welcome Inn, though—there was his wife too, but as far as I knew, she got sick and Charlie took over the business completely. Charlie had a flare in his eyes that reminded me of Lexi, as though he was ready to leap forward to defend everything he valued with his life.

He perched on the edge of his chair now, scowling and eyeing us like he was biding his time and working up a rant.

I wasn't late, but I was the last one who showed up, which made me seem late. Today's meeting was a private one that Dad wanted nobody but me to be involved in. There was a reason why the full-time employees hated me and called me 'nepotism baby' behind my back. They didn't know or care that the real reason I joined the company, even though I was barely out of school, wasn't to get an express ticket up the corporate ladder. Dad had grand plans to groom me into his successor, but I just wanted to offer some help so that he had one less person to stress over.

I muttered an apology now, avoiding Dad's baleful stare, and opened my laptop. My brain felt like it was running at half its usual speed, still saturated with dreams.

'I guess this is all we can expect today,' Dad said in the hearty voice he used exclusively with clients and stakeholders. 'Thank you all for being here today. Christopher, the updates please?'

I had, with the help of the operations and partnerships teams, incorporated the changes in floor plan and updated the list of franchises we planned to bring in for the shopping belt, as well as the alternative locations we had found for the establishments on Long Street. But my presentation flew right over Charlie, as well as Ben the dessert shop-owner and Mr Wang the antique store owner.

Charlie rose to his feet, cutting me off before I could get to the second half of my presentation. He was a tall man, especially when he held his back like that.

'Gerald Fang,' he said, glaring at Dad. 'I will not sell my inn for you to construct some over-commercialized, over-priced multiplex that will drive small local businesses to go bust. Haven't you destroyed enough neighbourhoods?'

Dad raised his brows. 'Destroyed? That's a bit harsh, Charlie. Some might say I've given those places a new life, replacing those outdated establishments with more lucrative ones. No business can stay the same forever.'

'Outdated?' Ben snarled. Despite looking sturdy for his age, he was the sort of businessman Dad would never take seriously, simply because he was dressed in a weathered T-shirt, slouchy jeans, and sneakers for a meeting.

'Gentlemen,' Dad said. 'Let's talk this over calmly, shall we? I assure you we have your interests at heart too.' Someone snorted. Dad gestured at Charlie's chair. 'Please, have a seat.'

Charlie and Mr Wang remained standing.

'I will not *talk this over calmly* when you just called Long Street outdated,' Charlie said.

'Hear me out, please,' Dad said, unruffled. 'We've found alternative arrangements for you. Long Street is but a street. You can take your business anywhere else.' Dad nodded at me. 'Go on, Christopher.'

Charlie cut me off before I could move on to my next presentation slide. 'No need. I'm saying this for the third and final time, Gerald. I'm not interested in selling, and I don't care if you come in with all your glitzy hotels and malls. I will not move out.' He tossed a look around the boardroom, his lip curled. 'I knew this meeting was a waste of time. To think I let my daughter convince me to come.'

He stormed out of the room with Ben and Mr Wang in his wake. Maude came around the table to apologize.

'Charlie's been on edge lately because of his younger daughter's accident,' she said. 'You gave a good presentation, Chris. Thanks for your time, both of you.'

After they left the building, I watched them from the floor-to-ceiling window of the boardroom. The men ranted, gesturing vehemently, before everyone packed into a dark blue van with Ben behind the wheel.

I waited until the van had passed the traffic light at the end of the road before turning back to Dad.

'They're gone,' I announced.

Dad shook his head, letting out a dry chuckle. 'A bunch of sentimental, myopic fools. This is the reason why their businesses are complete shambles. Charlie Lee's inn has more staff than backpackers, and that old man Wang's furniture is what will accompany him to his grave.'

'They might still come around,' I said quietly. When Dad got into such a mood, it was best to just let him vent.

'They will.' His voice stamped out any lingering trace of doubt. 'They always do. These people, all they really want is more money. We'll start low, then raise the bid incrementally until we reach a price we're all happy with.'

But I wasn't so sure Charlie would come around that way. He didn't seem like the sort who would wait for the price to be right before giving up his business.

'There has to be a reason why he's holding on to his inn so tightly,' I said. 'If we can find out what it is, we might be able to make a better offer.'

Dad nodded slowly, considering my suggestion. 'Christopher, I want you to find out the background of that inn—its history, occupants, everything you can learn. Get to know those people too, especially Charlie.'

I nodded.

'Is that demographic analysis ready?'

'Not yet. I—'

A sigh—one that was delivered so often I should be immune to it by now. It was the exasperated sigh Dad reserved for people who were more hindrance than help. You could hear all of my father's expectations crumbling in that one heavy breath. Never mind that he could easily get any of his staff to do this task; if he assigned it to me, it was solely my responsibility.

'I'm sorry,' I said. 'I'll get it done—'

'Send me the report by Monday,' he said, getting up from his chair.

'But today's Friday. We're visiting Mum.'

'I'm not going tonight,' he called over his shoulder.

'Again?'

Dad whipped around at my tone.

'I mean, this is the third week in a row you're not going.'

'I'm busy, Christopher,' he said, like I was the one being unreasonable. But this was not the first time I had heard this excuse.

'She misses you, you know.' I kept my gaze trained on the edge of the table.

'She understands I need to work. For this family.'

Was it really for this family, or for himself? Sometimes, I wanted to throw the question out in the open, just to see what happened.

But I had neither the guts nor the heart to question my father. Ever since Mum got sick, I had taken on the role of Dad's fallback person—someone who would never let him down. Before long, actions became habit, and the things we should have said to each other piled up like unwanted clothes in a dusty corner. Neither of us dared to look in that closet.

* * *

'Is it Friday already?'

She seemed to be in good spirits today. But with Mum, you just never knew.

'Like you haven't been waiting all week,' I replied, like I always did. The doctors said some regularity was good for her and familiar situations would comfort her. 'Hayley says hi.'

'When are you going to bring her to meet me already?'

'I told you,' I said. 'We're not like that. She's like a younger sister to me.'

She peered at me askance, a glint in her eyes. 'Better not let me find out you've been hiding behind this excuse all this while. If you have a secret girlfriend . . .' She wagged a finger in my face.

I set her hand back on her lap with a pat. 'I do not have a secret girlfriend, but I'll be sure to let you know if anything changes.'

'You do that.' She folded a page in the magazine she had been reading before I arrived and set it down. Her gaze roamed around the room. 'So . . . where's your father?' Her smile trembled, like she already knew the answer and was hoping I wouldn't give it to her.

I hated having to give it to her.

'Well, his work is important.' She forced the corners of her lips back up. 'Let's have dinner, shall we? I'm starving.'

She got out of the easy chair and left the reading room, abandoning her magazine. *Cosmopolitan.* And on the page folded down: 'How to Make Your Bedroom Your New Playground'.

The room suddenly reeked of disappointment and dashed hopes. I watched Mum's bird-like frame slip between the lounge chairs before catching up with her. She linked her arm with mine as we made our way to the dining hall.

Hopewood Sanatorium—though it preferred to call itself a 'health resort' and its patients 'residents'—was a sprawling facility next to a hill favoured by lovebirds and stargazers, complete with recreation rooms, surveillance cameras and its fair share of troubled occupants. For positive reinforcement, the long-term occupants received privileges like leaving the premises for a day, depending on the amount of progress, social interaction, and community contribution they had made in the week.

Mum often did well enough to get that out-of-grounds card, but she said it was the company, not the destination, that mattered.

We got our dinner from the dining hall and went up to our secret spot to eat. Not many people knew about the small balcony on the eighth floor of the north tower, where you could look out over the city uninterrupted. Mum and I took our usual seat at the bench next to the mini garden, staring at the lattice of skyscraper lights in the distance as we ate.

'Manda said you didn't want to attend group session yesterday,' I said, forking some of my salmon. 'Everything okay?'

I didn't intend to make this the conversation starter, but I had to get it out of the way.

Mum waved her fork in the air, her voice too buoyant for the topic. 'Oh, you know. Just wanted a little alone time.' She glanced up at me. 'Don't tell your father.'

'You know you can always call me, right? If you ever want to talk, I'm always available.'

'I'm fine, I promise. It's you I worry about. You're looking a little on the thin side these days.' She pinched my chin, ignoring my grimace. 'All work and no play make Chris a dull boy.'

'It's the multiplex,' I said.

'Ah, yes. The new project. How's the conquest going? How did the meeting go today?'

'Let's just say the locals are getting restless. But Dad's ready to go all out to win them over.'

She gave a tiny sad smile as she pushed her food around on her plate. 'I'm sure he will. Your father always gets what he wants.' She spooned a mouthful of mashed potatoes. 'So, what have you drawn this week?'

I usually showed her my sketches after dinner, but Dad's absence had left a space too noticeable without a conversation filler. So I set my fork down and pulled out my sketchpad, flipping to the latest drawings.

Mum's eyes lit up as she pored over each sketch. Unlike Dad, who had no idea about my hobby, Mum kept a copy of every single doodle of mine. If you quizzed her, she could tell you when and why I did each piece, and where in the city I hid them.

She came to a stop at the latest one. Her gaze flicked up. 'Who's this?'

'That's a … girl.'

Her eyebrows rose. 'That's no ordinary girl if you're drawing her.' Portraits were not my thing and Mum knew it. I preferred to sketch a hand here, a shoulder there, anything but a proper face because it felt too intimate.

Then why had I drawn Lexi without the slightest discomfort, almost as if I had seen her face a million times before?

'And I know for a fact that isn't Hayley,' Mum added.

She did know what Hayley looked like, thanks to the photo that Hayley had stuck in my sketchbook in the hopes that I would one day draw her.

What could I possibly say? That I had met Lexi in a dream and we had stolen bread together?

'Chris?' Mum prompted.

'Just a girl I saw on the street. I thought she was pretty. You know,' I said with what I hoped would pass for a sheepish shrug.

Mum squinted at me. The number of times I had felt compelled to draw a random girl on the streets was a grand total of zero. With school and work and art, there was barely time for anything else. Even if I felt a spark of anything with a girl, I was never in the headspace to pursue anything.

'She seems sad,' Mum said, turning back to the sketch.

'She is.'

I realized it was true as soon as I said it. Lexi *was* sad, no matter how hard she tried to disguise it. There were times when her gaze would turn wistful and a shadow of melancholy would flicker across her face. Plus, she ran a little too hard away from my questions.

'Any idea why?'

I stared at Lexi's portrait. 'Maybe she doesn't know where to go next.'

'She can come here,' Mum said, waggling her brows. 'I promise I'll be a good mother-in-law.'

I rolled my eyes. 'She's just some girl I saw, Mum.' Why did I still bother to lie?

Mum let out a dramatic sigh. 'How is it that my son, so handsome and so smart, is so tragically dull?'

'I don't have time for—'

'Oh, pffft,' she scoffed. 'You know those who deny themselves something are usually the ones who want it the most. All you do is work, and while I'm indescribably proud of your achievements, I've never seen you truly happy or doing something you're really proud of … something for yourself.'

'I'm painting,' I said. 'That makes me happy and it's something I'm doing for myself—'

'Undercover. I think Night is a lot more honest than you are.'

'You do realize we're essentially the same person.'

'Correction: Christopher is your father's son. Night is who you really are.' A sigh. 'Back when your father was chasing me, I thought I had all the time in the world to decide. It was when he decided to chase his career and let me go that I realized he was the one I really wanted.'

'He still loves you,' I said quietly.

Mum laid a cool hand on my cheek. 'All I'm saying is, don't wait to go after what you want. Sometimes, the longer you wait, the more you have to lose.'

Dear Night,

We haven't found an answer to everything yet, and maybe we never will. Sometimes, when we don't have an answer for something, we call it strange or inexplicable. But that's just because we haven't seen everything that's possible in this world.

You understand that. You look for the edges of possibility in your art—however hazy they may be—not to define them, but to find a space within that infinite realm that can hold you and your art, your dreams and desires. To safe-keep a living piece of you.

Maybe deep down, we're all looking for something fantastical, something beyond the boundaries of what we know. Maybe we want to believe everything is possible if we're willing to give it life.

And maybe your art can really give life to something magical and inexplicable.

A girl with horns curling to her waist standing at the edge of a red-bricked building, overlooking the grimy city. A reflection in a puddle of a couple dancing in rainbow-coloured rain. And the latest one I found: a boy perched on the edge of a boat floating in the sky, watching a house half submerged in the ground.

Your art is danger, a challenge issued to the universe. It's sometimes sad, sometimes defiant, and always unfathomable. Yet somehow, I can always find a piece of myself in it.

You made me believe in the magic hidden amongst reality, but the real magic lies in finding you at last.

Your believer,
Lexi

Chapter 3

Lexi

Getting lost in a dream was less fun when you had only your memories for company.

Still, at least I was wandering around Night's paintings. If my memories brought me back to places familiar and comforting, then Night's paintings took me to places wild and free, surreal and incredible. One minute, I was perched atop a white bird, big enough to send me pin-wheeling through the frigid night sky; and the next, I was back in the toasty bakery, drenched in warm lights and inhaling the scent of freshly baked goods.

However long this dream may last, I was going to enjoy it while I was here.

Even more so now that Chris was back.

'Lexi?'

I swivelled in the stool behind the cash counter. 'Hi, Chris.'

'You've been here all this while?'

'Looks like it, doesn't it? Scone?' I offered him a blueberry one, which he ignored.

'And I'm … back?'

'Clearly.'

His brows pulled close. 'But—but this is a dream. So I'm dreaming about the same place and the same girl. I didn't even know you, why would I dream about you?'

'Actually, the question is why we're both here and when we're going to wake up. But that's okay. I'm not after any answers.'

'You're not worried at all?'

I took a bite of my scone. 'About what?'

'Oh, I don't know, maybe that we're meeting here again? And—'

'And what?'

'And it's just bizarre!' He threw up his arms. 'Why am I suddenly having these dreams of you? Are we sharing a dream? Am I in your dream? Are *you* in mine?'

'You're getting hysterical. Have a banana roll,' I suggested.

'No! Stop giving me food. I don't want food. I want to stop thinking about you—'

'You've been thinking about me?'

He closed his eyes and took a deep breath, then let it out and fixed a grave stare at me. 'Lexi.' The look on his face made me fight to hold in my laughter.

'Chris,' I mimicked his tone. 'If this is a dream, are you going to waste your time freaking out over the how's and why's?'

'The how's and why's are necessary for moving forward.'

'No, they're not. They're just a distraction from what really matters.'

'And what,' he said, 'would that be?'

I eyed the tray of bread between us. 'Focaccia, fresh from the oven.'

He rolled his eyes. But maybe it was the smell of the focaccia that made him continue in a significantly calmer tone, 'I didn't mean to yell at you, I'm sorry. It's been a long day.'

'That's okay. I'm used to it.'

He raised a brow. 'You're used to people yelling at you?'

'Not yelling. Just … freaking out, in general.'

'Who?'

'Hmm.'

The words spilled out. Later, I'd pin it on the scone for loosening my tongue.

'I used to think it was normal,' I said.

Chris stopped glancing around. His eyes, the colour of the night outside, settled on me.

'It wasn't until I was invited to a friend's house for dinner when I was ten that I realized not everyone's mother had a panic attack every time they read the news or stepped into the kitchen.'

'Your mum….'

'Has anxiety. It's a response to a traumatic experience.' I had never spoken about this to anyone before. Only my family and the Long Streeters knew about Mum's condition. 'So, do you want to talk about your long day? We've got all night.'

Chris picked up on my unwillingness to continue with this topic. 'Seems like it. Maybe later.' He picked up the banana roll from the tray, shrugged and took a bite.

'I thought you were mad at me or something.'

'Why would I be mad at you?'

'Because I obviously got on your nerves the last time we met. And you're not the most mellow person around.'

'Thank you,' he said dryly.

'So, I didn't know if you'd be back. Thought you left in a huff.'

He peered at me, a strange look on his face. 'You do know that this is a dream, right? I didn't leave because I chose to. Someone woke me up.'

'Ah. That's too bad.'

He set down his bun and stared at me. 'You don't want to wake up.'

I snorted. 'Well done, Captain Obvious.'

'So, you're just going to hide here forever? Keep sleeping?'

'Say this is a dream. Then we'd only be here until morning, right?'

'Yeah,' he said slowly.

'So until morning comes, we have this whole place to ourselves. Shouldn't we make good use of the time we have here and live the way we want? No expectations, no consequences. Don't think, just do.'

Chris held my gaze as he considered. His gaze reminded me of Night's paintings, pulsing with a secret yearning for adventure, like colours waiting to explode on to canvas.

'And that includes bread-stealing,' he said at last.

I nodded. 'Among other things.'

'Just until morning.'

'Exactly.'

'I guess I can do that.'

'Good.' I hopped off the stool. 'What do you say we do some roaming?'

He blinked. 'Roaming?'

'Roaming,' I confirmed. It seemed like a waste to only stay in this bakery when we could go anywhere, and anything was possible in this strange, beautiful place. I grabbed Chris's hand and dragged him outside.

The night was as vast and empty as before, ours and ours alone.

Across the road was the playground Mum used to take me to after school. It had twin swings that creaked horribly the minute you climbed on. I made a dash for them.

'Chris!' I called over my shoulder. 'Push me!'

But he lingered by the swing post, watching me attempt to throw myself into the air. 'Did you have a deprived childhood or something?'

'Beats standing by the side, acting like I'm too cool for this.' I closed my eyes and felt the air part around me. The momentum of the swing lulled me back to the days when the thought of my mother didn't make me sick with guilt and helplessness. 'I used to close my eyes and imagine I was flying.'

Chris had his brows raised when I opened my eyes again.

'Haven't you ever dreamt of flying?' I said.

'Nope.'

'Never?'

'Never. And I never understood the fascination with flying. Gravity exists for a reason.'

'To pin us to the ground.'

He shrugged. 'Saves you from falling, at the very least.'

'Aha,' I said. 'So you're afraid of falling, not flying.'

'I never said I was afraid.'

'What's wrong with admitting you're afraid?' The image of Mum locking herself in the bathroom, refusing to come out for an entire day, flashed across my mind. 'It's when you deny your fear that it starts to take over you.'

Another image—Mum flinching every time a match was struck. She'd reach for my arm and her nails would always bite into my skin.

'Some people let their fears take over their lives, until they become defined by them and lose themselves,' I said, glancing at him.

Chris reached over and stopped my swinging. He leaned down and locked his steely gaze with mine. 'I'm not afraid.'

I matched the look in his eyes. 'Prove it.'

He parked himself on to the swing next to me and sent me a defiant look.

I grinned. 'Now fly,' I instructed, kicking off the ground and launching myself into the sky. My grasp on the metal chains of the swing loosened the higher I went, until it completely slipped off and I was airborne. I closed my eyes. Beneath me, Chris was calling out my name, but I was already weightless, floating off somewhere gravity couldn't reach me. I was the girl in Night's painting. The thought sent me soaring higher.

The painting was the one he had placed outside Maude's shop about a month ago. He was slick, placing a twenty-by-twenty-four in the compartment between the floral and stripes sections right under Maude's nose. I spotted the painting when visiting Maude and took it home, just like with the other paintings I'd found.

For nights, I had wondered what it would be like to be that girl in the painting—the one with the wind in her hair and stars in her pocket, sailing through the sky with her heart in her mouth.

And now I *was* that girl. Not the Lexi who stayed silent when her mother had an anxiety attack or the one who kept beating herself up for that mistake, but the girl whom Night thought of when he put his brush to the canvas and filled her with colours.

This no longer felt like a dream; everything felt surreal. I was starting to get the hang of flying. I was becoming one with the wind, and the air was yielding to me—

'Lexi!'

My eyelids flew open. I ventured a glance down. Chris was staring up at me from the ground, no bigger than my finger, but his voice rang in my ear as if he were right next to me. I gasped. A giddy laugh bubbled up from me. How had I managed to come this high?

As soon as I started considering the practicalities, I lost control. The air no longer buoyed me up; it released me like a cloud releasing rain, and I was plunging back to the ground before I could react. The sand pit loomed closer and closer….

Chris shifted into view with his arms outstretched, ready to catch me. I tumbled clumsily into his arms, and we crashed to the ground with our limbs entangled.

We lay side by side on our backs, long enough for the shock to wear off, spitting sand and waiting for our breaths to return. Being in a dream did nothing to soften the impact of falling. I stretched out my hand, my fingers reaching for the sky so far away now.

Chris turned to me. 'See? Gravity's your friend.' A beat. 'Or not?'

'At least now I know what it's like to fly and fall. You've been on the ground all this while.'

He shook his head. 'Why risk it when you know you have to come back down eventually?'

'Because I want to at least experience it. I don't want to stay on the ground and look up at the sky, wondering *what if.*' I got to my feet and brushed sand off myself. 'Come on, let's try it again together. This time, we won't fall.'

I offered him a hand. He sat up and parked an elbow on a drawn-up knee, but didn't take my hand.

'Fine. Stay on the ground, then.' I kicked off my shoes, preparing to take flight again.

Before I could lift myself off the ground again, he grabbed my hand and got to his feet. As soon as he took off his shoes, we were in the air.

We rose higher and higher, until the chilly night air seeped between our toes. The only warmth came from his hand around mine, but it didn't matter. We were now one with the wind.

'Beats being on the ground, doesn't it?' I said.

The smile on his face was answer enough.

We trailed shapes in the sky with the mist curling around us, then admired our handiwork from afar. They were ephemeral, barely leaving a mark. But for a moment, we had left *our* mark.

Time slipped by, endless and eternal, and our excitement kept us going. Far below us, the city was an intricate web of lights. The view from up here was even more beautiful than from Hopewood Hill, where my parents used to bring me and Eliza for Sunday picnics, way back when we still did things like that.

When the cold finally got to us, Chris and I drifted back to the playground to retrieve our shoes. We got more bread from Auntie Fong's bakery before settling on the rooftop of one of the shophouses to eat. Here, the bread was always warm.

Chris munched on his walnut rye loaf as he stared down at the dark silhouette of trees in the park across the road.

'Earlier, you said you don't want to be one of those people who let their fears define them.' He turned to me. 'Is that why you want to try everything here? Because you know there are no consequences?'

I didn't reply at first, just kept my trained gaze on the lights in the distance. It made me uncomfortable how he could read me like a book. How I wanted to believe I was fearless, but was I really fearless in a place where there were no consequences?

'You know who's truly fearless?' I said. 'Night.'

Chris snorted. 'Night? You think *he's* fearless? Why would you say that? What makes you think he's a guy, anyway?'

'I just know.' I took a bite of my croissant. 'You can tell a lot about a person from their art.'

'Sounds like you're just making him what you *want* him to be. What if he's really a coward who hides behind his paintings? What if he's a weirdo? I mean, his paintings don't make much sense.'

I turned to look at Chris. 'You've seen his work?'

'I … might have chanced upon it.'

'Really? Where?' I had collected, at last count, eight of his paintings, including the one at Maude's shop. But there had to be more out there that I hadn't found yet.

'Somewhere. Everywhere.' He waved a hand. 'Can't remember. The guy probably doesn't have much of a life if he's going around hiding paintings in public places. What is he even trying to achieve?'

I had thought long and hard about his purpose for doing this, too. Maybe, like the rest of us, he was just trying to leave his mark on the world, in some way or another.

'In my dreams, I'm chasing Night. I can't see his face, just his back, as he runs further and further away from me. No matter how hard I chase, no matter where I look, he remains firmly out of my grasp: a shadow, a shirttail, a puff of breath.' Faceless, elusive Night. Sometimes, I wondered if the reason why I sought him so desperately was because I wanted to believe in his magic, the escape and possibilities he promised.

'You really shouldn't get your hopes up. He'll probably end up disappointing you.' He leaned back on his elbows and stared out into the distance.

'Spoken like you know him. What would the son of an urban development tycoon know about a nocturnal street artist?'

He took a sip of his coffee, ignoring my question. We ate in silence, waiting for each other to break the ice.

'I remember one of his first few paintings that I found,' I said. 'It was the one with the birds. He'd hidden it in the back alley of a diner at Corner Street, stuffed it there between cardboard boxes and wooden crates like he didn't care about it.'

'Maybe he didn't.'

'Why not? Why paint them in the first place, then?'

'Maybe he just wants to leave a part of himself everywhere. Maybe he doesn't want people to find out he paints because they think it's a waste of time. Maybe he just wants something to call his own, a secret that only he knows, a piece of his life that belongs to him alone.' He took a deep breath and turned back to the park. 'Or maybe he just wants to escape.'

'You feel it, don't you?' I nudged him. 'That's the thing about Night's paintings. We find a piece of ourselves in them, any of them. It's like they can reach deep into your soul.'

Chris glanced at me. I expected him to be secretly laughing at me again, but he only stared at me like he was considering my words.

'Why are you so intent on finding him?' he asked quietly.

'Maybe I can't stop thinking about Night and his paintings because I feel like he knows me and I know him,' I said. 'We're both trapped in our own skin, becoming the people we have to be when we don't even know who we really are yet.'

'*You*? Trapped?' Chris snorted. 'You made me steal bread. You dared me to fly. I'm sorry, but a girl like that is the opposite of trapped.'

I liked that he thought of me that way, even if it wasn't true. 'Well, I can't do those things anywhere else, can I? It's only in here that I can be that girl.' I turned to him. 'So can you. I mean, I know you're probably happy being the heir to Kingdom Heights, but—'

'Why would you assume I am?'

'So you admit you're not fine?' I asked.

'Takes one to know one,' he retorted, getting to his feet. He took off into the sky, knowing I would follow.

We drifted on our backs through the clouds, our hands brushing against each other's. The night air sat on my skin, cool and damp. More than once, the fear that I might fall again seized me—it *was* a pretty long way down—but I turned my focus to the stars above us instead.

A salty tang wove its way through the air. Beneath us, the sea rippled like black silk. Somewhere to our left, the glow from a boathouse beckoned.

I signalled to Chris, and he offered me a hand. I slipped mine into his and we settled into a pair of lounge chairs on the deck of the boathouse. A gentle breeze curled around us. Stars winked overhead in the clear inky sky. It was easier to trace the constellations here.

Chris was staring up at the sky too. I watched his profile silently, wondering if he was happier here than in his waking life.

'Stop staring,' he said, without turning to me. 'It's rude.'

'What are you thinking?' I asked.

'Stop probing. It's rude.'

'You know, you can tell a lot more about a person from the things he doesn't say than the things he does.' I shifted on my side to face him. 'Just like you can tell more about someone from what he doesn't paint than what he does.'

'And what,' he said, again with that infuriating smirk, 'do Night's paintings tell you?'

'That he's lonely.'

His smile slipped.

'All his paintings—at least those that I've seen—are of wide, empty spaces and lone figures. He's good at painting skies, colours and light, but hardly ever does portraits. Even if he does draw people, they're almost always faceless or have their backs turned. Maybe because he's never really been close to anyone.'

'Sounds like you have him all figured out.'

'I don't know about that. What I do know is that he's my fourth constellation.'

'Your *what*?'

I pointed out Ursa Major with my fingertip. 'My fourth constellation. Dad's Aries the Ram, Eliza's Cygnus the Swan, Mum's Andromeda the Doomed Princess, and Night's Pictor the Painter. As for you . . .' I considered him. 'You could be the fifth—Pegasus, maybe.'

He shook his head. 'People aren't constellations. Besides, won't you run out of them eventually?'

'There are eighty-eight constellations to date. There aren't enough *people* in my life for all of them.'

'I'm sure Night would love having you label him as a constellation.'

'Is that a bad thing?'

'It makes no sense. No one is made up of a pattern of stars,' he said. 'They're made up of—'

'Dreams and fears and failings and triumphs—each one a star.' I shrugged. 'That's how I see it. The good, the bad, the ugly all coming together to create something special.'

'Huh.' He turned back to the sky. 'Never thought of it that way.'

The ghost of a smile worked its way to his lips. And I knew, despite everything he said, that he was a dreamer too.

Chapter 4

Chris

It didn't feel like a dream any more. I couldn't have dreamt all that up—the flying, the bread, Lexi as the girl in my paintings. These past two nights I spent with Lexi felt more real than any waking moment I'd ever experienced.

There were so many times I could have told Lexi that I was Night, but I didn't want her to be disappointed when she found out that the 'wildly talented phantom' she thought she could relate to was, in fact, a boy who donned a suit and tie to a cold office during semester breaks, who did everything his father planned for him and had to sneak his art in after hours.

But no dream lasted forever, and my day was already planned out—after my morning jog with Dad, I would head to Bobby's to tutor Hayley, then pay Long Street a visit.

Waking felt cruel after the night I'd had. Being on solid ground again felt strange now that I knew what it was like to fly, even if it was only in my dream. I still didn't understand why I kept meeting Lexi in a dream we apparently both shared, but that detail seemed trivial now.

My feet pounded on the pavement; each step was grounding, solid, but lacked the wild freedom of flying. At least the jog offered me some time alone with my thoughts. If Dad noticed my silence, he didn't comment on it.

He only spoke after we finished our last lap around the park. 'Make sure you record every shop and occupant's background. We'll start with the low-hanging fruits, Maude and Anitha. Have them convince as many of them to get on board. As for Charlie and the rest, I know you'll find a way.' He clapped me on the back.

I took a swig of water. 'Sure, Dad.'

A beat.

'I know you're still mad at me for not visiting your mother yesterday,' he said.

'She's doing great, you know,' I lied. 'No episodes, attending group sessions regularly. She's ready to come home.'

'That's for Doctor York to decide.'

I stared down at my running shoes. 'Are you sure you're not just keeping her out of your way while you work on the multiplex?'

His voice was sharp as a whip. 'What are you implying?'

'I'm just saying,' I said, 'she didn't really have a choice in going to Hopewood. You pretty much decreed that she stay there.'

'Your mother is sick, Christopher.' Another crack of the whip. 'She needs to rest.'

I didn't reply.

'You think I'm keeping her there against her will so I won't have to face her problem? You think I'm ashamed of her?'

I levelled my gaze with his. 'I didn't say that.' The implication rang loud and clear—*he* did.

Dad frowned at me. I wondered what he saw in my face then—if he could look past waking-Christopher to see dream-Chris. I kept my gaze fixed on him.

He got up abruptly. 'Have the report on all the occupants of Long Street ready by Monday morning.'

I watched him leave, stuck with my useless hope that he would—for once—look back and change his mind. But, of course, he never did.

* * *

A sigh.

Hayley tossed her pencil down on the table. 'This is pointless. Do you know the number of times I've used calculus in real life?' She formed a circle with her fingers. 'Ze-ro. Why do we have to put ourselves through something this meaningless just so we can pass a meaningless test and get meaningless grades that qualify us to do more meaningless things?'

I raised a brow. 'I thought you were too cool for existential angst.'

She shot me a look. 'Antagonism is not going to work here.' She turned back to her books and did some more lip-biting before giving up altogether. 'I need a break.'

She bounded out of the room and towards the kitchen, returning with a strip of Oreo cookies and two cans of chilled kombucha.

'So how's your mum?' she asked, tossing me a can. 'Your dad let her home yet?'

Funny how offensive it sounded coming from her when I had said the same thing to my father this morning.

'Her carer said she refused to attend group session yesterday.'

'You didn't tell your dad about it, did you?'

'Of course not.'

'Maybe it'll help for her to be around people. Real people. In real life. I mean, I would be borderline bipolar too if my family threw me in a sanatorium with no shopping privileges.'

I glared at her, and she muttered an apology.

'They do have shopping privileges,' I said. 'You just have to earn it.'

Hayley gave me her trademark dry look. 'The *point,* Chris.'

'I know.'

'For all you *know,* you're not really doing a whole lot about it.'

I didn't blame her for getting on my case about Mum. While Hayley's mother had passed away when Hayley was too young to remember anything, mine was all for sticking around. Except that Dad didn't seem to want her and her emotions in the house. And while I didn't see anything wrong with helping Dad with his business, leaving Mum in Hopewood for almost three years was starting to strike a wrong chord with me.

At noon, Bobby's students from his charcoal drawing class filed out of the studio in the adjacent room. After they left, Bobby popped in, dressed in his usual rumpled linen shirt and blue Levi's.

'I'm going to grab lunch,' he announced. 'Want anything?'

'Dad,' Hayley said. 'What did I tell you about knocking? Chris and I could've been making out.'

'If you were, you won't have a door I need to knock on any more.'

Hayley sent me a woeful look. 'The course of true love never did run smooth. Will you still take me, even with all the obstacles in our way?'

I leapt out of my chair. 'I will take lunch.' Hayley and I followed Bobby to his car. 'Do you have any lunch recommendations near Long Street?' I asked as I climbed into the passenger seat.

Bobby glanced at me. 'Why Long Street?'

'Kingdom Heights' new conquest,' Hayley said, sticking her head between me and Bobby from the backseat. 'His dad's sending him to pay lip service so the locals will give up their land willingly.'

Bobby frowned as he manoeuvred the car out of the parking lot. 'And going there for lunch will get the job done?'

'It'll take some time, as soft approaches often do,' I said.

'Yeah, a soft approach isn't something his dad is good at,' Hayley said. 'He offered money, but unlike him, some people aren't all about that.'

'Watch it,' I warned her reflection in the rear-view mirror. She sank back into her seat and stuck out her tongue at me.

'This is why I'm a teacher and not a businessman,' Bobby said as we cruised down the main road. 'Imagine having to chase people out of their homes. Most of them live there, right above their shops. If you take over that piece of land, they'll be as good as homeless.'

'We're offering them alternative residence *and* another place to set up shop. All they'll be doing is relocating,' I said, trying to keep the defensiveness out of my voice. 'It's not a bad thing.'

'Why don't you ask your mum if it's a good thing, being relocated?' Hayley piped up.

'This is business,' I snapped. 'What's it got to do with my mum?'

'All right, that's enough, both of you,' Bobby said as he made a turn. 'You know, Chris, I gave up my studio so I could look after Hayley full-time after her mother died. But I don't see that as a failure.'

I looked at him. He couldn't be more different from my father, with his salt-and-pepper hair, craggy face, and paint-spattered clothes, driving his trusty old Nissan. I had sometimes wondered what it would be like to be Bobby's son instead, but then I'd think of Mum and the reverie would end there.

'What's your point?' I said.

'My point is that there are other ways to measure success than just the number of deals you close.'

A snort escaped my mouth. 'You're not my dad. You're not me. You don't know what it's like in our family.' My words sounded harsher when they were out in the open.

Silence swelled in the car before Hayley put a pin to the bubble. 'Wow. Way to be a jerk, Chris.'

'I'm sorry,' I muttered. Bobby shook his head. 'But it's just business.'

'Not everything is a transaction, Chris.'

'It is to our family.' This was because business deals were easier to keep track of than the business of intangible things. 'Ever since Mum got sick—'

'Ever since your mum got sick,' Hayley interrupted, 'you've been well on your way to fulfilling your dad's dream by turning into Gerald Fang Junior.'

'That's not—'

'Besides, what twenty-year-old in his right mind would obsess over building his father's empire when there's a perfectly adequate girl sitting behind him right now?' Bobby shot her a look through the rear-view mirror. 'You're lucky you've got us, Chris. We make you slightly more normal.'

We spent the rest of the car ride in silence.

We arrived at a hole-in-the-wall café a fifteen-minute drive away from Long Street. Even after we had placed our orders, Hayley and I still weren't talking to each other. This wasn't the first time we had fought over this, but Hayley knew better than to pass judgement on the way our family worked.

It was only after Bobby reached for my sketchbook and flipped to my recent sketches that the ice thawed between me and Hayley.

'Worked on anything new lately?' Bobby asked. He came to a stop at Lexi's portrait. On the previous page was a half-finished sketch of her sitting on a rooftop, eating bread, and watching the sky. 'Well. I thought you weren't into portraits.'

'Who's that?' Hayley demanded, reaching for the sketchpad.

'She's … a girl from school.'

'You know her? Was it an "ooh-she's-so-pretty-I-have-to-draw-her" kind of thing?'

'When a guy draws a girl like that,' Bobby said, 'it's probably an "I-want-to-know-her-story" kind of thing.'

Hayley raised her brows at me.

'I don't know why I drew her, really,' I said, rubbing my brow.

'Whoever she is, she makes a good subject,' Bobby said. 'You're on to something here, Chris.'

Hayley was about to say something when our food arrived.

Like the café, the food was humble but hearty. Clearly, the chef didn't need fancy plating and trendy ingredients to attract its regulars. Unfortunately, this place fell within the area we had acquired, so it would have to make way for the multiplex. Dad would have no qualms about tearing it down, even if it meant robbing these patrons of their usual lunch spot—

No. *Robbing* was a harsh word. We were *replacing* it with a bigger and better alternative. Long Street, with some sprucing up, could become a vibrant dining quarter that attracted a wider demographic. If only those shop-owners could see that we were trying to help them.

'Speaking of your art, Chris,' Hayley said, taking a bite of her turkey burger. 'I checked out the places where you left your paintings and most of them are gone. Whoever's found them has been following you. Either that, or they know you well enough to figure out your hiding places.'

'Looks like you've got yourself a fan,' Bobby said.

Hayley smirked. 'Not so mysterious after all, Night.'

'I'm not trying to be mysterious,' I said. 'And it might not be the same person who found my paintings.'

Didn't Lexi say she had found the paintings? What if she was also the one who had taken them?

But then that would mean she was real. That Lexi was real. But she wasn't. She was just a figment of my imagination. Just a girl running around in my dreams.

I shook my head to clear it. I was here for a purpose—I needed to work.

After lunch, Bobby offered to drop us off at Long Street before heading home for his two o'clock watercolour painting lesson. But I figured a walk might help Hayley blow off some steam, so I told him we would make our way to Long Street on our own.

Hayley started walking ahead of me after Bobby drove off. I tailed her, keeping a two-metre distance between us, the way I always did when I wasn't sure what mood she was in.

'You're not still mad at me, are you?' I asked the back of her head.

She stopped, then spun around. I caught up with her in two strides. 'She's not some girl from school, is she?'

'*That's* what's on your mind? I thought it was the argument we had in the car.'

A shrug. 'About your dad, you and I both know I'm right. So there's nothing for me to be mad about. This girl, though, I don't know anything about her.'

'You wouldn't believe me if I told you.'

She cocked her head. 'Try me.'

'I met her in my dreams.'

Hayley looked ready to sock me one. She stuck one arm on her hip. 'Chris. I'm mortally wounded. Look, I understand that my crush is a one-sided thing, and you'll probably never realize that I'm your true soulmate, but since when have you not been able to talk to me about something?'

'I told you, you wouldn't believe me.'

'Explain.'

I walked absently, trying to buy some time to figure out how to explain. In the end, only the truth sounded right.

'Lately, I've been having these dreams.' Hayley kept pace with me, waiting for more. 'And in these dreams, there's this girl. Lexi. She—she seems to be living in my paintings.'

Hayley stopped, her brows furrowing. 'Come again?'

'I know it sounds bizarre.' My stride quickened as I mulled over the whole thing. Hayley jogged a little to catch up. 'But there were moments in my dream when I could swear I saw the exact image I had in mind when I created those paintings. The girl in my dreams is the girl in my paintings.'

Hayley laid a hand on my shoulder, forcing me to come to a stop. She looked me in the eye. 'Chris. I'm saying this in all seriousness. You should see a doctor.'

I rolled my eyes and kept walking. What did I expect?

'I bet it's your sleep apnoea, or whatever it is,' Hayley went on. 'All that oxygen deficiency is messing with your brain. Schedule that doctor's appointment. I'll go with you.'

But what I saw next convinced me it wasn't oxygen deficiency. Or stress. Or any other explanation I would likely get from a doctor.

In my dream, Auntie Fong's Bakery had a magical glow, but at two in the afternoon it looked just like any old bakery, with a dark green door and the day's specials written on a chalkboard placed outside the shop.

I came to a dead halt, spared half a moment's hesitation before bursting in.

The bakery looked exactly like it did in the dream—the wooden racks stacked with bread, the local corner with its jars of *kaya* jam and assortment of confectionary, and the display cake at the centre of the shop. The cake, however, wasn't the garden maze with the fountain in the middle, but a stone castle on a cliff by the sea. It was so exquisitely constructed, right down to the textured walls and the crests and dips of the waves, that there were more customers taking photos of it than shopping for bread.

'You're not hungry already, are you?' Hayley said next to me. She gasped when she noticed the cake on display. 'That is some cake.'

I got myself a walnut rye loaf, just to see if it tasted the same as it did in my dream. It did. Of course, how different could a rye loaf taste? But somehow, I knew it was the exact same taste, just like I knew this was the place Lexi remembered, the one she took me to in our dreams.

There was no doubt about it now. Even if she only appeared in my dreams, Lexi was as real as this place. But how? Why?

'Chris!'

I came to a stop, glanced around and found myself on the pavement several stores down the bakery, my half-eaten rye loaf in my hand. Hayley stood a few feet behind me, waiting for me to realize that I had zoned out and walked ahead without her.

'Sorry,' I muttered when she caught up with me. 'That's the bakery in my dream.'

Hayley narrowed her eyes at me, then sighed when I didn't back down. 'You're probably just overworked. Your mind's on overdrive.'

No one was going to believe me. A girl from my paintings I was seeing in my dreams? I was lucky it was Hayley I was telling this to. At least she wouldn't run in the opposite direction.

'You're right. I'm probably just tired. Forget it,' I said, turning to leave.

We reached Long Street a few wrong turns later and ended up in front of Maude's shop. It was one of the few shops I dared to enter on Long Street, only because I wasn't public enemy No. 2, right after my dad.

A month ago, I had slid my painting between the floral and stripes sections here. I didn't know why I'd picked this shop, but as soon as I stepped foot into it and heard Maude describing a quilt she had sewn to a customer, I decided this was the place to hide my painting.

According to Hayley, the painting I had hidden here—the one of the girl suspended in the air with stars in the pockets of her dress and the wind coursing through her hair—had been found.

Maude was attending to a customer when we entered, cutting up a few yards of printed silk while they chatted. I headed over to the floral and stripes section, rifling through the rows of fabric to find my painting.

'Told you it's gone,' Hayley whispered. 'Someone's on to you.'

'Chris?'

I spun around, retracting my hand like I had been doing something illicit. Next to me, Hayley jumped a little.

With the customer gone, Maude came over, her face lit up with surprise. 'It *is* you! What are you doing here?' She turned to Hayley. 'And this is…?'

'Hi, Maude. This is my friend, Hayley. We were just around the area, thought we'd pop by.'

She gave me a knowing look. 'You mean, you thought you'd drop by on behalf of your father.' She smiled. 'That's okay. I knew he'd send you eventually. You're a better negotiator than he is, anyway.'

'I think so too,' Hayley piped up. I shot her a look.

'Is there absolutely no chance that you'll sign the deal?' I asked Maude.

She sighed. 'Truth be told, I have half a mind to. My daughter wants me to retire, and it's not like business is booming these days. I'm just surviving on a few regulars.'

'We can offer you a bigger space to lease,' I said. 'Think of it as an upgrade.'

She shook her head. 'Newer, prettier things aren't always better. They take time to fill up again.'

A shop was a shop. What was there to fill up?

'Don't mind Charlie, by the way,' Maude added. 'He's just been really worried about his daughter.'

'You said she got in an accident?'

'Yeah, the poor girl's been in a coma for almost two weeks. It was a hit-and-run. As though Charlie doesn't have enough on his plate already, with his wife and inn. You can't really tell, but he is this close to breaking. Thank goodness he has his other daughter to keep him from falling to pieces.'

'What about the rest of them? What are they holding on to?'

'I think you should ask them that yourself.'

'I don't think I'm too popular with them. As long as I'm on my father's side, I'm against them.'

'But you are not your father.' She set about arranging the floral and stripes fabrics. 'Come and get to know the people here.'

The problem with getting to know people was the inevitable attachment that followed.

'We have our weekly barbeque at the rooftop of the Welcome Inn,' Maude went on. 'Charlie might not be the best company, what with the accident and all, but you should come anyway.' She gestured at Hayley. 'And bring your friend with you. More company's always welcome.'

'I'll … I'll think about it.'

'Sunday, seven o'clock. If you do decide to come.'

Dear Night,

I don't know if you know this, but you have a slight fixation with hands. This recent painting I've found is the third one that focuses on it. Who is that girl sprawled over the piano? Her eyes are closed—is she asleep or dead? More importantly, why are her hands scarred?

They remind me of my mother's hands. But unlike the choppy, petty slashes the girl in your painting has, my mother's is a dull pink patch of skin tissue that covers almost the entire back of her right hand. After the fire, I never dared to ask about her injury—did it still hurt? Was it going to be there forever? Did she blame me for it?—nor did she speak about it.

In the days and months after the fire, my dad used to apply—or tried to, at least—a medicated balm on those wounds, so that they wouldn't get infected. The balm was off-white, runny, and smelled like yoghurt left past its expiration date in the fridge.

The first time Dad spread it gently across Mum's wound, she hissed loudly and said she would never use that balm again. From then on, he would have to chase after her with the putrid tube of balm or her pills, his voice laced with exasperation, the way you would coax a child cheating on their bedtime. Mum would even lock herself in the bathroom just to avoid both types of medication. Dad and Eliza, at their wits' end, would send me to talk to her as a final measure.

I was the only one who could always bring her out. Not Dad, who applied balm on her wound and served her pills and water, or my sister, who was always ready to take her somewhere quiet whenever she became distressed. Anything could set her off—bright lights, loud noises, even the blast of heat from a bus exhaust.

She just always wanted me. Me, the one who caused that accident and gave her that scar. Me, who did nothing because there was nothing I could do. It was me she reached for whenever her breathing grew shallow and her pupils dilated. Me, whom she hugged a little too tightly before calming down again.

After unlocking the bathroom door and letting me in, she would pull me into her arms and rock me back and forth on the floor. She would let me brush my fingers over her wound.

Eventually, that patch of raw skin became a map of sorts, one that led me back to my mother, and my mother back to the world.

Markedly yours,
Lexi

Chapter 5

Lexi

At first, a dream had seemed like the best place to hide. Anything could happen, but no one and nothing could reach me here. I thought I wanted to hide out here forever.

But the truth was, I was starting to miss everyone at Long Street, even the gossips like Auntie Chang and grumpy Uncle Wang. Most of all, I missed my family. It was strange how I wanted time and space away from them, but also longed to be close to them.

Here in the dream, Long Street—and everywhere else—was empty. A street was just a street without the people in it.

I folded my arms close to me as a shiver ran through me again. Maybe it was the lack of people here, but the skating rink felt much colder than I remembered it to be.

Footsteps echoed in the skating rink. I glanced around wildly, eager for some company, and sure enough, found Chris wandering down the row of yellow plastic chairs. He quickened his pace when he spotted me.

'Hi again,' I said.

He spared no time for pleasantries. 'We can't keep meeting like this. It's unnatural.' But his eyes spoke a different greeting—a quiet excitement gleamed in his eyes under the lights of the skating rink. 'Why do I keep meeting you here? I'd never even met you before all this started.'

'Hey, don't look at me. I'm not the one bringing you here every night.'

'Yet, against all logic, I keep ending up here.'

The words stung. Granted, I wasn't as fun as my sister, or the best at small talk like my mum on her best days, but I still liked to think that I managed to keep those in my company well-entertained with my sparkling wit and soulful eyes.

'You're welcome to leave,' I told him.

He sank into an adjacent plastic chair and looked me in the eye. 'That's the thing. *I don't* want to leave.'

I wasn't sure if he meant it. But when I tried to read his face, I realized we were staring at each other in a way two people who had just been arguing never would. A shiver rippled through me.

Chris's gaze slid towards the arena of ice before us. 'Maybe Hayley's right. Maybe I *am* losing it.'

'Who's Hayley?'

'Friend of mine.' He turned to look at me. 'Are you really happy to just stay here forever?'

I shrugged. 'I'll wake up when I do.'

'And have you woken up so far?'

'No, but—'

'So basically, you've slept for at least three whole days? That's a whole lot of nothing being done.'

There's our good old Chris.

'I know *you* get a whole lot done, helping your dad build his empire and all, but not everyone's aspirations are as grand as yours.'

He just looked at me. 'What are you running away from, Lexi?'

'Your intrusive questions.'

'Did you know your fingers dance when you're feeling uncomfortable?' He glanced down at my hands.

I stilled my tapping fingers and clenched my fists. 'No, I do not.' I placed my hands primly in my lap. 'But thank you for the observation.'

A chilly gust of wind swept by, bringing with it memories of Dad taking me and Eliza to the skating rink when we were kids. I could hear our skates scratching against ice (I loved that sound), Eliza and I laughing and squealing whenever Dad grabbed our waists and spun us around.

'This place...' I said.

Chris glanced at me. 'Another place your mother brought you to when you were young?'

'My dad, actually. He brought us all here, taught me and Eliza how to skate. Eliza started out as the better skater; I fumbled all the time. Mum would cheer us on from here.'

The memory brought a smile to my lips. I could see myself with Dad and Eliza in the rink, her in her high-water jeans and pink sweater and gloves, me in my red ones, navigating the treacherous arena filled with older kids whizzing about, kicking up ice by skidding on their skates.

'But as we got older, the skating rink became a place for Eliza to meet boys,' I said. 'She'd pair off with some guy or other while I practised my jumps.'

'What about your parents?'

'Mum got sick after that, and Dad had to take care of the business. It was just me and Eliza. And then, later, just me. My parents would fight sometimes because of her sickness—he'd want her to get treatment, but she'd resist.' Chris was watching me intently. I turned away. 'Once, she didn't even dare to move an inch, just stayed frozen to the spot.'

'Why?'

'She was afraid that her movement might cause friction with the air and cause a fire. Fire's her biggest fear.'

'I'm sorry.' He seemed to mean it, too. His flinty gaze had softened a fraction, but it wasn't the usual obligatory pity I saw in people's eyes when they found out about my mother. 'It's not easy.'

'You say that like you know what it's like.'

He leaned in his seat. 'I do know a thing or two about sick mothers. I know how hard it can be for everyone in the family.'

'You never mentioned your mum. Is that why you're working for your dad?'

A beat of silence passed, where Chris seemed to be internally debating whether to share. I waited, neither backpedalling nor prodding.

'Someone has to help keep things together,' he said at last. 'My dad doesn't show it, but I know part of him is just using work as his crutch. So, if me inheriting the company someday is what my dad wants, then I'll do it.'

'So you rose to the challenge.'

He shrugged, but I knew it had to be a big decision for him to make, choosing obligation over what he wanted to do. But what *did* he really want to do?

'Sounds a little like you chose work over your mum though,' I said.

'That's not true,' he snapped. 'She knows I didn't choose work over her. We're all doing the best we can.'

It sounded like a refrain he had uttered many times before.

He must have caught the look on my face, since he retorted, 'You're the one hiding in a dream. Who's abandoned her mum, now? At least I'm doing something. All you're doing is running away.'

I almost hit him. I really did. But my dream was not a place for anger.

'I'm cold.' My words came out clipped. 'Let's move.' I got up and left.

'Sure, avoid the conversation,' he called after me.

'Either shut up and join me at the rink, or keep sitting here with your unsolicited opinions,' I yelled back.

Without waiting for his reply, I headed down to the lower deck, where the skating equipment was kept behind the counter.

Chris followed.

'Please tell me you can skate,' I said, pulling out a set of socks, skates, and gloves for myself.

He chose his gear, then sat on the wooden bench next to me to put on his skates. 'Probably not as good as you. I don't do fancy jumps.' We laced up our skates in silence, still sulky from our argument earlier.

As we entered the rink, Chris caught my elbow. 'I was being a jerk earlier. I'm sorry.'

He looked so earnest it was impossible to stay mad at him. 'Turn those puppy eyes away, Chris. You're forgiven.' I patted his cheek twice, then made for the rink. Behind me, Chris protested against my description of his eyes, but I ignored him and glided away.

It felt good to fall back into a familiar momentum, to hear our skates scratching against the ice and feel the cold air on my face. We were the only ones in the rink, but with Chris with me now, the silence didn't feel quite as hollow. Sometimes, all it took was one person to fill up the emptiness.

I spun and glided, leapt and skidded, feeling my muscles stretch into fullness as they eased into the motions.

Chris was also getting into the momentum, gliding in circles for practice. I skated over to him and gave him a nudge.

'Race you!'

He careered past me, smirking. 'I never lose!'

I sped up, lengthening my strides and kicking off harder, my body pressed low. We zigzagged in and out of each other's paths round and round the rink until Chris finally called over his shoulder, 'How do we know who wins if we don't set a finish line?'

'Does it matter?' I yelled back.

'It matters if the winner gets something. Or if the loser has to forfeit something.'

I slowed to a stop. 'A confession. The biggest, darkest one you've never told anyone. That's what you'll have to give up when you lose.'

He grinned. 'Well, then. You'd better start thinking.'

I kicked some ice on to his jeans in response before skating over to the double doors, flinging them open and cruising out into the night.

Outside, the ground had frosted over, and the chill from the rink followed us out the door. The world was now our skating rink, boundless and free for us to roam. A chill hung in the air, but within me sat a gentle warmth. A hush settled over us like a silk blanket, and the streets in the distance felt emptier than before. But the silence was no longer terrifying.

Laughter bubbled up in me, a strange, almost foreign sound. It had been a while since I had laughed like that.

Chris appeared next to me. 'What's so funny?'

'Nothing, I just love this dream.' I pointed at a faint orange speck in the distance, sitting against the wall of trees. 'See that spot of light over there?'

'Yeah?'

'That shall be our endpoint.' I dropped my hand. 'Remember our deal. Last one there dishes out a mind-blowing confession. Ready?'

A smile crept across his face. 'Go!'

We tore through the wind.

The world rushed by in a blur. There was only the sound of my skates slicing through ice and the blood rushing in my ears. This felt almost as magical as flying and just as intoxicating. I kept my gaze fixed on the orange glow in the distance, not sparing a backwards glance.

Only when the orange light—which turned out to be a lone streetlight that wasn't obscured by trees—finally loomed close did I look around for Chris.

But all that greeted me was an expanse of frosted ground and a row of trees in the distance. Far behind me was the skating rink, its neon lights illuminating the pavement.

Silence crept back in, bringing along its abject emptiness.

This felt painfully like the dream where I was chasing Night, where he was always just an inch beyond my grasp.

'Chris!' I called, only to have my voice tossed back at me. Several more tries yielded the same result. 'Dammit, Chris!'

This was the third time I was left in the wake of his impromptu disappearance, and frankly I'd had enough of it. The next time I saw him, he owed me more than a confession.

'Lexi!'

I whipped around in the direction of his voice.

He appeared no further than five feet away under a tree lit by a street lamp.

He raced towards me before I could do the same, and somewhere in the middle we collided into each other. I threw my arms around him and felt him stiffen. But before I could pull away, he wrapped an arm around my waist and pulled me close to him. I didn't know if he was catching me or hugging me, but I leaned into him anyway.

We stayed like this long enough to chase away the cold.

'Thought you'd pulled another disappearing act,' I said.

'I thought *you'd* left me here.' His voice sounded muffled in my hair.

'Of course not. I'm not the one who leaves every time, am I?'

'This is your dream,' he said. 'If you leave me here, I'll never be able to find my way back.'

'You can always wake up.'

He just shook his head like I wasn't getting it. But his presence had already altered the landscape here somehow. If he disappeared for good, it would be like abandoning me here, in a dream that no longer belonged to just me.

'By the way,' he said softly, 'you lost.'

I pulled away and looked up at him. His misty breaths came out in ghostly puffs. A tiny smile played at the corner of his lips.

'You cheated,' I protested.

'I won fair and square. You saw me at the endpoint.'

'That's because I was looking for you,' I said. 'That doesn't count.'

'Doesn't change the fact that I won. And now you owe me a confession.'

'Fine. But first, can we please get toasty?'

As soon as we kicked off our skates, the frost around us thawed and disappeared. In its place was just grass glistening with dew under the moonlight. The air turned balmier by the minute as we lay on our backs and gazed at the star-speckled sky.

I waited until every shard of cold had left my body before speaking. 'I admit that I'm a coward.' Chris gave me a sidelong look, ready to apologize, but I shushed him. 'This is my confession. I admit I'm hiding here so I don't have to go back to my mum.'

Chris folded an arm under his head. 'Well, that's obvious.'

'When I was younger, when I first learnt that she was sick, I used to be afraid of her. After the fire, she had these scars on the back of her hands. Burn scars.'

'What fire?'

I turned to and propped myself up on an elbow, looking him in the eye. 'I was eight years old when I almost burnt down our house. Eliza was at school and Dad was at work. Mum and I were the only ones at home. She got burnt trying to save me.'

He was silent, waiting.

'I thought I was in for it, that Mum was ruined and no one was ever going to forgive me. But not only was she not mad at me, she....' I couldn't find a way to describe the shift in our relationship.

'She what?' Chris asked.

I lay back down, buying some time to think. 'She sort of ... needed me more than before. I was the only one she wanted, the only one who could bring her back to us again, even though I barely did anything.' A small smile found its way to my lips. "Que Sera, Sera" always works. She said her mother used to sing that to her when she was a kid, and me humming it helped calm her anxiety.'

Chris was watching me intently when I looked at him again. He sat up. 'If this isn't reason enough for you to wake up, I don't know what is. She's waiting for you. She needs you.'

I turned away from him and plucked on a blade of grass. 'Maybe a small part of me is still afraid of her.'

I had never told anyone this. My confession came out shaky and quiet, but the words kept spilling out of me.

'It's been years since the accident, but it feels like we haven't quite moved on completely. Sometimes, I wish we could just lay it all out in the open—all our struggles and fears and doubts—instead of pretending everything is okay. Why is that so hard?'

'Because the fear multiplies when we give voice to it,' Chris said. 'Everyone's doing the best they can.'

'You keep saying that. Do you really believe that?'

He didn't reply. I turned around, expecting him to have fallen asleep. But he was gone, leaving me all alone in my dream again.

'Dammit, Chris,' I said softly.

Chapter 6

Chris

It was the buzzing on my bedside table that woke me up this time. I fumbled for my phone and checked the time. Three forty-five in the morning.

My chest felt tight, like I'd held my breath for too long. I sat up, wheezing like an asthmatic. The phone continued ringing. Hopewood. This could not be good.

'Hello?' My voice came out thin and raspy.

'Chris?' Manda's voice was just as tense. Someone was crying in the background. My heart pounded harder.

'Is she okay?' Stupid question. Would Mum's carer be calling me in the middle of the night if everything was okay?

'She had a nightmare and now she's crying for her family. It would really help if you and your father could come over and be with her for a bit. You know we don't want to sedate her unless we absolutely have to.'

'I'm on my way,' I said, already slipping into a shirt. I raced down the hallway to Dad's room, not bothering to knock.

Dad was asleep. A part of me felt guilty for waking him up. Maybe I should go to Hopewood alone and let him get some rest—

No. Mum needed us. Both of us.

'Dad.' I tapped his shoulder. 'Dad, wake up.'

He rolled over, murmured something.

'Dad,' I tried again. 'Hopewood called.'

'I know. They called me. It'll be okay in the morning—it always is. Go to sleep.' He turned back on his side.

My hand flopped back to my side. 'So you're not going?'

I had wondered before how many middle-of-the-night events like this it would take for Dad to finally stop making the trip down to Hopewood, but I never thought he would actually leave me to deal with this alone.

'She'll be fine,' Dad said, pulling the covers over him tighter. 'It's just a nightmare.'

I straightened up, trying to shake off the feeling of being deserted. Trying to shake off my bristling anger. Dad needed his rest, after all. This was not a big deal, nothing I couldn't handle on my own.

* * *

I was no stranger to an episode, having witnessed Mum go through it one too many times, sometimes in the middle of the night. This was, after all, the hour where we lay alone with our own thoughts. I could understand why Lexi would rather stay in the dream, where night-time came with none of those intrusive thoughts, only magic and whimsy.

Dad had upgraded Mum to a private room after the last episode, so the only people witnessing her breakdown this time were me, Manda, and Dr York.

Dr York was dressed in sweatpants and a T-shirt, which meant he had rushed here like I had. Manda had her arms around Mum and was rocking her back and forth gently. When she spotted me, Mum tore out of Manda's grasp and lunged towards me.

'Chris.' Her eyes were swollen and red, and tufts of hair stuck to her face. 'You'll take me home. Right, Chris?'

'It's all she keeps saying,' Manda said as I stroked Mum's hair and shushed her gently.

'Where's your father, Chris?' Dr York asked.

'He … he couldn't make it.'

Manda's brows shot up, disappearing behind her bangs. 'He couldn't make it?'

'He's busy. He's tired. I . . .' I didn't know how else to explain it, so I said instead, 'I'll handle this.'

Mum was still sniffling, but at least she had calmed down a little. I rubbed her back and apologized to Manda and Dr York. This scene felt like a repeat of the others that had come before it—the crying, the apologies, the hushed voices, Mum shaking in my arms—and a part of me was tired of it. I didn't want to be the one handling all this every time. But I couldn't afford to feel tired.

'Chris,' Dr York said. 'We need to talk. Will your father be available for a meeting in the morning? My office, ten o'clock?'

'I'll let him know.' I gestured at Mum. 'I'll take it from here.'

'Keep us updated,' Manda said before leaving with Dr York.

I nodded and turned to Mum. 'It's okay, Mum. I'm here. Get some sleep.'

'I love you so much, Chris,' she said as I helped her up.

'I know.'

'I'm sorry for all this. So sorry.'

'Shhh,' I said, reaching for a tissue from the bedside table to wipe away her tears. 'Come on, let's get you back to bed.'

I helped her back to bed and set the covers around her, then sat in the sofa and waited for her to go back to sleep.

Her voice came out tiny in the dark. 'Chris?'

'Yes, Mum?'

'Your father….'

'He was really tired. I thought I'd let him rest.'

She didn't reply. Her gusty breaths fell steady after a moment, and I let myself relax just a fraction.

I tried to get back to sleep, to return to the dream. I had left Lexi there all alone again, this time with her confession. Hopefully, she would spare me her wrath when I returned.

But I couldn't return to the dream. My sleep came in fits and starts, and I woke up just a couple of hours later. Real life was calling; the dream would have to wait.

* * *

'Mr Fang, it's been two years and ten months since you brought your wife here.'

Dr York's office was a direct copy of an interior design catalogue, from the cream-coloured leather sofa to the teak desk and bookshelf. Designed to comfort and assure yet doing anything but that. Being in here never boded well.

I took a sip of the tea Dr York offered, just to have something to do. Dad had brought me a change of clothes and I had freshened up in the guests' bathroom. He looked well-rested and composed, the opposite of Mum last night.

'We're concerned about her progress,' Dr York went on. 'Or rather, the lack of it.'

'I thought she's been doing well lately,' Dad said. 'Save for the occasional breakdown in the middle of the night, she's been doing well enough to earn those out-of-grounds privileges, no?'

Dr York frowned. 'No, actually.'

'But Chris told me….' He shot me a look.

'She calmed down pretty quickly. I didn't want to worry you,' I explained.

Dr York cut in. 'I called you here today to discuss how we can provide more attentive care for Mrs Fang.'

'She's staying in a health resort, with carers on 24/7 duty. How much more attentive can you get?'

'It's not simply the amount of attention, Mr Fang, but from whom the attention is received. We've had residents whose conditions improved immensely when they returned to a familiar environment.'

Dad frowned. 'I don't follow.'

'Home, Mr Fang.'

I stole a glance at Dad. His jaw started to tighten.

'If I knew what to do with her at home, would I have sent her here?' His voice was even, but that only meant he was more enraged. 'If I had any idea how to treat her problem, would I be sitting here talking to you?'

'I'm just saying,' Dr York replied coolly, 'that perhaps she isn't getting the attention she *prefers*. Yours, specifically.'

Dad folded his arms. 'Are you saying that I'm neglecting my wife?'

'I'm saying it might help to reassure her that she is not being abandoned here if you put up a more regular appearance.' He went on before Dad could work up a response. 'There are two options: in-house surveillance or monitored integration. I recommend the latter, but the choice lies with her immediate guardians.'

'What does either of them entail?' I asked.

'In-house surveillance means your mother will live at home with a personal carer who will provide a weekly report of her condition. Monitored integration means she will join external communities of her choice and expand her social circle, and we'll do a biweekly assessment of her progress.'

'So you're saying she needs to get out more. Meet people,' I said.

Dr York smiled. 'We believe in holistic, organic approaches at Hopewood, as you know. The most natural remedies sometimes work best.' He turned to me. 'Chris, what do you think?'

I chose my words with care. 'It'd be nice to see my mum more often.'

Dad leaned forward in his seat. He had his hands clasped before him and his elbows on his knees, the way he did when he was thinking hard. The silence in the room was deafening, and my tea wasn't helping much. Still, I took a sip. And another.

Dad unclasped his hands, and finally uttered the words I thought I would never hear him say.

'We'll take her home.'

* * *

Mum was still in shock even after we got home. It didn't take long for the paperwork to be completed and for her to pack her things, but by the time we arrived at our doorstep, sunlight was slanting in low through the windows. She didn't say much on the drive home, just listened to me and Dad talk about work like it was the most fascinating topic she had ever heard.

I was afraid Mum would start crying when she saw the house again, because I'd caught her eyes welling up from the rear-view mirror. She looked sated, if a little worn out, her eyes still puffy from all that crying last night.

While Dad unloaded the bags from the trunk, I went over to her and wrapped an arm around her shoulders. 'I hope those are happy tears,' I said.

'Of course they are.' She grasped my hand. 'This is a fresh start for all of us, Chris.'

I wasn't a superstitious person by any count, but declaring something as a fresh start was like begging for it to go wrong. For her sake, I kept my mouth shut.

With Mum's bags in hand, Dad stopped outside their bedroom, where he hardly slept these days, preferring to spend most nights in the study instead. 'You and Amanda can take the whole room. I'll sleep in the study. I figure you probably need some getting used to … being home.' He seemed almost unsure of himself, as though he needed a roadmap to navigate his relationship with Mum again. I had never seen this side of him before.

I stepped in. 'I'll help Mum settle in. Manda said she'll be coming tomorrow morning.'

Dad hesitated for a moment, glanced at Mum, then turned to me. 'Dinner tonight—all of us?'

I almost didn't want to say it. I didn't want to tell him about the gathering at Long Street. When was the last time we had a meal together as a family? And this time, Dad was the one proposing it. I wanted more than anything to have dinner with my parents again, just like old times. But work was work; I knew Dad would rather have me attend the Long Street gathering than have dinner as a family after so long.

'I have plans,' I said. 'At Long Street.'

Dad understood right away. He nodded. 'Go.'

'But you two could still have dinner together,' I suggested.

Dad glanced at Mum, who said, 'We don't have to if you don't want to. I know you're busy.'

As though on cue, Dad's phone rang before he could reply. He glanced at the screen. 'I have to take this. Go ahead without me,' he said before ducking into his room, phone pressed to his ear, already in business mode.

Mum watched the door to Dad's study slide close. I hated the look on her face.

I fired a quick text to Hayley telling her I would pick her up in half an hour, then gave Mum a nudge. 'Join us?'

She smiled and took my hand, then began to spin in gentle circles down the hallway. Dad got nervous whenever she behaved erratically—dancing one minute, crying the next—but I was happy to indulge her. I didn't shush her when she burst out laughing. After last night, it felt good to hear her laugh.

We waltzed into her room, where I helped her unpack. I put on some Beatles on my phone, and we belted along while unpacking. I felt a weight I hadn't realized I'd been carrying lifted off me, if only for a while. Despite her condition, Mum was the only person who could unknot the tension inside me.

Apart from Lexi.

My hands stilled as my thoughts drifted to her.

'Hey, Mum,' I said.

'Yes, dear?'

'Have you ever had dreams where you kept meeting the same person?'

Mum joined me on the bed, taking her toiletries bag from my hand. 'All the time,' she said softly.

I looked up at her. 'Really?'

'Of course. I dream about you and your father almost every night. Night-time is the worst. I miss you both so much sometimes I can hardly sleep.'

That would explain the eye bags she tried so hard to conceal.

'No, I mean someone you've never met before.'

She raised a brow. 'Someone like … that girl in your sketchbook?'

'How did you…?'

'Please. I'm your mother. Give me some credit. My son who never draws portraits is suddenly sketching a girl.' She peered at me. 'Did you really meet her in your dreams?'

'You don't think it's weird?'

She gave me a wry smile. 'Chris, I just came back from Hopewood. Nothing is too weird for me.'

On the drive to Bobby's, Mum appeared to be in a good mood, but I could tell she was a little disappointed even as she hummed along to Nirvana on the radio.

'I know you were hoping we could all have dinner together tonight,' I said.

She shook her head. 'I'm just happy to have your company.'

'Tell the truth, Mum. You're not even the slightest bit mad at him?'

'Mad? For what?'

'Oh, I don't know, for putting you in a "health resort" for almost three years, forgetting your anniversaries, and not making it for Friday night dinners because of work.'

'Your dad doesn't have to do anything special to show that he cares.'

'That's not anything special, that's the bare minimum.'

She just shook her head again, like I wasn't getting it. And I didn't. They were so different, almost polar opposites, that it seemed inconceivable they could have fallen for each other. Lexi, like Mum, was a free spirit. What if I was more like my dad than I thought?

Must. Stop. Thinking. About. Lexi. What did it matter if she was like Mum? She was just a girl I could only meet in my dreams.

Mum and Hayley went for each other like long-lost sisters and couldn't stop exchanging stories about me all the way until we reached Long Street. By then, Mum was already planning for our wedding.

'You do realize she's barely eighteen, Mum?' I said.

'Never too late to plan a wedding,' Mum said.

Hayley grinned. 'Words of the wise.'

I gave up on the two of them and navigated my way around the back alley parking lot. Long Street was plenty of things, but roomy was definitely not one of them. The street itself was no wider than ten feet, not counting the five-foot ways on either side, and the pavements were cluttered with handwritten signboards and vendor carts. Yet somehow, the clutter here felt comforting.

We made our way towards Maude's shop, one of the few shops still open, even though it was only seven o'clock. Apparently, Sunday night gatherings were a big deal at Long Street.

'Why are we here?' Mum asked. 'Everywhere is closed.'

'Remember that multiplex I told you about?' She nodded. 'This is the street Kingdom Heights is planning to develop into an F&B stretch.'

'Including the skating rink?' she asked, gesturing at the building behind the parking lot.

I had never paid much attention to the skating rink since it was in the other wing of proposed multiplex and not under my purview. But now that I took a good look at it, it looked exactly like the skating rink from the dream Lexi and I shared. I stared at the sliding glass doors, half-expecting her to burst through them on her skates, her wild hair flying behind her.

'Chris?' Mum said. She and Hayley were peering at me, and I realized a smile had crept up my face.

I dropped it right away. 'I just thought it might help to come here and play nice with the locals.'

'Chris!' Maude cried when she spotted us. 'You came!'

'I hope we're not imposing,' I said.

She waved a dismissive hand. 'Of course not. You may be Gerald Fang's son, but tonight you're all friends of mine.'

After getting introductions out of the way, we waited for Maude to close her shop, then followed her to the Welcome Inn. She kept up a steady stream of pleasantries and small talk, which Mum was happy to engage in.

Generosity was something I was wary of, and something Dad was always leery of. No one, according to Dad, could possibly want nothing in return for something they gave. The world existed on a balance between give and take, profits and losses. The fact that Maude would welcome us so easily into Long Street meant, to Dad, that she had an agenda in mind.

Wow, what a cynic, Lexi would have scoffed.

Must. Stop. Thinking. About. Lexi.

We had arrived at the Welcome Inn by the time I managed to pull myself out of my head. Something about the inn looked forlorn, like a wistful gaze on the glory days. Dad would be doing them a favour—what we offered had to be worth way more than the inn. It was a good deal, despite what Bobby said.

Maude looked a little nervous as she ushered us into the lift. 'Just go easy on Charlie, okay?' she said as the lift doors slid open. 'He might get a little cranky, but it's nothing personal.'

'I bet she regrets inviting us now,' Hayley whispered in my ear. I shot her a look.

Maude sighed. 'But I guess I would be too if my spouse is sick and my daughter just got into a car accident.'

'That's terrible,' Mum said.

The panic bell inside my head went off. Some days, it didn't take much to send Mum into an emotional trough, and she had been overwhelmed by enough feelings lately. I squeezed her hand, willing her not to start crying. *Not tonight, please.* She squeezed back like she could hear my plea.

We stepped out into the rooftop garden, a cosy space no bigger than my living room, with an al fresco bar overlooking the street. Fairy lights strung around the periphery lit up the entire area. The barbeque was already under way, if the aroma was anything to go by. There were about twenty people present, and we were the last few to arrive.

'Everyone,' Maude announced, 'this is Chris and his mother, Clare, and his friend Hayley. I thought I'd invite them over tonight.'

Most of them waved and said hi, but one voice piped up. 'Chris? Christopher Fang?'

At that, the chatter died down. Charlie stepped to the front, a spatula in his hand. If he came after me with that, I hoped Dad got his multiplex in the end.

He came up to me and levelled me with a stare. 'Here to get me to sell this place?'

'No, sir,' I said, looking him in the eye. 'Just here to—make friends.' The words fell awkwardly off my tongue. I raised the two bottles of wine I had thought to bring. 'Red wine?'

'Friends.' He snorted. 'You can tell your father this inn will last longer than that company of his,' he said, then went back to the grill.

'Charlie,' Maude said. 'These are my guests tonight. Be nice.'

As Maude sat Mum and Hayley down and went to get food for them, a girl slightly older than me edged her way through the crowd towards me. People were already starting to keep a wider berth from me, which made me notice her long before she sat herself next to me. She had eyes that reminded me of Lexi, except that Lexi's were brighter and rounder. And unlike Lexi, who wore her hair loose, this girl had hers tied up in a messy bun.

Must. Stop. Thinking. About. Lexi.

'Sorry about my dad,' she said, offering me a plate of meatballs.

'That's okay. I'm just glad he didn't chase me away with that spatula.'

She cracked a smile. 'I'm Eliza.'

'Chris. But you already knew that.'

I watched as Anitha engaged a group of ladies in conversation, including Maude, Mum, and Hayley, while Ben tried to balance four cups of beer before handing them to a group of men. A few of them went up to Charlie, but Charlie only nodded or paid them no attention as he tended to the grill absently.

I had been to my share of social functions, but none of them was anything like this. Dad had never allowed me to attend school functions or class gatherings, calling them a 'pointless waste of time'. I had other things to do anyway, like study the terms of an acquisition contract or follow Dad to board meetings and observe how he presented to trustees and stakeholders, learn the ropes of managing a business like Kingdom Heights. I had no time for friends. 'Friends,' Dad once said, 'only have your back if you can give them what they need—and sometimes not even then. Family, though, family you can always trust.'

But being here tonight, even with an awkward introduction, I felt a terrible urge to cross that line, the one that had always separated me from everyone else. To stick my head out from behind the door that had long shut me inside my tiny world. To try, just for one night, to connect with people other than those my father introduced to me.

Eliza was watching me as she chewed on a meatball.

'What?' I said.

She shook her head. 'You could not look more out of place if you tried.'

Had she heard my thoughts?

I ignored her remark and gestured around us. 'So this seems to be quite the big deal. You guys go to town with carcinogenic food every week?'

She rolled her eyes at me. 'If you must know, we usually do potluck nights.' She glanced around. 'Dad didn't want to do it this week. Said he'd rather be at the hospital with my sister. To be honest, none of us wanted to.'

'So why do it?'

'Routine is what my mum needs,' she said. 'The folks here want to give her a sense of normality.'

'I heard about your mother. I'm sorry.'

'See that woman over there?' She nodded at a willowy woman sitting in a far corner, placidly munching on a sausage as she watched Charlie at the grill.

'Yeah?'

'That's her. These gatherings mean more to her than it looks. Besides,' she added, tossing me a sidelong—almost accusatory—look, 'better do it while we still can, right?' A beat. 'You're probably wondering why we're still holding on to this inn. Why not join half the occupants of Long Street and give up the space?'

'Our offer is pretty generous, if you think about it,' I said. 'Even if you're not a fan of the new location, the amount we offer as an alternative is enough for you to buy another plot of land to rebuild your inn. It's not like we're the bad guys out to rob you here.'

'To my dad, anyone who tries to take this inn away from him or chase him out of it'—she shrugged—'is bad.'

'I don't get it. It's just a building. Shouldn't what's inside matter more than the location?'

She considered me. 'You know, you kind of remind me of my sister. She said the same thing once. That a building is just a building without the people in it. But this street is where my parents first met, so this inn being here means everything to them. Dad thinks keeping the inn here will always remind Mum of her life before the fire.' She gestured at the scene before us. 'This all started when Mum got sick a few years ago. The neighbours decided to organize weekly gatherings for her, hoping some company will do her some good.'

'Doesn't seem to be working.'

'Most of the time, it does. Really. But after what happened to Lexi, she seems to have gotten worse.'

At her name, I gasped so hard that I choked on my food. Eliza thumped me on the back as I coughed, until I held up a hand to tell her I was okay.

'Lexi?' I rasped once I had gotten over my fit.

Eliza handed me my glass of wine. 'Yeah, Lexi. My sister. Are you okay?'

No. It *couldn't* be.

Except … didn't Lexi mention her sister too? Could it be Eliza?

I stared at the Eliza before me, who was in turn peering at me with her brows creased.

'Lexi's your sister,' I said, letting the reality sink in. Lexi, the girl from my dreams, the one who flew and danced on ice. 'Lexi is your sister.'

'You know her?' Eliza asked, her frown deepening. 'Lexi never mentioned you. I didn't know she had friends outside of Long Street.'

Lexi, a recluse. Who would have guessed? 'We are … acquainted,' I said.

'How?'

I scrambled for a convincing answer. 'Night,' I blurted.

'You know about his paintings, too? Lexi is obsessed with that artist.'

I made a gesture that could be interpreted as a nod or a shrug. 'Eliza,' I said, fidgeting with my fork. When I looked up at her, she was watching me with her brows raised. 'Can you take me to see Lexi?'

Dear Night,

There are times when all the magic in the world seems possible—in dreams, in a story, in a painting, in the hour between night and day when the light at the corners of the world appears the softest. I call them the soft hours, the ones that you cling to long after you wake up.

Your art is the soft hour I can't seem to pull myself out of. My sister thinks I'm obsessed, and maybe I am. Maybe you're the magic I desperately want to believe in, the cure to reality. Some days, my loneliness lives inside me like a disease. And when I look at your art, I feel like you're sitting next to me, as though to say, I know. I'm here too.

No one gets what I mean. But I feel like you're someone who not only understands what I mean by soft hours, but who looks for it too, and tries to preserve it on your canvas.

Maybe I'm the loner girl who dreams too much and can't live with my feet on the ground. After all, the kids at school use to call me and Eliza 'the girls with the weird mother'. They would laugh at us when we were younger and whisper behind our backs when we got older.

Once, Eliza marched up to the girls who whispered about us with a pair of scissors in hand. 'Then I guess weird runs in the family,' she said before grabbing a handful of one of the girl's hair and snipping it off. Dad sure had his hands full with her.

Maybe Eliza had taken all the bravery and left none for me. All I did was dream of another world, another life, my old life. The one before the fire. Or a new one, where I find you and we walk towards that light at the farthest corner of the world.

In your paintings, strange is the official language. In your paintings, strange isn't met with whispers behind your back, slanted glances, or pointed fingers. In your paintings, that's where I can live forever in those soft hours.

Strangely yours,
Lexi

Chapter 7

Lexi

I stood before the gates to the Wild Ride amusement park, no longer wondering how I got here or how the mechanics of this never-ending dream worked anymore. The gates weren't as imposing as I remembered, although the sight of the carnival lights against the sky, the bear mascot, and the ticket counters at the entrance still sent a zing of excitement through me like I was a kid again.

Chris appeared just as I was about to enter, staring at the *Help Wanted!* sign flapping in the breeze on the notice board.

'Hello again.' I pointed at the sign. 'You should try out for the mascot. I'm sure you'll look very adorable in a bear costume.'

He didn't reply, just stared at me with his brows furrowed.

'What's wrong?' I asked.

'Your sister told me what happened to you.'

'My sister? Eliza?'

'Unless you have another sister, I'd say that's the one,' he said.

'How did you—I don't—wait, *what?*'

'Long story short, you were in a car accident. And now you're lying in the hospital in a coma. It's been five days.'

I stared at him for a long while. 'Sure. And you're the reaper who's come to collect my soul.'

He rolled his eyes. 'I'm being serious, Lexi. You don't remember the accident at all?'

I shook my head.

'What's the last thing you remember before appearing on that road?'

Memories came back scattered—a flash of light here, a voice there. 'I was picking up some stuff from the pharmacy for Mum. It was late evening, and I was two streets away from Long Street. And then I was just there on the empty road where you found me.'

'And you never wondered how and why that happened?'

'I was just glad I didn't have to go back so soon, okay?' I snapped. 'Who knew I'd be here this long?'

He said nothing.

I nodded at him. 'Now, your turn. You said you talked to Eliza. How'd you know who she was?'

'I didn't, until I met her at the gathering. At the Welcome Inn.'

A snort escaped me. 'What were you doing at our Long Street gathering? Thought your dad couldn't wait to get rid of us.'

'Don't change the topic.'

'You were there as a spy, weren't you? Find out what offers we've been receiving from other companies so you can buy us over?'

'No. Lexi, focus. I'm trying to help you remember.'

'Why?'

'Because the sooner we can make sense of this, the sooner our lives can go back to normal.'

'Normal is overrated.'

'Not if it means having a regular sleep cycle.'

'So … you don't have enough sleep because you're dreaming too much?'

His expression was wry. 'Yes.'

'So what do you want me to do? I'm not a sleep therapist.'

'I want you to wake up. Didn't you say this was your dream? If you wake up, we'll stop meeting here, then I can sleep in peace and you can go back to your family.'

'You said I'm lying in the hospital?'

He nodded. 'Eliza's agreed to bring me there. I'll visit you in the morning.'

'Great. I look forward to it, then.' I reached for his hand. 'Now. Candy floss and Ferris wheel time.'

He resisted when I gave his hand a tug. 'Seriously?'

'Look,' I said. 'We're not going to solve anything right now. I couldn't wake up even if I wanted to—I don't know how. So let's just have some fun here for one more night, okay? Humour me.'

He shook his head. 'You go ahead. This is not really my thing.'

'How can amusement parks not be anyone's thing?'

'My dad doesn't believe in commercialized thrill.'

'That's rich coming from someone whose family is in the business of creating these sites of commercialized thrill.'

'I handle the real estate logistics, not marketing.' He brushed the flapping *Help Wanted!* sign away from his face. 'And even though I have access to those places, I don't have time for them.'

'That is just sad. So you've never had an amusement park experience?'

He shook his head, frowning when my pitying look deepened. 'It's not a big deal.'

'Of course it's a big deal. What did you spend your childhood doing? Tracking the stock market? Counting money?'

He cast me a sidelong glance. 'Something more productive than sleeping.'

'Touché.' I linked my arm with his. 'Well, my friend, let this be an education in having fun.'

* * *

We went on each of the rides at least thrice, sharing two sticks of candy floss and a huge cup of strawberry yoghurt smoothie in between—until all that was left was the Ferris wheel. The last time I'd been on one, a broken nose was involved. But I was willing to give it another go now that I had different company.

'I never got the point of a Ferris wheel,' Chris said as I dragged him towards it. 'What's so fun about being trapped inside a glass box that spins at the speed of death on the same spot? At least the roller coaster goes somewhere.'

I shoved him into the capsule in front of us. 'You must be fun at parties.'

'No time for those either,' he muttered.

Like all the rides, which came to life once Chris and I were strapped in, the Ferris wheel shifted into motion after I shut the capsule door.

'That's the sound of the gates of hell closing,' Chris said.

'Don't be a drama queen.'

He leaned back in his seat and didn't offer any more smartass comments.

'I love Ferris wheels,' I said, staring out the window. 'The world feels like it's moving right below you, and you feel like if you stood on your tiptoes you could reach the sky. My last ride was awful, but at least I have better company this time.'

That got his attention. 'What happened on your last ride?'

'Bad date. He zoomed in for the kill before I was ready and slobbered all over me. I accidentally broke his nose while pushing him away.'

'Good move.'

'I bet Night wouldn't do something as predictable and low as that. There would be no leering or slobbering, and I wouldn't be compelled to break his nose. Instead, we'd lie on our backs and pretend we have the sky at our fingertips.'

When I turned to him, Chris was watching me with an odd look. I decided that if he kissed me then, I wouldn't pull away or break his nose. But all he did was get up from the seat and lie on the floor of the capsule, facing the sky.

I stared at him. 'What are you doing?'

'Being Night for five minutes. Are you getting down here or not? Because I'm starting to feel like an idiot.'

I grinned and lay down next to him.

On the ground, the rocking of the capsule felt stronger, like an adult-sized cradle. When we reached the peak, I stretched out my hand above me. He glanced at me askance, then did the same without saying a word.

'Admit it,' I said, nudging him. 'Deep down, you like being Night, don't you?'

He didn't reply.

'I bet he loves Ferris wheels too.'

A snort.

'What's it like being Gerald Fang Junior? Is your life really as miserable as it sounds?'

He rolled his eyes. 'Thank you, but my life is not miserable. At least I don't spend my time digging through back alleys and old cardboard boxes for a bunch of worthless paintings by someone I've never met.'

'See, this is where you and Night are different. He sees the magic in everything, while you only see the purpose.'

He turned to me and raised his brows. 'You don't think I can be Night?'

The thought made me laugh. 'You? Night? I don't think so. I mean, where would you find the time to paint?'

'I could paint late at night. Or in that hour just before sunrise, when the light is the softest and your heartbeat is all you hear.'

The ground shifted beneath me as the Ferris wheel dipped. My breath caught. He was the first person I had ever met who talked about that soft hour before dawn. Other than Night, I didn't think there might be anyone else who would understand.

Chris laughed at the look on my face. 'See? Told you I could be Night. Just spout a bunch of crap like that and anyone can be Night.'

I scowled. 'Do *not* make fun of Night.'

'Don't hold your breath for him, is all I'm saying. You know what they say about putting all your eggs in one basket.'

'Night deserves all of my eggs.' Wait. What was I saying?

Chris chortled, then pursed his lips together at the look on my face. I tried to salvage the remnants of my dignity and directed my attention back to the sky.

Chris sat up and rested his elbow on his knee. 'Now that I've done the one thing I've never tried, it's your turn.'

I remained where I was. 'What do you mean?'

'Fair's fair. I stepped into an amusement park; I'm even on a Ferris wheel. What's *your* poison?'

There was one painting of Night's that I found—the only one I couldn't relate to—of a boy cutting through the deep blue water, heading towards a waterfall splashing against the gilded horizon.

Before I could decide whether to tell Chris about it, the air rushed past us. And then we were no longer in the Ferris wheel capsule. Instead of the star-dappled sky overhead, giant spotlights glared down at me. Cold metal pressed against my back.

I scrambled to get up, almost tripping on the bleachers. The smell of chlorine hit me, along with the sight of bright blue water rippling before me.

'Oh,' I muttered. 'No….'

Next to me, Chris quirked his lips. 'You can't swim?'

'Yeah, keep laughing. You weren't so cocky when we were flying.'

'You're the one who fell,' he pointed out.

'Are you begging for a broken nose?'

He held out a placatory hand but didn't drop his smirk.

'The pool's closed.' I pointed at the sign hung on the railing next to the pool. 'Today's not our lucky day, I guess.' I scurried down the bleachers towards the exit.

'Oh yes, it is,' Chris said, steering me towards the pool.

'We're trespassing.'

'So? We've already stolen bread. What's trespassing on an empty natatorium?'

'Look at you, rebel without a cause now.'

'Fair's fair,' he said again.

'Fair is the place we just came from.'

'Yeah, the one you dragged me to. If we're going to be stuck in the same dream, the least we can do is make good use of it. Swimming is a very important skill.'

'Which I won't be able to use in real life, since, according to you, I'm in a coma. Some other day, Chris.'

'But you're already dressed for the occasion,' he said, gesturing at my outfit.

I looked down to find myself in a swimsuit indeed, a navy-blue one-piece Dad had bought for me in the hopes of one day teaching me how to swim. But after Mum got sick, everything fell by the wayside.

'Trust me,' Chris said. He was dressed in just a pair of swimming trunks now, revealing his lean, well-muscled body. I turned to face the water so he couldn't see me blush.

'Jump in,' he said from behind me. 'You'll be fine.'

I took a deep breath and crashed into the water with a scream. As I burst back through the surface, Chris splashed in next to me with significantly more aplomb.

'It's cold!' I cried, gasping and slipping under again.

Chris took my hand and led me over to the wall. I clung on for dear life. 'Let's start with the basics.'

'Now? Here?'

He shrugged. 'Where else? If I can't teach you how to swim, I'm going to at least make sure you don't drown.'

Chapter 8

Chris

Someone was shaking me awake.

If only I could wake up when I chose to, instead of being interrupted every time. But would I choose to wake up any more, given the choice? Life was much easier—happier—in the dream. I was starting to see what Lexi meant by escape.

I cracked open my eyes; the person before me came into focus. 'Mum,' I murmured.

Breathing got more difficult when I woke up these days. My chest felt like it was caving in on itself. I sat up in bed, a little lightheaded, and reached to turn on the bedside lamp. The alarm clock read 3.05 a.m., and it was still dark outside.

She smoothed the hair off my face. Cool air settled on my sweaty forehead. 'Were you having a nightmare?' she asked.

'No. I was having a pretty good dream, actually. Why are you up?'

'Well, your body doesn't seem to agree with you.' She peered at my face. 'I thought you were dead. You were definitely not breathing just now.'

Hayley said the same thing the last time. Was this something I should be worried about? There were cures for sleep apnoea or whatever this was, weren't there?

'I'm fine, Mum.'

'It's that girl, isn't it?' Mum said.

Should I be relieved or worried that my mother believed in Lexi's existence as much as I did, even though she had never met her? But how could I explain to her everything that had happened this past week? None of this made any sense.

'Mum, why are you awake?' I asked instead.

She sat down on my bed, chewing her lip. 'Can you help me?'

'With what? What's going on?'

A smile broke upon her face. 'I want to make breakfast for your father.'

'Mum, it's three in the morning.'

'It's just … I'm finally back after so long, I just want to do something nice for him. Prove to him I'm completely well, that things will only get better from here.' Her wide eyes shone with desperate hope.

'No offence, Mum, but making him breakfast at three in the morning is not going to prove to him that you're completely well. Why don't you go back to bed now, and we'll talk about breakfast in a few hours?'

I didn't want to tell her that Dad and I didn't have a habit of having breakfast at the table. Most of the time, Dad wolfed down whatever his secretary bought for him at his desk.

'Okay,' she said after considering my proposal. 'Can I sleep here tonight?' She lay down on the other side of my bed. 'Maybe it's because I've been in Hopewood for too long. I can't get used to the bedroom again.' Neither of us mentioned that she was sleeping in their bedroom alone. 'Besides, I should make sure you don't die in your sleep.'

I rolled my eyes and pulled the covers over her.

* * *

I didn't get to return to Lexi after that. Mum made sure I didn't sink too deep into my dreams, shifting in bed whenever I drifted off, which meant that she slept lightly too. At seven o'clock sharp, she sat up in bed and shook me awake.

'Breakfast time!' she chirped.

There were no proper breakfast options in the kitchen, save for a jar of raspberry jam a business partner had sent from Germany and an emergency bag of bagels.

I closed the refrigerator. 'You know what they say about the best-laid plans, Mum. Let's just order in breakfast.'

Her face fell. 'Oh, that's right. I forgot you work on weekends too.' She looked up at me sharply. 'And about that sleep thing, I'm scheduling a doctor's appointment for you.'

'Mum, really. I'm sure it's nothing.'

Dad came downstairs, dressed and ready to head out, just as Manda arrived.

'I was going to make us all some breakfast,' Mum said, her voice painfully bright.

Dad stared at her, measuring his words. 'But we don't eat breakfast at home.'

Manda glanced at Mum, whose hopeful gaze was starting to falter, and told him, 'Well, now you do.'

* * *

'Christopher. *Christopher.*' Dad stood at the doorway of my office. 'I hope the project is what's on your mind.'

'What's up, Dad?'

'Your mother called to ask if you want to have lunch together.'

I checked my cell phone on the desk but didn't find any text or phone call from Mum asking about lunch. It was odd because I had already told her that I'd be visiting Lexi at the hospital today on my lunch break. Besides, if she was going to ask us out for lunch, she would have asked me first.

'I'm meeting a—friend for lunch,' I said.

Dad frowned. 'Who?'

I couldn't blame him for being suspicious. Aside from Hayley and Bobby, I had never had lunch with any friend. Eliza wasn't even really a friend. I didn't know what to call her—an acquaintance, maybe? What I did know was that we both cared about the same person.

'Just a friend from school,' I said. 'We thought we'd catch up for a bit.'

Dad made to say something but settled for a conclusive nod before leaving. Later, when I passed by his office on my way out, I found him munching on a sandwich his secretary had most likely got him. I ducked out of sight, my guilt weighing on my chest, and made my way to Long Street.

Eliza was already waiting for me at the front steps of the inn when I arrived. She pushed her sunglasses up her head and got to her feet as soon as she spotted me.

'Before I take you to see her, I think you owe me some answers,' she said, dispensing with the pleasantries.

'Fair enough.'

'Let's talk inside.' She turned and led me into the inn, then out the sliding screen doors to the backyard, where wrought-iron tables and chairs, along with a large trash bag filled with banners, party streamers, and bunting lay strewn around.

Eliza followed my gaze. 'Some guests organized a birthday party here a couple of days ago.' She gestured at one of the chairs under a faded yellow umbrella. 'Have a seat.'

I sat. 'What do you want to know?'

'You said you knew Lexi through Night?'

'I—came across his paintings. So did Lexi. She took the paintings, even though they're not really for the taking.' I barrelled on before I could change my mind. 'And lately … I've been seeing her in my dreams.'

She raised her brows. 'Excuse me?'

There was no going back now. 'I don't know how this is happening. But I've been meeting her in my dreams since the accident.'

Eliza stared at me for a long moment. 'Uh huh.' She was probably already regretting this meeting.

A third voice came. 'You've seen Lexi? You've seen my daughter?'

Eliza and I spun around in our seats. Lexi's mum stood leaning against the door frame, her forlorn gaze fixed on me.

'Mum.' Eliza hurried over to her. 'This is Chris. He was at the gathering last night.'

'I know,' she said, her attention still pinned on me. 'You said you saw Lexi? My daughter Lexi?'

'Mum. Lexi's in the hospital,' Eliza said gently.

'But he just said—'

'Eliza?' called another voice.

Charlie. Not good. The last thing he needed to know that I was acquainted with Lexi, or that I was seeing her in my dreams—if he'd even believe that.

His gaze volleyed between his wife and Eliza. 'What's going on?'

Lexi's mum pointed at me. 'He says he's seen Lexi.'

Charlie turned to me and folded his arms. 'Christopher Fang.' His tone was stern, almost challenging. 'What are you doing here, besides upsetting my wife?'

'I….'

I could lay out an entire proposal to a packed boardroom *and* defend it against any detractors. But now I couldn't find the words—*any* word—to explain this phenomenon. Probably because they all sounded ludicrous, even though I knew now that it wasn't just a dream.

Eliza rested a hand on Charlie's shoulder. 'Chris is a friend of Lexi's, Dad.'

'A friend of Lexi? How did they even know each other?'

'I'll explain more when I get back, but Chris and I are late for a lunch reservation.' She nodded at me as Charlie continued with his questions. 'Let's go, Chris.'

Eliza and I didn't exchange a word until we slid into my car parked at the back. She nodded at the bouquet of pink gerberas in the backseat. 'Those are for Lexi?'

'I didn't know what kind of flowers she liked, so....'

'Those are her favourite, actually.'

A smile crept up my face, as though my heart was in bloom. 'Good.' I pulled out of the parking lot. Eliza kept her gaze out of the window while I drove. 'I see your dad's impression of me hasn't improved.'

'It takes a lot for him to warm up to someone. Lexi's a lot like him, actually.'

'Really?' Not the Lexi I know, then. 'Lexi said she's closer to her mum.'

She narrowed her eyes at me. 'Look, I don't know what your relationship with Lexi is. For all I know—'

'For all you know, this is just a ploy to persuade you to sell the inn?' I finished, sending her a sidelong glance.

She pursed her lips. 'So you admit that's what you're doing?'

'Look, Eliza. I appreciate you taking me to see Lexi. But what she and I share has nothing to do with my work.'

'What she and you share,' she echoed. 'What *do* the two of you share?'

What *was* it we shared? Friendship, yes. That's what it was.

'Friendship,' I said.

Eliza made a scoffing noise. 'Friendship. Christopher Fang talking about friendship?'

I turned to her when we reached a stoplight. She seemed completely different from the person I had spoken with last night.

While she had been merely wary during the rooftop gathering, now she was downright mistrustful of me.

'Don't look so surprised, Chris. I did some checking up on you.' She levelled a stare at me. 'So tell me, what kind of special friendship do you share with my sister?'

One that even I didn't understand. I didn't know why I looked forward to returning to the dream every night, except that whenever I was with Lexi, I felt calm and excited, peaceful and restless all at once. When I was with her, I felt the same way I did when I was painting. Free.

I didn't realize I had said all that out loud until I noticed Eliza regarding me with a frown. 'You mean to say,' she said slowly, 'that you really met Lexi. In your dreams. Spoke to her.'

'I know it doesn't make any sense, but yes.'

A wry smile. 'Stranger things happen every day.'

At the hospital, Eliza led the way to Lexi's ward in the east wing. This part of the hospital was significantly quieter than the others, almost as though it had been forgotten. Remote or private, depending on how you looked at it, just like the colour white was a combination of every colour there was or the rejection of it. So much of art, like everything else, came down to perspective.

Eliza pushed open the door and gestured for me to enter. I stepped in, and there she was. The girl from my dreams.

Only, she wasn't. Not quite.

The Lexi I knew wasn't this still, sleeping girl, so sapped of life, pinned to a bed in a room with stark white walls. In my dreams, Lexi was filled with every colour imaginable. She was always on the move, whizzing around so quickly that she left trails of starbursts behind her. There, she was alive, larger than life. But here she looked so small, as though she was drowning in that bed.

My feet felt leaden as I walked towards her. My hands itched to spill colour on the walls. Lexi would hate it too. I stared hard at the one sleeping before me, half-expecting her to wrinkle her nose at the bare walls.

What was she doing now? Was she still in that pool, learning to breathe? I had left her there last night, just after she had gotten the hang of breathing techniques and synchronizing her movements.

Or, was she somewhere else now, living out some other scene in Night's—*my*—paintings, wishing for Night to appear and be the answer to everything?

I could feel Eliza watching me, even though she hung back and let me take the seat next to Lexi's bed. 'How … how is she? In the dream?' she asked.

I thought of how best to describe her. Every adjective I knew seemed to fall short when it came to Lexi. 'Free. Happy. Able to talk someone's ear off. Impossibly persistent. Funny.'

Her brows rose. 'Really?'

I nodded.

She stared at Lexi's sleeping face, a million emotions crisscrossing her face. She looked like she was about to cry, but no longer had the energy to do so. 'She'd probably rather be in there than here then. I know I would.' A sigh. 'Truth is, we're all tired. Tired of not knowing how to help Mum get better. Tired of holding on to an inn we know is not going to bring in the dough for much longer. Tired of hoping and trying and waiting and failing.' She shot me a wry smile. 'Sorry, I'm not usually like this. But you become all doom and gloom the older you get. I'll, uh, leave you with her for a while.'

I nodded. She backed away from the bed, and I waited until I heard the click of the door behind her before taking Lexi's hand. It was as soft as I remembered, though not as warm and slightly dry.

'Hi,' I said, feeling like an idiot. The only response came from the beeping monitor. My phone buzzed in my pocket before I could say anything else. Mum.

'Chris,' she said as soon as I picked up. 'Where are you?'

'I'm in the hospital. Eliza brought me to see Lexi, remember? Thought I told you last night.'

'Yeah, you did.'

'So why'd you ask us out for lunch? If you want to have lunch with Dad, you should just tell him—'

'I didn't ask you out for lunch,' she said.

I stopped. 'But Dad said you called to ask if we wanted to have lunch together.'

'No, I didn't.'

'So it wasn't you who asked to have lunch together with Dad?'

'No.' She sounded as perplexed as I was. 'I'm having lunch with Mandy and her sister now.'

So that meant … Dad was the one who wanted us to have lunch together? Could it be that the one time Dad initiated having a meal as a family, both Mum and I had other plans?

'By the way, I've scheduled an appointment with Dr York for you. Meet me at Hopewood after lunch.'

'Mum….'

'Mandy's sister's father-in-law has the same symptoms as you, and he almost died in his sleep. I'd rather be paranoid than lose my only child. You're going, no arguments.' She hung up.

I stared at Lexi. Whatever else I wanted to say to her would have to wait.

Chapter 9

Lexi

'We need to fix an alarm or something on you,' I said as Chris stalked down the beach towards me this time. 'In case you disappear without warning again. You can't leave a girl hanging like that. It's just not good manners.'

He didn't even crack a smile at my joke. Granted, he had a pretty much non-existent sense of humour, but this was too grave, even for Chris.

'Another long day?' I guessed.

'You're in a phone booth,' he pointed out. 'On a beach.'

'Like you said, Night paints some weird stuff,' I said with a shrug. This was a scene out of another of his paintings, one that I still couldn't fathom. What was he thinking when he painted this? Why a phone booth? Why was it by the sea?

But even as I asked those questions, Chris just continued staring at me. The wind tousled his hair as the waves rolled behind him. I stepped out of the phone booth and sat down on the sand.

'Well, don't just stand there,' I said, patting the space next to me.

He took his place next to me. 'Lexi. Why are you here?'

'I told you, we're in Night's paintings.'

'No, I mean why are you still here? Aren't you ever going to wake up?'

'Are we talking about this again? I told you, I don't know how to wake up even if I wanted to. It's not as easy as opening your eyes. Besides, I like it here. That's all that matters.'

'Is that really all that matters? It doesn't matter that you've been asleep for as many nights as I've met you? Or that your family's out there worried sick about you?'

I frowned. 'What's your point, Chris? That I'm running away? Because I'm not the only one who doesn't want to leave. You're coming back every night too, aren't you?'

He shook his head. 'This isn't about me.'

'Do you hate it here that much? I think it's a lovely place.'

'It's also a lonely place, and you know it. I get that you'd rather *hide* here—'

'Antagonism, Chris? Doesn't work on me.'

'I'm not trying to antagonize you. I'm telling you that right now, you are lying in a hospital bed and your family is falling apart without you.'

'Stop it,' I snapped.

This was everything I was trying to avoid. I didn't want to be reminded of it here, especially by someone who knew nothing about my family. This was the only place where I didn't have to feel guilty or afraid or sad—

The world started spinning, the edges darkening. Before us, the sea roiled and roared and crashed as the wind screamed in my ears. I tried to pick myself up but tumbled to the ground before I could get to my feet. Chris leapt up and picked me up.

'Lexi?' His hands cupped my face. I tried to focus on his eyes, but his face was blurry. 'Lexi, what's wrong?'

Maybe the sea breeze was getting to my head.

But then I wasn't at the beach any more. The world was now dark and still. I was prone, immobilized. The air smelt like antiseptic. It was quiet, save for a slow and steady beeping noise next to me. One beep. Two beeps. Three—

'Lexi!' Chris yelled.

And then I was back on the beach again. Cold sand between my toes, wind threading through my hair. The sea had subsided to a rustle. Chris hovered above me, peering down at my face.

I blinked. Chris helped me sit up and held me against his warm, firm body. 'What happened?'

'You just … disappeared,' he said, frowning in confusion.

Where had I gone? The beeping, the darkness, the smell…. It had to be the hospital.

'You said I'm in a coma?' My voice came out shaky and small. 'I'm in a hospital?'

He nodded, reaching for my hand. I grasped it gratefully, keeping my head down and my eyes closed. The night suddenly seemed big enough to swallow us whole. Just three seconds of being awake was already terrifying. I wanted more than anything to stay in this dream bubble, in the comfort of Night's paintings. But how could I continue to leave Mum and Dad and Eliza—and everyone on Long Street—hanging?

My breath caught in my throat at the thought of them.

'Lexi.'

I opened my eyes to find Chris peering at me.

'Take a deep breath,' he suggested. I drew a deep, shaky breath. 'Good. Now one more.' I inhaled again, drinking in the cool, salty air. Then twice more for good measure. 'Better?'

I nodded. 'Thank you.'

'Wow, she *can* be polite. Who knew?' He laughed when I rolled my eyes. It wasn't a sound you heard very often.

'And he *can* laugh. Who knew?' I said.

A beat passed between us. I was suddenly aware of his arms wrapped around me, the heat of his breath against my skin.

'So what was that about?' he asked, breaking the moment.

I poked the crease between his brows and told him everything I had just experienced. His frown deepened until I was done talking.

'So you can hear what's going on out there?'

'Not for long,' I said.

'That's great. A few seconds of consciousness is an improvement.'

I rolled my eyes. 'You and I have very different ideas about improvement.'

'Maybe next time you'll be conscious for good.'

'Wonderful,' I said dryly.

He sighed. 'There must be something worth waking up for.'

I said the first thing that came to mind. 'Night.'

'What?'

'I need to at least find out who Night is before I go gently into the good night.'

'Glad to know you've got your priorities straight.'

I shrugged. He wouldn't understand that Night's art made me believe in magic and happy endings, that his art felt almost like a lifeline for me. We watched in silence as the waves crested and fell in an endless rhythmic dance.

'Lexi,' Chris said. I turned to look at him. 'I know it's easier to stay here. But your family needs you. If you're brave enough to fly, you're brave enough to wake up.'

Waking up was easy. It was living through the waking moments that was hard.

Chapter 10

Chris

I couldn't focus on anything all morning. All I could think of was Lexi's terrified face when she regained consciousness for just a few seconds. That was how she really felt. Not blithe and uncaring, but scared. What would she be like when she woke up?

'So…' Hayley said, interrupting my thoughts. 'She's real? Not some horny fantasy of yours?'

I gave her a withering look.

'I don't know, Chris. You say you've been sitting on Ferris wheels with her and teaching her how to swim in your dreams. What am I supposed to think?'

I deepened my look.

'Okay, okay,' Hayley said, getting up to pace. She went back and forth eight times with her head dipped before finally throwing up her hands. 'I give up. This makes absolutely no sense. So what, you entered her dream? Or do you two share the same dream? Either way, how does that work?'

'Who knows? Stranger things happen every day.'

'Like what? Name something that's weirder than this.'

'You eat pancakes with salad dressing. Can't get any weirder than that.'

'Chris. Be serious.'

'I always am, I'm told.'

'I can't believe I just told you to be serious. Who are you and what have you done to my friend?'

I rolled my eyes, Lexi-style.

'And … Eliza believed you?'

'It's not that much of a stretch.'

'Except that you're frolicking with her sister in a dream.'

'We were *not* frolicking.' Although I did come close to kissing her the other night when we were lying in the Ferris wheel capsule, and last night by the beach….

No, Chris. Don't think about that.

'I beg to differ,' said Hayley. 'What you two had was a date. Multiple ones, in fact.'

'I'm going to see her again today. I'm going to visit Lexi at the hospital.'

'Alone?'

I shot her a wry look. 'You can come too, if you want. But if Charlie appears, run and save yourself.'

Hayley blinked. 'Is that … humour from you?'

I left her marvelling at my newfound sense of humour all the way to the car. Before we left, I double-checked my bag for my sketchbook, which I came to collect from Bobby's house before heading to the hospital. If I didn't have the guts—or heart—to tell Lexi the truth in our dream, I would tell her in the real world, where I didn't have to face her directly.

'Hey, do you think your sleep apnoea symptoms are caused by you being too deep in your dreams to pull yourself out?' Hayley asked, buckling up as I pulled out of the driveway. 'Think about it. It's almost like you're in a coma yourself—your body shuts down and you stop breathing while you're trapped in that dream.'

'No scientific basis for that.'

'And there is for meeting someone in a dream?' she retorted. 'Stranger things happen every day, like you said. But, hey, at least you met a fan. To collect your art is one thing, but to dream about living in it? That's hardcore.'

'She doesn't know I'm Night,' I reminded her.

'Still, you have to be slightly flattered.'

'I'm mostly worried.'

She snorted. 'Of course you are. You should tell her, though, if you regard her as a friend. Disappoint her sooner rather than later.' She punched my arm to let me know she was joking, but it didn't feel like one to me. I had to tell Lexi soon.

* * *

Apart from Lexi, the hospital ward was empty when we arrived.

'Why isn't anyone around?' Hayley whispered as we approached Lexi's bed, as though she was afraid of waking Lexi up.

I shrugged. 'Maybe they're between shifts.'

Lexi seemed, as always, peaceful, like she was right where she wanted to be. I settled into the chair next to her and picked up her hand. The dead weight in mine almost made me retract, but I remembered how Lexi's hands felt in the dream and clasped it tightly now, hoping to infuse some life into it. I thought I felt a twitch in her finger, but I might have been mistaken.

'Sorry I left you at the beach last night,' I told her. 'I'll see you again tonight.'

I felt like an idiot talking to someone who wasn't going to respond, but what happened last night proved that there was a chance she might hear what I was saying.

'I can't believe she's real,' Hayley whispered, like she might wake Lexi up. After I introduced Hayley and Lexi to each other, Hayley raised a hand in an awkward sort of wave. 'Chris has told me a lot about you.'

I shot her a look.

'Okay, not that much,' Hayley said.

I shot her another look.

'What?' she demanded, then rolled her eyes and flopped on to a chair at the foot of the bed.

I turned to Lexi. 'Hope I'm not catching you at a bad time. Maybe you're in another one of my paintings.' I paused to let that sink in. 'That's right. Night's paintings are my paintings. I'm Night. I just didn't know how to tell you that before.'

'Oh, sure,' Hayley said. 'Telling her now totally counts.'

'Will you please—' I made a zipping motion over my lips.

Hayley raised her hands in defence and pursed her lips.

I turned back to Lexi. 'Have you ever considered that Night does what he does because he doesn't want to be found? To know that someone out there appreciates my work is enough for me.'

'Now you sound like a phony celebrity artist,' Hayley muttered.

I ignored her. 'Maybe you think Night will come and save you or whatever, but what if he's as trapped as you are? What if he has a role to play that he can never break out of?'

Hayley didn't have a comeback for that. She was poking at her phone, pretending like she wasn't listening.

'I wish I could stay in that dream too and not care about what happens out here,' I went on. 'But there are people waiting for us here, people who care about us. Which is why I can only be Night after hours, when there are no expectations and obligations, and that's why you need to wake up. Your family is waiting for you.'

The door to the ward swung open, cutting me off. Charlie stood at the doorway, his gaze darkening when he spotted me. I let go of Lexi's hand.

'Christopher Fang.' He took a step towards me. 'What are you doing here? How did you—' He glanced down at Lexi's sleeping form. 'Eliza brought you here, didn't she?'

'She did, yesterday. I came here on my own today. I didn't realize you—'

'If you and your father think this is going to work, don't bother.'

I blinked in confusion. 'What?'

'This whole act with my daughter. Isn't it just to get me to move out?'

'I'm not here because of my dad. I'm here just to see Lexi.'

He narrowed his eyes at me. 'Since when were you friends with Lexi? She doesn't have many friends outside of Long Street, and I've never heard her mention you'

I had no good answer for him.

'You wouldn't believe it if he told you,' Hayley muttered.

Charlie narrowed his eyes at her. 'What's that?'

I tugged on Hayley's arm. 'We were just leaving,' I told Charlie, dragging Hayley out of there before she could say anything else.

'If I see you here again….' Charlie called after us.

At the door, I turned back for another glimpse of Lexi. But all I saw was Charlie gently pulling the covers tighter around her.

* * *

It was just a little over a month before Long Street would be cleared, and things there were already starting to look different. Half the shops were boarded up, and the remaining ones were having clearance sales.

How would Lexi feel coming back to an empty street and what used to be her home? Would she want to return to the dream?

'What does that guy have against you?' Hayley kicked a stray can out of the way. 'I mean, I get why he hates your dad's guts. But *you* haven't been up in his face. Talk about shooting the messenger.'

'Except I *have* been up in his face,' I said. 'I attended that gathering and showed up at the hospital.'

'Big deal. You're just a concerned friend. Where's the crime in that?'

'According to her sister, Lexi doesn't have a lot of friends outside of Long Street,' I said.

She jabbed a finger at me. 'That doesn't count, by the way. Telling her when she's unconscious is as good as not telling her.'

'I'll tell her when I see her tonight,' I said.

'You're going to see her again?'

'It's not like I can control what I dream.'

She shot me a look. 'I'm sure there are ways to not go back to that dream. Didn't your mum make you go see a doctor? Be honest, you *want* to go back, don't you?'

I didn't reply.

'I heard what you said, about wanting to hide in that dream.' Her gaze sharpened. 'You don't really mean that, do you?'

'Of course not.'

'Good. Because you might stop breathing altogether if you linger too long in your dreams. It's not funny,' she huffed when I let out a snort. 'It's a matter of life and death.'

'Melodrama becomes you, Hayl,' I said.

We came to a dead halt in the middle of Long Street.

'Oh, no,' Hayley breathed.

One of the shops—a café, from the looks of it—was on fire. The charred chalkboard and wooden chairs outside came into view as we got closer. Firefighters were already at the scene, halfway through putting out the fire, but the shop seemed beyond rescue.

Harold Go, the shop-owner, stood before the wreckage, staring dazedly as it crumbled into cinders. A firefighter told him to stand back, but he remained where he was until Charlie towed him away from the fire and into Ben's dessert shop, where they were joined by others. As soon as they sat Harold down, a couple of police officers approached them.

Hayley tugged on my arm, holding me back. 'I think we should leave.'

'Why?'

'What if they think your dad did this?'

'He wouldn't,' I snapped. 'What do you take him for?'

'I'm just saying, you're not their favourite person right now. Anything can be blamed on you or your dad.'

'I'm sure this is just an accident.'

'Still, let's get out of here.'

'Don't get too close to the fire,' said a voice next to me. Hayley and I turned to find Lexi's mother staring at the shop in flames. I had seen the same look in Mum's eyes often enough to know that something was amiss.

'Mrs Lee?' I said, carefully approaching her. 'Maybe we should get you somewhere else.'

She raised a shaking hand to clutch my arm. 'Stay away from the fire,' she hissed, pulling me away.

I recognized the signs—shallow breaths, dilated pupils, heightened emotions.

Hayley sprung to action and steered her away from the burning café. But Charlie, having spotted us, leapt up from his seat in Ben's shop.

'Christopher Fang!' he called, looming towards me. The police officers, Harold, and Ben followed in his wake.

'Not good,' Hayley muttered.

'Take Mrs Lee somewhere else,' I told her. 'I'll handle this.' Hayley started to argue, but I gestured at Mrs Lee, who was shaking more violently now, and she relented.

Hayley had barely begun to lead Mrs Lee away before Charlie and the rest caught up with us.

'Stay right there,' he ordered. Hayley stopped. 'Where do you think you're taking my wife?'

'She's upset, can't you see? The fire's upsetting her,' I said.

'In any case,' Charlie said, reaching for his wife's hand, 'she's not yours to take anywhere.'

Harold rounded in on me. 'It's strange, isn't it, that you should show up here when a fire breaks out? My café is a smoke-free zone. None of my staff smoke, and they've always been careful. There's no reason for the café to catch fire unless there's foul play involved.'

'I knew this would happen,' Hayley muttered. She stuck out her chin at Harold. 'What evidence do you have that Chris planted the fire?'

'Did I say he did?' Harold retorted.

'This is a serious allegation, Mr Go,' one of the police officers said. 'If you suspect foul play, you need to be able to justify that.'

'What's there to justify?' Harold demanded. 'This boy and his father have been trying to take over this place for ages. Now a month before the land lease is up and I'm still not gone, Gerald Fang is getting antsy. I'm not surprised he would resort to something this dirty.'

As I was about to protest, but Hayley grabbed my arm and started to drag me away.

'If this is how Gerald Fang is going to play, I'm all in!' Harold Go roared.

In the thick of the commotion, Mrs Lee collapsed to the ground. Her breaths were short and shallow as shudders racked her body. I knelt before her, propping her up by the shoulder. Charlie tried to pry me off, but Mrs Lee clutched my arm. Her fingernails dug hard into my skin.

'It's okay, it's okay,' I murmured, ready to start humming a Beatles song that usually calmed my mother down. But 'Que Sera, Sera' popped into my head, and I started humming that before I realized what I was doing.

Mrs Lee drew deep shaky breaths and rubbed her arms like she was self-soothing. Charlie stared at us, incredulous. I ignored him, focusing on Mrs Lee. Charlie looked torn between hauling me off and letting me finish placating his wife, but he obeyed when I gestured for everyone to give her some air.

Mrs Lee took slightly longer to calm down than Mum usually did, but managed to get back on her feet after a while.

'The fire's under control, don't worry,' I said. She let go of me, apologizing for the fingernail marks she left on my skin.

Charlie narrowed his eyes at me. 'She doesn't respond to anyone but my daughter.'

'Flying off the handle doesn't help,' was all I said as Charlie reached for his wife's hand and gently drew her close.

I looked at Hayley. 'Let's go.'

As we turned to leave, Harold Go began charging as us. But Charlie held a hand to stop him, and watched us go without another word.

Dear Night,

They call it an episode, these unpredictable bouts of incongruence, like they're a rerun of something on cable TV for the world to watch. And maybe they are a repeat spectacle, one that's overplayed to the point where the actors, seasoned, know their places and recognize their cues way ahead of time.

The first time my mother had an episode, I didn't recognize it for what it was. It started out gradual but grew worrying. In the days after the fire, we were stranded—no house, no inn—but what left us all truly helpless was my mother's breakdown. We lived in fear of the next episode, the next second we would lose her to her fear.

An episode to an eight-year-old is one of the most terrifying things ever. Some days she was my mother, in spirit and in flesh, and other days she was a ghost.

So, I learnt to notice the signs sooner. A shift in my mother's expression, a non sequitur remark, a twitch in her finger, or a shaky touch. Pretty soon, I could catch the sprite before it became unruly and took over my mother's mind.

When I showed her your paintings, she observed every inch of each one, from the gradual shift in colours to the silhouettes of each figure. Like me, she seemed to lose herself in them. In your world.

'I wish I could meet him,' I told her once.

'You've met him often enough.' She pointed at the painting of a man standing in a forest of stoplights at night. 'In there.'

At times like this, it feels like she never left.

Apprehensively yours,
Lexi

Chapter 11

Lexi

I hated that Chris was right.

I hated that I couldn't stay here forever, and I hated that I *knew* I couldn't stay here forever. Being here only meant something when I had company. All this time I had been here, it was his presence that had made this dream a much better place than reality. When it was just me, this remote landscape was lovely but lonely, like an abandoned painting.

But what if both of us stayed here?

Chris wasn't happy in his life. People who overused the word *fine* were usually anything but. I caught glimpses of the waking Chris at times—snappy, impatient, and cold. But then the magic of this dream would get to him, seep through his skin, and turn up the light in his face, his eyes. I saw that light when we were flying, when we pulled on our skates and did figure eights on ice, when we shared bread on the rooftop under a blanket of stars.

But when Chris appeared that night, I got the sense that he wasn't staying long this time. His face was as tense as the first time I saw him, when he wandered down that street towards me, but less confused and more resolute.

His footsteps were drowned out by the sound of the waves, but I could feel his presence—a relief and a comfort—before I turned around to find him approaching me. The floorboards creaked as he came closer.

I didn't question how he always knew where to find me. At the skating rink, the beach, and now the lighthouse. Who was I to question how the dream worked?

Here in the upper deck, we were buffeted by stone walls against the waves below. Chris slipped into the space next to me wordlessly. His thundercloud expression matched the storm-tossed waves outside. I drew my knees to my chest and made space for him. We sat like that in silence, watching the waves and clouds roll in. I could tell something was gnawing but figured he'd tell me when he was ready.

'I've always wanted to live in a lighthouse,' I said. 'I wonder what it's like to look out at sea every night and see those ships trying to come home? Seems like a terribly important job, to guide ships towards you and bring light to them.'

He watched me silently until I turned to face him. 'What if you're one of those ships? What do you expect to see when you come back?'

I considered his question. 'A light. That's all I need.'

He didn't reply, just looked out at the sea. When he spoke at last, it was in a voice so quiet I thought I had misheard him. 'Harold's café burned down today.'

'Uncle Harold? How? What happened?'

'The cause is unclear … but some of them think my dad's behind it.'

'Why would they think that?'

He sent me a scathing look. 'Can't you think of a reason why?'

'Fine. What's the damage? Are Uncle Harold and his wife okay?'

'They're okay. It's just the shop.' He shook his head. 'Just when you think things aren't complicated enough.'

I didn't want to think about this. It seemed like all I could do when I was awake was worry. For once, I wanted to break out of that never-ending loop of cause and effect so that the slightest action didn't set off a butterfly effect. But everything led to a consequence; there was no breaking out of this loop.

I took a deep breath of salt-streaked air. 'At least none of that matters here.'

Chris observed me for a second. 'Did you know that every night the person you tried so hard to be when I first met you slowly falls away?'

'Funny,' I said, hefting myself on to the parapet. 'I could say the same for you.'

He climbed onto the parapet next to me. It was a pretty high drop, but I didn't worry about falling. Here in the dream, I felt safer than I did anywhere else. 'You know all this is temporary. This Manic Pixie Dream Girl persona, this freedom, this isolation, this *dream* itself. You know these won't last.'

The MPDG label made me bristle, but I pushed that aside. 'I can sleep forever,' I retorted.

'You wouldn't.' But he didn't seem entirely sure.

'You don't think I will?'

The moonlight reflected in his eyes dimmed. 'So you're just going to give up? One car accident and you're just going to leave everything and everyone behind?'

'You think I'm selfish and a coward,' I said. He started to protest, but I cut him off. 'It's okay. *I* think I am, too.'

He turned back to the sea, his jaw tightening. 'If you do decide to keep staying here, then this will probably be the last time we see each other.'

'What do you mean?' I stared at him, waiting for him to look at me again, but he kept his gaze fixed on the foamy sea before us.

'I came here to tell you that I'm not coming back.'

'Like, ever?'

'Ever.' There was no room for hesitation in his voice.

'I thought it wasn't within your control.'

'It is now. I'm undergoing therapy.'

'For dreaming?'

'For breathing,' he corrected.

'So, what? You don't breathe or dream now?'

He rolled his eyes. 'So I don't stop breathing in my sleep.'

My brows slid towards each other. 'I don't understand.'

'Sleep apnoea. Heard of it?'

I nodded. 'I didn't know it was that dangerous.'

'It can be. But the doctor isn't entirely sure. My case is … unusual. I'm not middle-aged or obese and I don't have a history of respiratory problems.'

'Why then? How come you're stuck in a dream that's making you lose your breath?'

He smiled, making the corners of his eyes soften. It was a moment I ached to capture. 'You're the one asking the why's and how's now?'

'I was going to ask you to stay here. With me.' My voice was almost drowned out by the roaring waves.

'Lexi.' He took my hand and looked me in the eye. A deep sadness lay in his. 'I can't. My family needs me.'

'But you're not happy there, I can tell.'

He shook his head in frustration. 'It's not about avoiding the difficult moments; it's about finding joy in spite of them.' Letting go of my hand, he stared resolutely ahead. 'We can't expect to be happy all the time, and I'm not going to fear living just because there will be times where happiness is in short supply.'

Could I bring myself to return to what I was so happy to leave behind? Find joy in spite of everything?

'WWND,' I said softly.

Chris frowned. 'What?'

'What would Night do?'

A pause. 'What do *you* think he would do?'

'I'd like to think I know him well enough. But I never have an answer for that question.'

'What if you can meet him if you wake up?' he asked suddenly. 'Would you wake up for that?'

'You know where I can find him?'

'I … might be able to arrange a meeting.'

My heart raced at the thought of finally meeting Night. No longer just a mirage, slipping out of reach. It would be me and Night, walking down Long Street, my hand in his, just like that couple in his painting. Night would no longer be faceless. He would be real, right next to me, and he'd turn to me with a smile….

But when I looked up, it was Chris by my side. And instead of a paint-splattered hand, it was his hand grasping mine.

'How?' I demanded. 'How can you arrange a meeting with him? You know him personally?'

He shrugged. 'I have my ways.'

That figured. Gerald Fang Junior could probably track down a nocturnal artist with the snap of a finger.

'I bet Night would love it at Long Street.'

Chris frowned. 'Why?'

'Because—'

'If you say because you're one big happy family, I may vomit,' he warned.

'*Because,* Tin Man, no one's invisible on Long Street. Not sure if that's a good or bad thing, but at least Night wouldn't have to hide behind his art there. If I ever see Night, I'd take him to Long Street.'

'Does that mean you'll wake up?'

I hesitated. 'What if I wake up and you're not there?'

'I will,' he said. 'I *will* be there, I promise. You won't be alone.'

I hopped off the parapet and lay on my back on the cool wooden floor. The full-bellied moon hung above us. I raised my hands, formed a frame around the moon with my fingers.

Chris stared down at me. 'What are you doing?'

'I'm taking a piece of the sky with me.'

'That's corny. Even for you.' But he joined me on the floor anyway.

'I just want to see if it's any different when I wake up.'

A smile crept across his face. I counted the seconds our gazes held. It was five seconds later when he leaned over and kissed me.

It didn't feel like that stupid, impulsive one my last date planted on me. This one made my skin buzz and my body pulse along to the swash and backwash of the waves.

I wondered briefly what colours Night would use to paint each type of kiss before realizing that Chris's kiss felt the same as Night's paintings—sublime and sweeping, enough to throw me off-kilter but also bring me back to earth.

When we pulled away, all I could hear was the rushing in my ears. Chris seemed a little surprised by what he'd done, but he remained where he was. Still next to me.

We huddled close, listening to the crash of the waves beneath us and the sound of our hearts beating in tandem. This moment felt too large to fit into the frame of my fingers, so I closed my eyes and hoped to take a piece of it with me out of here too.

Chapter 12

Chris

When I finally opened my eyes, chaos exploded around me. My head felt like a helium balloon ready to drift into the sky, while a bag of lead sat on my chest. I filed this away for a possible painting. A balloon head and a lead heart pulling me in two directions.

Lights—cruel brightness—and a tangle of voices reeled me back to where I lay. Above me, a blurry face shifted into focus. Mum.

'Chris?' She brushed the hair off my face.

'Give him some room, Clare,' Dad said.

When Mum shifted away, I let my gaze rove around the room. This wasn't my room or Bobby's studio. Fluorescent lights threw everything into clarity. I tried moving my neck, but that only made me dizzier.

'What happened?' I mumbled, attempting to sit up again.

'Oh, Chris,' Mum cried, throwing her arms around me. I caught a glimpse of Dad's face pinched with worry.

I repeated my question.

'You stopped breathing,' Mum said, cupping my face with her hands. 'I couldn't wake you up. You would've died if you got here too late.'

'Your mother says you went to see Dr York for your sleep condition,' Dad said.

'I—I fell asleep,' I said.

'Yes, we know that,' Dad said impatiently. 'But what—'

'No, I mean I fell asleep. In my dream. I was lying next to….' I glanced at Dad, whose frown was deepening by the second, then at Mum, who I could tell was trying to make sense of my explanation.

'Gerald,' Mum said. 'Will you let the doctor know Chris is awake?'

Dad's gaze shuttled between me and mum. He nodded once and left the ward. We watched him shut the door behind him, then sat for a while in silence.

'You gave me a big fright there, Chris,' Mum said. Her eyes were shining as her lower lip trembled dangerously. I realized then how hard she had been holding it in for Dad's sake. 'I thought I'd lost you, too.'

I took her hand in mine. 'Sorry, Mum. It won't happen again, I promise.'

Manda wasn't as kind. 'You could've died, Chris. Your mother was worried sick. She almost—'

Mum shushed her, but I knew what Manda meant. The last thing I wanted was for Mum to go through what she did after Grandpa's death.

But I said, 'Because there was something I needed to do.'

'Like what, die in your sleep?' Manda quipped.

Mum glanced at her sharply. 'Mandy,' she said, just as Dad returned with the doctor and a nurse.

The check-up didn't take long; what did, though, was the diagnosis of my sleeping problem. I didn't display the usual symptoms sleep apnoea sufferers did, nor did I fit into the typical description of sleep apnoea sufferers. Yet, my brain just didn't receive enough oxygen when I sank into deep Lexi-filled sleep.

It was past lunchtime when I was finally declared out of risk and left alone with Manda and my parents again. Hayley burst into my ward with Bobby and, in the same fashion as Mum, threw herself at me like a human tornado.

'Hayley,' I choked, patting her on the back as she threatened to cut off my oxygen supply for good. 'Nice to see you, too.'

'How are you feeling, Chris?' Bobby asked.

'Just fine, Bobby. Really,' I added, more for Hayley's benefit, since she was still reluctant to let me go. She only did, at last, when Bobby said, 'Let the boy breathe, Hayley.'

Dad stood by the side, watching all of us in heavy silence, before sparing a glance at his watch. He came over and laid his hand on my shoulder.

'I'm glad you're okay,' he said. It sounded like a rehearsed line to those who didn't know better, but Dad hardly ever showed affection, and this was the closest he got to it.

'Sorry if I worried you.' Something came to mind. 'Did you know about Harold's shop?'

His grip tightened before he let go of my shoulder. 'I heard. Harold's looking to press charges.' A dry laugh. 'But of course, there's no evidence that I did it.'

'Of course you didn't,' I said. 'It was an accident.'

He nodded. 'If you're feeling better, I'll be heading back to the office.'

'Right. The board meeting.'

'Take the day off, get some rest, but remember to have that risk report ready when you come back.'

'I will, don't worry.'

'Good boy.' He patted my shoulder once more, then left without noticing the look on Hayley's face.

Hayley's lip remained curled even after Dad left. 'Really? His son is in the hospital—you almost *died*—and all he cares about is a board meeting and risk report? Are you his son or his business partner?'

'Hayley,' Bobby warned.

'Heaven forbid his business charges on without him for one day,' Manda agreed.

Amid Hayley and Manda's shared rant, my memories caught up with me. Had Lexi meant what she said last night? Had she finally decided to wake up? Without the comfort of night-time, nothing seemed certain now. What if she changed her mind? What if she decided all this wasn't worth waking up for after all, especially with the tension escalating between Dad and the Long Streeters? Panic started rising from my gut.

'Where's my phone?' I asked.

Chapter 13

Lexi

The voices came first, then the light. Just a shaft of it between the curtains was bright enough to make me squeeze my eyes shut again. The room was so quiet I could hear the air hum—signs of life, signs of reality.

When I cracked open my eyes again, Eliza's form shifted into view. She and Maude were reclined on the couch by my bedside, fast asleep. The sight of them made my eyes well up at once. Tears spilled out faster than I could catch them.

I tried moving a finger, then my hand, and finally tried to sit up. The bed creaked slightly, jolting Eliza awake. She leapt up from the couch when she spotted me moving.

'Lexi!' She shook Maude awake before rushing over to help me sit up. 'Hey, you,' she said, tearing up too as she tucked a tuft of hair behind my ear, then pulled me to her and squeezed me in her arms. Maude came over to hug us both. When we pulled apart, all our eyes were wet and shining.

'It's morning,' I said, staring at the pink-gold light that slid in through the gap between the curtains.

'Yes, it is,' Maude said. '7.27 a.m., to be exact.'

'It's morning,' I said again.

It was finally morning. The air carried colours that night didn't, beautiful and soft. I remembered one of Night's paintings, *Spectrum of A Day,* that carried this colour. He had filled up the entire canvas with glass jars, each containing light of a different colour, one for each minute of the day. The hues varied in the subtlest way, but you could see the gradual shift from morning to night, dawn to dusk, with each jar that receded into the background.

'It's morning,' I said again. This time a sigh escaped me.

Maude and Eliza exchanged a look. 'I'll go get the doctor,' Maude said, just as Eliza said, 'I'll call Dad.'

In the day, the hospital ward didn't feel quite as daunting as it had at night. At least I could move now, feel the life pulse through my body—though not in the way it did when Chris and I kissed.

Chris. He promised he'd be here when I woke up.

But there was no one else in the room apart from me and my sister. Did Chris even exist? Chris, who knew me better in a few nights better than I had ever known myself. Maybe he really was just a figment of my imagination, a boy my mind had conjured up to turn my dream from interminably lonely to magical.

Corny or not, I was glad I had managed to take a piece of the dream with me.

'Maude and the rest have been on shift duty for the past few days,' Eliza was saying. 'Dad wanted to stay, but….'

I nodded, hearing her unspoken words. 'How's Mum?'

She shook her head. 'Not good. She had another episode after she found out about your accident. We can barely get her to talk these days. She needs you. She always has.'

'I know.' I just wished I didn't feel that weight in my gut every time someone told me that.

Dad and the rest hurried here soon after the doctor looked me over and announced the all-clear. For the better part of an hour, I was caught up in hugs and pats on the back from Dad and the Long Streeters, as though I had achieved a remarkable feat by waking up.

'You've been asleep long enough, young lady,' Anitha said. 'But if you need some time to regain your memory, we'll understand.'

'Do you even recognize us?' Ben demanded. He pointed at himself and enunciated the following words slowly: 'I … am … Ben. Remember?'

I rolled my eyes. 'No amnesia, no brain damage, everyone,' I said. 'I'm fine.'

'You don't go into a coma for two weeks without some damage, is all I'm saying,' Anitha said. Next to her, Min, Auntie Fong's niece, nodded vigorously.

'Don't worry, Lexi. We'll find out who ran you down,' Ben said. 'We'll make sure we do some damage to him too.'

'People,' Dad roared at last. 'Can you please keep it down and let my daughter rest?'

* * *

During lunch, Anitha and Min updated me on the investigation of my accident—no leads, though the police were asking for witnesses to come forth.

After lunch, most of the Long Streeters either left or were chased out by the nurse who declared that only family could stay. Dad left with them to bring Mum to the hospital. It was while everyone was saying their goodbyes that I overheard Eliza's phone call.

'Where are you? Get over here *now,*' she was saying.

Did Eliza get a new boyfriend while I was in a coma? I wouldn't put it past her, although given that she wasn't entirely over Ryan yet, a new flame might not be the best idea.

Eliza went on. 'Lexi's—how did you know?' She shook her head like she didn't care to know. 'My dad's gone to fetch my mum here, so you have about half an hour to see her if you're quick. Where are you now?'

'Who's that?' I asked.

Eliza perched on the edge of my bed and took a deep breath. 'This is going to sound really weird,' she began.

I had seen weird, *lived* in it. 'Try me.'

'As weird as some guy claiming to have met you in a dream?'

My breath caught in my throat.

It was real. Chris was real. I hadn't just dreamt him up, nor did he only belong in my dreams. He existed in the flesh.

I couldn't hold back the grin that split across my face as I seized my sister's arms. 'You met Chris?'

Eliza stiffened. 'You are kidding me. He was actually telling the truth?'

I threw the covers off me and prepared to leap off the bed, but Eliza shoved me right back down. 'What do you think you're doing?'

'Going to see him. Where'd you say he was again?'

Eliza pinned me to the bed. 'Don't ever run to a guy like that. Not even in your dreams.'

I thought about how Chris and I had run—okay, skated—towards each other that night, how it had felt like two worlds colliding in the best way possible. Not one that led to destruction and heartbreak like in my sister's case.

'Oh, E,' I said. 'Chris is not like that. He's a good guy.'

'Do you know his dad's the CEO of Kingdom Heights?'

I stuck out my chin. 'I know that.'

'And that he's working with his dad to chase us out of Long Street?'

'They're not….' But I knew my argument wouldn't stand against the facts. Kingdom Heights wanted us out, and there was no way Gerald Fang was going to relent.

'What are you saying? That Chris is using me to get through to Dad? To make him give up the inn?'

'I'm just saying,' Eliza said, 'that you can't rule out the possibility that he's making use of this weird dream thing to get us to move out.' She acknowledged the look on my face. 'Yeah, he told me about the dream. Looks like you two were having too much fun in there to want to get out. I don't know exactly how this dream thing works, but for all we know he might have had a hand in manipulating it—'

'Did he tell you he was the one who convinced me to wake up?'

'Right. Because you wouldn't be much help with his quest if you were running around in the dream.'

Irritation prickled inside me. 'What do you have against him?'

'I just think it's strange that the boy you met in your dream—which, you must admit, already sounds weird on its own—happens to be the same boy whose dad is trying to take over our property.'

'This whole thing is beyond weird, okay?' I snapped. 'Who knows how it happened, or why it did? Strange things happen every day, and we explain them away with what we understand.' I shrugged. 'Maybe this just falls outside the parameters of common logic.'

'So you never questioned the connection between you and Chris?'

'Our dreams didn't require answers. Just our presence.'

I hated the look of pity she sent me.

Chapter 14

Chris

Sleep came in fits and starts that night. At times, Lexi's face appeared, but the dream never fully materialized, and I was left searching for her in the dark. I awoke at the first sign of light. Time trickled by before I was finally discharged and could rush down to Mount Colleen Hospital.

I couldn't care less about Charlie seeing me in the hospital or the risk report I was supposed to prepare for Dad. What did any of that matter when I was finally going to see Lexi, in a place other than my head? While in Bobby's car, both he and Hayley hounded me about why I was going to Mount Colleen. I was glad Mum was away at her twice-weekly visit to Hopewood. It was one less person I had to explain all this too.

'Wait, I'm confused.' Bobby sent me a sidelong glance as he turned a corner. 'When you said you met her in your dreams, you meant figuratively, right?'

'Nope,' I replied. 'I mean it in the most literal sense.'

Bobby glanced at me again. 'Seriously?'

'Look, I don't know how it happened,' I said. 'It just did. And yes, I know it sounds unbelievable, but I swear it's the truth.'

Silence lapsed. Whether or not they believed me no longer mattered. Seeing Lexi would put all their doubts to rest.

Hayley only spoke as we turned into the lane leading to the hospital parking lot. 'What are you going to do when you get there? Happy reunion, hugs and tears and kisses?'

That was exactly what I had in mind, but I made no reply to Hayley. I had hoped that Lexi and I would take one look at each other and all the cosmos and whatever would align the moment our eyes met. That we would be that boy and that girl from my painting who found a piece of themselves in each other and now walk hand-in-hand down the street, silhouetted by the setting sun. That there was someone around whom I could just be Night.

But of course, that was not possible, seeing as how she didn't even know I was Night. I wasn't entirely sure I wanted to tell her anyway. The longer I withheld the truth, the more disappointing it would be when I finally revealed it.

'Something along those lines,' I muttered in response to Hayley.

Hayley knew me better than that, though. She had seen all of my paintings, all the sketches. She knew I was Night, and that I dreamt of silhouettes and sunsets. She knew that was exactly what I was looking forward to when I saw Lexi.

'You're not really going to barge in there and expect her to receive you with open arms, are you? What if the dream was all part of your imagination and she doesn't even know you?'

I shot her a look through the side mirror. 'It's not part of my imagination.'

'Fine. Even *if* it isn't,' Hayley asked, 'what if she doesn't remember you? She was in a coma, after all.'

Then there was that.

'Didn't cross my mind,' I admitted.

'Hayley's right,' Bobby said. 'If Lexi has no recollection of all the times you two frolicked around in dreamland, then to her you'll just be the stranger trying to chase her out of her home.'

'We did not frolic,' I insisted, but my anticipation was already dying by the second. Even if the dreams were real and she did remember me, what were the chances of us having what we had in our dream? Right now, I was Chris. Not the Night she never knew, not Pictor the Painter. I counted in numbers, and she counted in constellations.

'So you think I should turn back?' I said.

But I couldn't do that. If I did, I would never know for sure if what Lexi and I shared was real.

'I just think you should take it slow,' Bobby said. He seemed to have digested the whole dream thing well, all things considered. 'Give her some time. Temper your expectations.'

Dad always told me to *raise* my expectations because that was the only way we could ever go higher. Falling—*failing*—was out of the question.

I didn't know what to expect any more, much less what to do with my expectations, as I navigated my way towards the east wing of Mount Colleen.

My feet turned to lead the closer we got. I was glad Hayley had, in her usual manner, insisted on coming along with me. Was this how Mum felt when she met Dr York and Dad for her progress assessment meeting? A thousand board meetings could not have prepared me for this.

Eliza was getting a cup of coffee from the vending machine when we rounded the corner.

She jabbed her thumb in the direction of the ward behind her. 'She's in there. But make it quick. My dad's on his way back.'

Hayley was about to follow me in, but I gave her my best beseeching look. She rolled her eyes. 'Fine. But I'll be right outside. Call for help if anything goes wrong.'

'Might be a little hard to call for help if I'm being tackled by a five-foot-five girl who just woke up from a coma,' I responded.

She scowled in response. 'Just remember what we talked about in the car.'

How could I forget? It was all I could think about as I knocked twice on the door and pushed it open.

'Come in.' The voice was too tiny for me to determine if it was indeed Lexi's.

I stepped in, letting the door click softly close behind me. And there she was, sitting up in bed dressed in loose-fitting scrubs. Splayed open on her lap was the book she was reading: *Alice's Adventures in Wonderland.* I would have expected nothing less from her.

She looked every bit like the girl I saw and kissed last night—beautiful and alive. I couldn't describe it, the *rightness* that filled me up at not just the sight of her but the look in her eyes. She knew, just like I did. She remembered. Just like I did.

'Hello, stranger,' she said softly, a tiny smile curling around her lips.

It took all I had to stay where I was and keep my cool. *Take it slow,* Bobby had said. Even with that look in Lexi's eyes, I needed to take it slow. Temper my expectations because falling was a lot more painful in the waking world.

I gestured at her dog-eared book, even though blood was buzzing through my veins and I wanted more than anything to cross that space between us. 'Not your first time reading it, I'm guessing.'

She frowned, like I had missed my cue and she was going along with my ad-libbing. She glanced at the paperback in her hands. 'How do you figure, Sherlock?'

I started babbling like an idiot. 'Well, it can't be a second-hand copy, given how careful you are with it. But it's well-thumbed, which means you must have read it many times.'

Her brows quirked, like she was secretly laughing at me. 'Immune to rhetorical questions in real life, too, I see.'

My witty comeback got lost in the mire of words I wanted to say to her. Finally, I settled for the obvious. 'So, you made it.'

'Yes,' she said, her gaze resting fully on me. 'We did.'

We. That word made me break free of the hesitation holding me back. I rushed forward and pulled her into a hug. She squeezed me back just as tightly.

'Sorry I wasn't here when you woke up,' I said against her hair.

Her voice came out muffled against my shoulder. 'You even promised.'

'How has waking up been for you so far?' I asked when we pulled away.

'I wouldn't know. I've only been stuck in this room until you came.' She leaned back against her pillow. 'It's been nice seeing everyone again, though.'

'Now you can go back to your old life.' And I had to go back to mine.

She shook her head and flipped through the book, finally landing on a page. '"I can't go back to the person I was yesterday because I was a different person back then,"' she read out from a page. 'Do you think Lewis Carroll had been in a coma before, too? Because that sounds like what someone who's been there and back again would say.'

'Or a dream.'

'Or a dream,' she agreed.

'Everyone thinks we're mad,' I said.

'Maybe we are. But everyone is a little mad. Who's to say who's mad then?'

'I would have to be half-mad to dream you up.'

'That you are,' she said with a glint in her eyes.

I kissed her then. I wasn't sure how much time we had left before the realities of our lives edged between us. Before I became the person trying to chase her family out of their home and she became the person who had, for the briefest period of time, showed me a piece of the chaotic, beautiful universe outside my careful, tidy, preordained world.

But for now, apart from the painfully white walls, we could still pretend we were in an extended version of our dream.

'I can't stand these cold white walls,' I blurted after we pulled away.

She gave me a commiserating look. 'I know. Imagine what Night would do with it.'

Now was the time. Now that we were finally face-to-face, it was time to come clean about Night. To tell her that I was the one behind those bizarre, pointless, incomprehensible paintings that had served as the backdrop to her dreams. To tell her that I was the 'wildly talented phantom' she had been trying so hard to catch hold of.

But I couldn't get the words out. *I am Night*—why was that so hard to say?

Because she was only in for disappointment if she found out.

Would it even matter that I was Night? It didn't change the fact that I was also Chris. Night only existed in his paintings and could never be realized as a person. He wouldn't last a day in Chris's life.

So I joined her in describing how Night would fill up the walls, carefully skirting the issue of his whereabouts.

We were on the third wall when Charlie burst into the ward, Hayley in his wake. I leapt up from Lexi's bed as he approached us.

'Not you again,' he said. 'What are you doing back here?'

'Chris is just here to visit me, Dad,' Lexi said.

'You know him?' Charlie said, keeping his eyes on me. 'I thought I told you not to come again. Is this what Gerald Fang is resorting to?'

'My dad is not resorting to anything,' I said evenly.

Hayley jumped to my defence, although she kept a clean berth of Charlie. Smart girl. 'Chris is not plotting against your daughter, if that's what you mean.'

'Dad,' Lexi said. 'Be nice to my friend, please.'

'Friend?' Charlie echoed. 'He's your friend now?'

'Yes,' Lexi said. 'And I believe him.' She ignored the incredulous look Charlie sent her. 'I believe him,' she repeated. 'I know who he is. But we knew each other even before he learnt about us and the inn.'

'Since when?'

Since I met your daughter a few nights ago in a dream would probably not go down too well, so I kept my mouth shut. Lexi obviously thought the same thing, since she didn't reply either.

But we were spared from eking out an answer when Lexi's mother entered the room with Eliza. Charlie and Eliza exchanged a look, but they didn't stop her from pulling Lexi into what seemed like a bone-crushing embrace.

Lexi patted her back repeatedly before her mother pulled away, gingerly raising her hands like something might erupt in flames any second.

'It's okay, Mum,' Lexi said. 'We're in the hospital. It's safe here.'

It struck me as an odd thing to say at first, but then I saw the burn scars on the back of Mrs Lee's hands and remembered.

Now that Lexi's mother was in the room, Charlie seemed more careful with his temper. It was the kind of thing people did around my mum—no sudden movements or aggression—in case it set her off. It annoyed Mum to no end. 'I'm made of flesh and bone, not champagne glass,' she would mutter.

A tentative truce now settled amongst us, but Lexi chose to break it.

'Mum, Dad, Eliza,' she said, reaching for my hand and grasping it firmly. 'This is Chris, the boy I've been seeing in my dreams.'

Dear Night,

Sometimes you don't realize there is an empty space next to you until something or someone comes along to fill it. You're just drifting around in your bubble until you find that there's a whole world beyond it.

I thought my space was complete with just me and you. But someone as abstract as you can never settle into that space next to me, much less fill it. You're not so much a person as you are a concept, a fantasy. You are space itself, space for me to squeeze someone in your likeness next to me.

When I first met Chris, I thought of all the ways he was not like you. He was uptight, obedient to a fault, and had no dreams of his own. He wasn't supposed to fit in the space next to me. We were two odd shapes colliding into each other. He was all angles and planes; I was amorphous. But somehow, we clicked right into place.

One of the reasons I was afraid of waking up was that Chris might not be real. That he was just someone I'd conjured up and I would be left with an irrevocably empty space next to me the minute I opened my eyes.

But then he walked into my ward that day, breathless and lost for words, and I found myself stepping into the best kind of chaos. My heart was all wings and flight and colours and light. He fills me up the way you fill the canvas, even though our encounters so far have only been surreal—though who's to say what's real and what isn't?

Still, I'd like to think that Chris and I have both been indelibly marked by our dreams. The dreams you created that we ran off with. In a way, you and Chris gave life to my dreams. It's funny how you and he can be so different yet so similar.

Concretely yours,
Lexi

Chapter 15

Lexi

'Is this really necessary?' I said.

'Of course it is!' Maude cried. 'You don't know what this past week's been like for all of us, especially your father. We *must* celebrate! And be sure to invite Chris. I heard the poor boy was hospitalized, too, for overwork. Oh, invite his mother as well. She seemed to enjoy the last gathering.'

'She came for the last gathering? What was she like?'

'A little guarded, but we made her feel right at home. If you asked me, I think all she needs is better company. So, remember to invite your mother-in-law.' She wiggled her brows. I rolled my eyes. 'Oh, don't be shy. The whole street already knows about you two.'

'Dad would probably throw him out of the inn.'

'No throwing guests out of the inn,' she said. 'That's the first rule, remember?'

'I thought the first rule was, the food isn't going to cook itself. Or, date night can wait until after Friday.'

She chuckled. 'Ah, well. It's one of them anyway.'

I let a moment of hesitation slip by before changing the subject. 'Chris told me Harold's suing Gerald Fang for the fire.'

'Oh, that. They found out the cause of the fire. Not arson'—she shot me a pointed look—'as you can guess. As ruthless as Gerald Fang may be, he doesn't seem like the sort to play this dirty. It was a stray cigarette that burned up a stack of old newspapers in the back alley. Harold's ban on cigarettes only extends to within his shop.' She shook her head sadly. 'No one could have anticipated that.'

'How is he now?'

'His son wants him to retire and move to Melbourne with him.' She shot me a rueful look. 'He's leaving at the end of the month.'

I sighed. 'Feels like everything's changing already.'

'Change isn't necessarily a bad thing, Lexi,' Maude said. 'We stop living when we get too comfortable. Sometimes, we need something—or someone—different from everything we know to shake things up a bit.' She raised her brows. 'Chris is different.'

'Dad says he's *too* different,' I said. 'From us.'

'He also thinks keeping your mother in the inn is best for her. You are not your father; you don't have to think like him.' She patted my shoulder. 'Make the call, Lexi.'

So I did.

Chris picked up on two rings, just as I was done writing my latest letter—and the first since I woke up—to Night. I slid it into my bedside drawer, along with the others I had written before my accident.

'Hey, you.' His voice sounded familiar and foreign at the same time.

'Kind of sucks that we're not telepathic now, huh?' I said. 'Communicating through dreams is way cooler than using phones.'

'Do you think we'll ever find out how we did that?'

'Maybe it's something we both ate,' I suggested. 'Or maybe it's the magic of Night's paintings.'

'Uh huh.'

'Speaking of magic,' I said, 'you are cordially invited to hang with us at the rooftop garden this Friday. Maude and the rest have planned a celebration, for, you know, us getting discharged. Apparently, it's a big yay and all.'

'Okay. Not seeing the link between magic and a Long Street party.'

'Because contrary to what my dad thinks, you're not the one with a motive. I am.'

His brows furrowed. 'You're losing me.'

I didn't care how corny I sounded. 'I'm about to show you the magic of Long Street, and how kicking us out is the worst idea ever.'

He sighed. 'It's not up to me, Lexi. The multiplex is already under way. All of you *have* to move out.'

'Not until a month later. Until then, we have every right to be here.'

'Lexi….'

I didn't like the turn this conversation was taking. 'Even if you don't want to make friends, we have a raffle at the end of the night. You could win … a yard of satin from Maude's store.'

'And what,' he said, 'would I do with that?'

'What about a week's supply of dessert from Ben's shop? Dessert always comes in handy. Or—'

'Lexi.' Another sigh. 'I don't want your dad to think I'm using you to fulfil some business agenda.'

'He doesn't….' I didn't bother finishing the lie. After my slightly preposterous introductions yesterday, Dad was almost convinced I had been brainwashed by Chris in some sort of mental kidnapping and was now experiencing Stockholm Syndrome.

Still, I told Chris, 'He'll come around.'

'He and Harold Go and, I'm sure, many others would love to have my head on the grill.'

'They found out that it was a stray cigarette that caused the fire. No one's pointing fingers.'

'Lexi, come on. I'm probably one of the top few people they don't want at their private gathering, right after my dad. The last time I went, your dad almost threw me out.'

'Then don't go as Christopher Fang,' I said.

'What?'

'Pretend you're Night.'

'*What?*' he said again.

'You're my immensely talented painter friend.'

'I'm not going as Night,' he said.

'So what, we're not even friends now that we're both awake?'

Chris let out the third sigh on this call. 'Fine. If it means that much to you, I'll be there. But if I go, I either go as someone else's guest—Maude's maybe—or I go with a purpose other than socializing.'

'What's the difference if you're my guest or Maude's?'

'Because then it won't seem as though I'm making use of our relationship to be a part of Long Street. Maude and I knew each other even before the multiplex plan came into conception.'

'You overthink too much, you know that?' Something he said caught up with me. 'Wait, since when did you and Maude know each other?'

'Since I went to buy textiles from her a couple of—'

'You bought textiles from her? For what? An art project?' The thought made me chuckle. Chris slaving over arts and crafts.

Chris stayed silent. I heard his dry look translated as static over the phone, and my laughter died.

'All right. Geez. Was your sense of humour cut off at birth?'

That got a brusque hmph, the closest semblance of laughter Chris spared. 'Listen, I have a meeting in ten minutes. Can we—'

'Got it. Maybe we could give that dream another go tonight. See if we can reach the same spot.'

'Maybe we could,' he said. And I got the sense that he, like me, would much rather be in the dream right now.

* * *

In the days leading up to Friday, the business at the inn kept me busy enough. Not because it was a hothouse of check-ins, but because the accounts and maintenance that the inn had fallen behind on because of my being away. Eliza was no good with balancing figures, and Dad had been too preoccupied with the turn in Mum's condition to take care of anything else. But Mum was getting better by the day, although she would sometimes panic when I left her sight.

I fell back into the familiar rhythm of work, and at times it felt like nothing had really changed. Except that it had. I had woken up from that dream as a different person. It was as if the landscape there had altered me in ways that only I could detect.

The party on Friday evening was where Mum and I could sit down properly to talk for the first time ever since I got discharged. Maude and the rest streamed in with their trays and pots of food, while I sat by the bar with Mum, spearing prawns and kebabs. Long Street was the only place she dared to move around freely without fear.

'This feels nice,' she said as she speared a prawn. She glanced at me with a small smile.

'It does.'

'I thought I'd never have the chance to sit down with you again. Things were different without you around. You and me, we're even more alike than Eliza and your father are alike. Without you, I felt like I was always skirting around them.'

'They're family too, Mum,' I said.

'I know. But promise me you won't leave me behind like that again.'

If only she knew how close I had come to doing just that. 'I promise,' I said.

'So,' she said, sending me an impish smile. 'You and that boy. What's the real story?'

'I told you.'

'A dream.'

I nodded.

She squinted at me, trying to figure out if I was telling the truth. I focused on spearing—cucumber, chicken cube, bell pepper, chicken cube, pineapple. Finally, she said, 'Your father thinks he's using you to make us give up the inn. Is that true?'

'You're not supposed to know that.' Dad had told me and Eliza that we were not to concern Mum with anything related to the business in case it made her anxious.

A wry smile. 'It's fire I'm afraid of, Lexi, not the truth. I know how the inn's been doing lately.'

'No one can make us give up the inn if we don't want to.'

'They can if they've already bought over the land.'

I took a deep breath. 'I'm sorry.'

'For what, sweetheart?'

'I know how much this inn means to you and Dad.'

She smiled. 'Lexi, you're always saying sorry to me.'

'I'm sor—'

She sent me a look. 'You're sorry for these'—she flipped her hands and showed me the scars—'you're sorry for not doing enough, sorry for the poor business, sorry for us being chased out. But what do you have to be sorry for?'

'I just feel like there's a lot more that can be done. That *I* could've done.' I was spearing harder than necessary.

Mum reached over to take my hand. 'You've done your best. You always have.'

That familiar guilt curled in my gut again, a reflex reaction to her kindness.

'Sometimes, I wish you were more like your sister,' she said. 'Back in her heyday.'

I grimaced. 'Nobody uses the word "heyday" any more, Mum.'

'Whatever the term you young people use these days, then,' she said. 'I wish you were a little more selfish. Go out, have fun, do what you've always wanted to do. You're only young once, you know.'

'You don't think I'm selfish enough? I almost chose not to wake up,' I blurted.

Her brows slid towards each other. 'What do you mean?'

'It means I would've stayed on in that dream forever until Dad decided to take me off life support.'

She dropped the prawn she was about to spear. 'You don't mean that.'

'I'm afraid I do.' I didn't dare to look at her, didn't want to see the fear and disappointment in her eyes.

'What made you change your mind?'

'Chris.'

She blinked. 'Chris?'

It sounded stupid, like something a lovesick teenage girl would say, but it wasn't like that. I didn't wake up just for Chris, I woke up because he helped me find the courage to.

'Speaking of whom,' I said, as Maude stepped out onto the rooftop with Chris and a woman who had to be his mother, given the resemblance in the eyes and nose. It wasn't hard to see where Chris got his good looks.

He made a beeline for our table as soon as he spotted me, leading his mother along too.

'You came,' I said.

'Well done, Captain Obvious,' he said, mimicking me.

'Where's Hayley?'

'She had a school project to work on.'

After the introductions were made, Maude led Mum and Chris's mother towards her table, where Anitha, Min, and the others sat. That left me and Chris alone with a plate full of kebabs and prawns waiting to be skewered. I did a quick count of the people present—twenty-four, excluding Chris and his mother. Full attendance.

'My being here changes nothing, you know,' Chris said.

I ignored that statement and handed him a skewer. 'We have twenty-four people to feed, so start spearing.'

He stared at it for a moment, then got to work.

We fell into a comfortable silence, occasionally making small talk with the few Long Streeters who popped by our table to congratulate me on my discharge. Most of them left us alone, although their gazes flicked towards us more than once. Chris and I tried our best to ignore them.

'I was half-expecting you to chicken out in the face of my dad,' I said.

His lips curled into a slanted smile. 'Who do you think I am?'

'A very nervous boy meeting his girlfriend's dad.'

He stared at me, and for a moment there I thought he might correct me on our relationship. But he only said, 'Why do you believe in me so much? What makes you think I'm not actually here on business? A lot of them seem to think so.'

'Because I'm the only one who's seen you in the dream. I've seen you when you're not Gerald Fang Junior.' I nudged him. 'Deep down, you're actually enjoying this.'

'What, driving metal sticks through cold, slimy prawns?'

I gave him a look. 'You know what I mean.' He didn't reply, so I nudged him again. 'Admit it.'

He jerked back when he saw the stain I had smudged on his shirt. 'Oh, no you didn't. This is war,' he declared, reaching for me with his prawn-soaked hands.

I squealed and dodged out of his reach. Soon, we were embroiled in a food fight that would probably have gone out of hand had Dad not appeared behind me then. While trying to evade Chris's prawn-stained hands, I took a step back that sent me colliding into Dad.

He glanced down at me, then at the mess we had made with prawn juice and some leftover pineapple cubes. Finally, his gaze landed on Chris.

'You're here,' Dad said, his voice as tight as his jaw.

This time, Chris didn't get snarky with his *Well done, Captain Obvious*. 'As Maude's guest,' he said instead.

I rolled my eyes. Dad caught that and said, 'Lexi, come and help with the punch bowl.'

I shot Chris an apologetic look, then headed over to the punch bowl table with Dad. Eliza was there, adding more water to the syrup.

'He was very insistent about not being here as my guest, Dad,' I told him. 'Said he didn't want you to think he was using me to get here. Be nice to him. His dad's the one you're against, not him.'

'Not if he's working with him.'

Sometimes, Dad could be so mule-headed.

'Well, tonight he's not just Maude's guest, he's also my friend. So please at least be civil if you're not going to be nice.'

'I'll pretend he's not even here. Okay?' That was the best he could do, for my sake. I nodded.

Dad ruffled my hair and returned to the grill, leaving me and Eliza alone with the punch. Eliza raised her brows at me, a loaded look in her eyes.

'What?' I demanded.

She shook her head. 'Not getting involved.' A beat. 'Although,' she added, 'you remind me of myself. Back when I was with Ryan.'

I made a face. 'Why are you bringing up that miserable piece of—'

'I'm just saying, I used to argue with Dad for Ryan's sake. This feels like a familiar situation, except I'm the audience now instead of you.'

I glanced over at Chris, who was now engaged in a conversation with Ben and his wife Mel from the dessert shop. It didn't seem like a very spirited one, but at least they were trying.

Dad kept a close eye on Chris (so much for pretending he's not even here) while cooking, so I stayed where I was with Mum, Eliza, Maude, and Chris's mother, who insisted that we called her Clare. Music drifted from the speakers next to the punch table—some surf rock from the sixties—and the food, like the people, made its rounds.

Was this what I had almost given up? The voices and laughter of the people I had grown up with, this view from the rooftop—the lavender twilight and red-bricked walls of shophouses lining the street—and the possibility of meeting Night someday?

What if Chris hadn't persisted in making me wake up? What if he had left me cruising the skies to my heart's content, let me continue living that semblance of a life in my dream?

I had the sudden urge to go over to him then. But what would I say to him? *Thank you*? That didn't feel right. The dream wasn't a terrible place to be, not when we were the ones living in it, when it belonged to just us.

At least for now, Chris seemed preoccupied with some of the Long Streeters, so I didn't have to worry about neglecting him. His gaze flitted over to me like he could sense me staring at him. A tiny smile slid across his face. I liked that I was getting used to seeing him smile.

Mum caught us exchanging looks. She gave me a nudge. 'Go over and talk to him.'

'That's right,' Maude said. 'Don't worry about your dad. He can't chase out my guest.'

I shared another glance with Chris, then got a plate of food and joined him at the corner of the rooftop. Everyone gave us our space without us having to say a word. I set the plate of food between us on the parapet and picked up a smoked salmon-wrapped asparagus.

'So have you been convinced to leave the Dark Side?' I said.

He shot me a look. 'Hilarious. Good and bad depends on which side you're standing on, though. Right now, where I'm standing, you're in the dark.'

I turned around and leaned against the parapet on my elbows. 'Really?'

He nodded. 'You're not seeing what our project can do for you.'

'This inn means everything to my parents. They built a life and a family around it. What's going to happen to them—to us—if it's gone?'

'A relationship can't be tied to a building. Your family isn't going to fall apart just because the inn's gone. Besides, we're offering an alternative location for you to rebuild your inn.'

I looked at him askance. 'So you're really here to persuade us to move?'

'That's not fair. You brought it up first.'

I smirked. 'Fair is where you buy cotton candy.'

He snorted. 'Sounds like what my dad would say.'

'Oh, no. I'm starting to sound like Gerald Fang? Must be all this hanging out with his son.' I laughed when he gave me a playful nudge.

A Beatles song came on and we started humming along. At the punch table, Clare started swaying along to the music, a can of beer in her hand. Pretty soon, she and Maude were dancing off with each other. Some Long Streeters, including me, stared but most of them looked more bemused than anything else.

'Chris!' Clare called. 'It's our song!' She twirled around clumsily, spilling some beer, and Maude steadied her. Clare shook her off and continued spinning and twirling, almost knocking into Ben on her way towards us.

'Your mum's quite the life of the party,' I remarked.

Chris's jaw tightened but he didn't reply.

'I'm guessing this isn't regular behaviour for her?' I said slowly.

He headed towards his mum. 'That depends on how you define regular behaviour.'

Some of the Long Streeters, like Ben and Uncle Harold, watched Clare like they didn't know whether to stop her, but most of the others joined her in singing and dancing, cheering her on.

'Chris,' Clare called again as she joined us. She had a spot of ketchup at the corner of her lip, and her eyes were bright and shining. She took Chris's hand and pulled him away before he could say anything.

I expected Chris to tell her to stop, but Chris placed a hand on her back and led her back to the corner of the rooftop, where it was less crowded. I watched his unfaltering smile, his firm but gentle hands holding on to his mum, and wondered if that was how I looked around *my* mother. As though this were a performance we had put up countless times before and we were just falling into character.

When the song ended, Chris let go of Clare's hand and tried to lead her back to the punch table. But Clare came over to me and helped herself to a clam from my plate.

'Mum, you're allergic,' Chris said, but Clare waved his concern away, keeping her eyes on me.

'So you're Lexi. The girl from Chris's sketchbook,' she said.

'Sketchbook?' I turned to Chris. 'You draw?'

Chris looked like he was desperate for a hurricane to sweep him away right then. 'I....'

'Can I see it?'

'You should see the things he draws,' Clare went on. 'Chris is more talented than he lets on.'

'Mum, let's get you something to drink, shall we?' Chris said, steering her towards the punch table. 'You must be thirsty from all that dancing.'

I popped a clam into my mouth while waiting for Chris to return. When he did, it was with a couple of cups in his hand.

He handed me a cup of punch as he gulped down a mouthful of water.

'Sorry,' he said. 'My mum's not used to large social gatherings. They get her all keyed up and—'

'That's okay.' I glanced over at Clare, then turned back to him. 'So you never told me you draw.'

'I just dabble. It's nothing.'

'When did you start?'

'A few years ago.'

'Do you paint?'

He cast me a sidelong look, and I knew he knew what I was thinking.

'I mean,' I explained hastily, 'if you know about Night and you draw, you might dabble in painting too. That's the … logical assumption.'

'Do *you* paint?'

'Me?' I snorted. 'I wouldn't know what to do with a paintbrush if it danced in front of me.'

'So you agree that painting is not exclusive to those who know about Night.'

'Whatever. So can I see it? Your sketchbook?'

He rubbed his neck. 'There's nothing to see. Just some doodles.'

'Your mum said you drew me. Doesn't the subject get to look at the drawing?'

Before he could come up with another excuse, Clare reappeared next to us. 'Chris.'

'Mum, what's wrong?'

She showed him a text message on her phone. 'It's your father. He wants to know where we are.'

'I thought Manda was supposed to tell him we're going for a movie if he asked.' He pulled out his own phone and swore softly when he saw the missed calls and text messages. 'What's so suspicious about a movie?'

'It's suspicious if you're lying,' I pointed out, only to have him throw a look at me. 'I don't get it. Why can't you be at a party? Besides, this is Long Street. Shouldn't your dad be happy that you're here, playing nice with the locals?'

'Not if I'm here, too,' Clare said. 'I'm not supposed to attend something this rowdy.'

I glanced at the Long Streeters. *Rowdy?*

Clare must have noticed the look on my face. 'Gerald's … protective,' she said.

'That's one way to put it,' Chris muttered, furiously tapping out a text message. This was the first time I heard him say something against his father. When he slid his phone back into his pocket after sending the message, there was a crease between his brows that hadn't been there before.

'Don't worry, Chris,' Clare said. 'Come on. Let's dance.'

Chris listened to the song that was currently playing. 'To Nirvana?'

'Why not?' Clare turned to me. 'Did you know? Chris plays a mean air guitar.' She laughed and set her phone down on the parapet, then bounced back into the party before Chris could stop her. Kingston, furniture shop-owner Jeffrey's son, joined her in belting out the song and headbanging.

Another text message came in through her phone. Chris glanced at it, the crease between his brows deepening.

'She looks like she's having a good time,' I said, trying to divert his attention.

He turned back to her, his jaw tensed. 'For now.'

'Why the long face? She's having fun.'

'For every action, an equal reaction,' he said, not taking his eyes off his mother. 'The higher she gets, the harder she crashes.'

'Why bring her to a party, then?'

His reply was terse. 'Beats keeping her at home.'

I wondered if his words were directed at me. But what if he was right? What if, like Clare, Mum needed to ease into the outside world instead of hiding in this 'safe house'?

As the music swelled, more people started getting into it. A heady mix of voices and laughter, food aroma and music threaded through the evening air. In this pocket of time—as least until the song ended—it didn't smell like teen spirit; it smelt like freedom and bliss.

Clare apparently thought so too. She took a swig of beer from a can on a nearby table—possibly Kingston's—then slammed it down on the table. 'This is the look of a free woman,' she yelled. 'No more Hopewood, no more out-of-grounds privileges, no more stupid group therapy sessions.'

She got up on a plastic chair, her face flushed as she looked down at all of us.

Chris and I rushed over. He reached for her hand. 'Okay, free woman. Come on down before you hurt yourself.'

'Gerald won't be able to control me any more. Right, Chris? We can live our own lives. You can make your art and I can travel the world.'

She wobbled a little on the chair. Chris's grip tightened and he tried tugging her down, but gently, in case she lost balance and fell backwards against the ledge. A couple of Long Streeters stepped forward to help while others stared.

'Mum, come on.' Chris's voice was low, patient, but I could detect the stormy undercurrent of fear. 'Dad's not going to be happy about this.'

Clare made no effort to lower her voice. 'How will he know?'

Maude rose from her seat and came over to us. Chris shot her an apologetic look, but Maude only patted his shoulder. To Clare, she held out both her arms. 'Come on down, dear,' she said. 'You're going to miss the raffle.'

'There's a raffle? I love raffles!' She turned back to face the street. 'But the view's pretty from here.'

'Well, the prizes for the raffle will beat even that view.'

Clare glanced back at Maude with a mischievous smile. Her face was flushed, her eyes shining and wild. 'You won't tell my husband, will you? He hates raffles.'

'Why would I tell him, dear? I hardly know him.'

'One time, he threw away a quilt I won at a raffle that the community centre held. I liked that quilt.'

'We won't say a word,' Maude assured her. 'Now, come on down. Everyone's waiting.'

'Okay,' Clare said simply, stepping down as though that option had always been within reach.

Maude beamed, like Clare had achieved a commendable feat. It was the look she gave Mum whenever her efforts to calm her down from an anxiety attack paid off.

Flanked by Maude and a few other Long Streeters, Clare returned to the punch table near the raffle box. Chris was about to follow her but decided to hang back. I reached for his hand and found it slick with sweat. He held on tightly.

Maude clapped her hands twice, waiting for the chatter to die down before saying, 'Now, the highlight of the night.' She raised the raffle box, and some of us clapped. These past few weeks have been hard on everyone, especially Charlie, Sara, and Eliza. But Lexi's back now'—more applause and cheers—'so our homecoming girl gets first pick of the raffle! Lexi?'

I set down my punch and made a beeline towards her. I grabbed the first piece of paper my fingers touched inside the raffle box and handed it to Maude.

'Congratulations!' Maude chirped. 'You've won!' She peeled open the folded piece of paper. Her face fell as she read out, 'A teak rocking chair from Jeffrey's shop.' She shot Jeffrey a look, like it was his fault. Jeffrey shrugged helplessly.

'I guess a teak rocking chair will look good in the Welcome Inn foyer,' I said.

Maude sent me a helpless smile before moving on. 'Chris and Clare, as our guests, will you pick next?'

Chris waved a hand at Clare, and she went forward to pick out another slip of paper, biting her lower lip like a child picking out candy.

'A week's supply of dessert, courtesy of Ben,' Maude announced, folding up the piece of paper.

Eliza leaned over and nudged me. 'Guess we know where you'll be having your next few dates.'

Chapter 16

Chris

In the end, it was the shellfish that gave us away.

Never mind that Mum was in better spirits than she had been in ages. When we returned home at quarter to ten—a reasonable timing for movie night—Dad took one look at Mum and rose from the couch, tossing his phone aside. He stormed towards us, and I fought the urge to put myself between him and Mum.

'Where have you two been?' Dad demanded.

'Didn't Manda tell you?' I said. 'We went to catch a movie after dinner.'

Dad's gaze sliced towards me. 'Unlike you, Amanda is more partial to telling the truth.' He glanced at Mum, took in the rash that was starting to form on her arms. She pushed her arms behind her as far as she could, as if that would make Dad un-see the rash. 'You were out of control,' he told her.

'Dad,' I said. 'We didn't go to a rave club. It was just a small gathering. We ate, we talked—that's it.'

Dad's stony gaze remained on Mum. 'You drank alcohol and ate shellfish. Did you forget that you're allergic, or did you just not care?'

Mum stayed silent, averting her eyes from Dad. On the drive home, her euphoria had slowly flaked off like chipped paint, and a sense of gloom had settled into the car like an extra passenger.

'We didn't do anything wrong, Mum,' I kept telling her, although I found a part of myself clinging on to that refrain too. 'It was just a party.'

But apparently, a party like that was out of control. Out of whose control, I wasn't sure.

'Allergies aside,' I said, trying for a jauntier tone, 'we had a pretty good time.'

'A good time *where?*' he asked again, still looking at Mum.

'The Welcome Inn.'

He turned to me at last. 'The Welcome Inn again?'

'Maude from the textiles store invited us.' I didn't want to mention Lexi; there was no reason to involve her in this. 'Not all of them were as hostile as Charlie.'

'What makes you think that this strategy doesn't work both ways, that they're trying to make us reconsider too? This nice act, what if it's their ploy?'

'It's not like that, Dad. They're not like that. The Long Streeters made a genuine effort—'

'Long Streeters. Is that code for *friend* now?'

'You're being unreasonable, Dad,' I snapped. I tried to remember the last time I said this to his face and came up blank.

Dad's eyes widened, then narrowed. 'Excuse me?'

I tried again. 'I just think that you might be projecting your own intentions on them. All you've seen of them is through the few representatives in the boardroom the other day. Sure, they're overly attached to their shops, but they each have a reason to hold on to it.'

He jabbed a finger at me. 'I did not send you there to become their spokesperson.'

'I'm not speaking up for them. But did you know, not once did any of them try to convince me to rethink our plans for Long Street? Charlie almost threw me out of his inn—but he didn't.'

They could have thrown me and Mum out of Long Street, after her antics during that Nirvana song, but they didn't.

Dad remained a stone wall. 'You need to rethink your priorities, Chris, if you think helping a bunch of strangers keep their outdated shops is more important than the family business.'

'Family *is* my priority,' I said. 'And so is our business. That's why I took Mum there. She regained something of a social life, made new friends there—'

'Those people are *not* her friends.'

'At least they don't treat her like a disease.'

The silence that followed rang louder than a slap.

Dad's stare burnt into me. 'What?'

I couldn't take back what I said now. So I barrelled forward. 'When was the last time you saw Mum really happy?'

'When I brought her home.'

'Yes, she was happy then, wasn't she? Over the moon. But then she found that her being home was no different from being in Hopewood. You're just as cold to her, and you avoid her even more now. But now that she's met some people she can have a bit of fun with, she has to feel guilty about it?'

'So I'm in the wrong for looking out for her?'

'Stop it.' It came as a whisper, so quiet it was almost inaudible. Mum squeezed her eyes shut and clamped her hands over her ears. 'Just stop, both of you!'

I fell silent. Dad threw me a look. When he spoke again, his voice was frosty. 'This conversation is over.'

I gently pried Mum's hands away from her ears. She was shaking. Manda, who had been hovering at the entrance of the guest lounge watching us, rushed towards us.

'Sorry, Chris,' she said. 'I had to tell.'

I shook my head. Dad had a way of forcing the truth out of people, and Manda was not obligated to lie for us. 'Take her to her room, will you? And get her something for the rash.'

Manda nodded and coaxed Mum up the stairs.

I was about to follow them when Dad snapped, 'Where do you think you're going?'

'I have some more work I need to finish by tomorrow,' I said, matching my tone with his. When was the last time I snapped at Dad, if ever?

'You should have thought of that before you went to some party,' he said. But this time, he didn't stop me when I headed for my room.

* * *

That night, I pulled out my sketchbook and let my thoughts spill on to the page. My hands worked fast and furious, pulling in shadow and light to create the face I was growing familiar with. The tufts of dark choppy hair she would brush off impatiently whenever they got in her face, the curve of her cheekbones, the spark that brought her sad gaze to life.

By the time my eyes started clouding over with sleep, I was almost done with the sketch. At work the next morning, I pushed my files and laptop aside to make space for my sketchbook, then set about completing the drawing.

Shortly after I was done, Dad called me into his office.

After last night's unprecedented fight, I wasn't sure what the situation was between us any more—how to react to him now or how he would regard me. We'd had disagreements before, especially when it came to Mum, but this one felt different somehow. This time, I had—unwittingly or otherwise—chosen a side. And I wasn't sure if I was even entirely comfortable with this side.

Dad wasted no words.

'I don't care what kind of relationship you have with those people on Long Street,' he said. 'But I don't want you to attend any more parties on Long Street. Our relationship with them is strictly professional. The more you hang out with them, the more clouded your judgement becomes.'

'My attending those gatherings won't affect how the multiplex plans play out anyway. You're going ahead with it no matter what, aren't you?'

'Chris.' My name came out as a weary sigh. 'I don't understand why this is coming between us. It's just a street.'

'If it's just a street, then why not just let it go? We've got the rest of the area.'

'Let it go? Do you know how much we stand to gain from redeveloping that street?' A pause. 'Is this because of the girl?'

My gaze flicked up from the desk.

'Your mother told me.'

'You spoke to Mum?'

'Contrary to what you believe, we do talk.'

'I'm sorry about what I said last night.' But I didn't know if I really meant it.

'So is it because of Charlie Lee's daughter? You're seeing her, aren't you? Is that why you're defending those people? Chris.' He gave me a look I wasn't sure I liked, something like pity. 'Don't tell me you're serious with her.'

I offered no denial.

'Can you really picture the two of you together?' he said.

I didn't have to. My dreams were pictures after pictures of us being together.

'Even if I leave Long Street alone, abandon my plans for our redevelopment project, so what? Are you certain you two will remain relevant in each other's lives? Right now, you two are involved with each other because you each have an agenda—you want her to give up the inn, she wants you to let it go—but once you are no longer tied together by that, you'll go back to your own lives.'

'We don't have to become strangers,' I said quietly.

'But you are. What makes you think she can understand how we work, how we live? What makes you think you can fit in with *her* way of life? What do you two really have in common, other than sick mothers?'

Words failed me completely. I stood there dumbly with only a sinking feeling in my gut. What would Mum think if she was here listening to this conversation? If she knew that her husband defined her with just one word?

And although a part of me was mentally battling his argument, another part had already accepted the rationality of it.

'Chris,' Dad said. 'I'm not stopping you from seeing her, but you must be rational about this. Don't get led into thinking she's the girl of your dreams.'

If only he knew.

'There are a lot of things to consider, given who you are and who she is. It's not just a simple matter of mutual attraction.'

He waited for me to think through his words, expecting me, like always, to see his point of view. To agree with him like I always did. But my thoughts were now one big jumble.

'Mum isn't sick,' I said at last.

'I don't think you're seeing my point, Chris.'

'I do see your point.' And I did. It was, by some measure, a valid point. 'But you're not giving them any option here. Is Kingdom Heights really going to throw its weight around and back a bunch of tenants into a corner?'

'You want options? This is the option I'm giving them: either move out or quote me a number that's higher than what the land they're sitting on is worth, because I will pay whatever price necessary to realize the multiplex vision.' He rapped the desk twice. 'This is business, Chris. There's no room for sentimentality here.'

That was what he had always told me, and what I had always accepted. But things were different this time round.

'Convey that to Charlie Lee the next and last time you see him,' Dad said, returning to his computer screen, signalling the end of the conversation.

I left his study, my fingers leaden as I tapped out a text message to Lexi.

Can we meet? I hesitated for only a split second before sending it out.

Her reply came soon after: *Sure. Time and place?*

7 p.m. outside Auntie Fong's Bakery?

Just so we're clear, no Oliver Twist heist this time, she replied. *We're in the real world now.*

We're in the real world now. Funny how *she* was the one saying that this time.

* * *

'Oh, no,' Lexi said, pushing off from the wall when she spotted me heading down the pavement. 'There's that face again.'

'What face?' I asked.

'That brooding tragic-hero face.' She squinted at me. 'What's the tragedy? Your dad gave you a hard time for being at our gathering last night?'

'Why do you automatically assume it's my dad? Can't there be another reason I'm in a bad mood?'

Her eyes widened and she raised her hands in defence.

'I'm sorry,' I muttered.

'So you *are* in a bad mood.' She cocked her head at the bakery we stood in front of. 'Well, bread will cure you of that.'

I pushed the door open and she stepped through, taking in a deep breath. A smile spread across her face, lighting up her eyes. Sometimes, she seemed so much like that girl in my dream, carefree and irreverent; at other times, when she thought no one was watching, the light in her eyes would dim and the corners of her lips would slip. No matter how many times I tried sketching her, I couldn't quite capture who she really was.

Lexi turned and caught me staring. 'Well, make yourself useful. Grab a tray.'

Bakeries had never been to me what they had been to Lexi. I had no memories of my parents taking me to one on a regular basis, nor did the smell of bread send me into some sort of carb-induced euphoria. But Auntie Fong's Bakery *was* a place I'd experienced something close to a happy memory. *Close to,* only because it was a place I couldn't seem to return to any more.

After paying for our bread (I handed the cashier a fifty and told him to keep the change, just to ease the guilt of stealing bread in my dream, a gesture Lexi found hilarious), we strolled hand-in-hand down the pavement, looking almost like the couple in my painting.

'Shame we can't fly here,' Lexi said suddenly, staring up at the sky. 'We could eat on a rooftop. Bread might taste different at this hour.'

I remembered the sensation of flight, the gathering of air at my feet before I rocketed off, weightless and wild.

In the end, we settled on a park bench across the street from the bakery. We were in that space between day and night when the light had that hazy dreamlike quality. If I tried hard enough, I might even be able to convince myself I was back in that dream. Back where time was suspended and nothing else mattered but the two of us in our little world.

'Did you know,' Lexi said, diving into her cinnamon breadstick, 'you can see the evening star around this time if you know where to look.'

'Where?'

She pointed somewhere to my right. 'You can't see it from here, though. It's pretty low in the sky, blocked by the trees.' Lexi peeled off another strip of bread and popped it in her mouth. 'So, now that we're fed, can you tell me what's on your mind without biting my head off?'

'My dad.'

She raised her brows. 'I figured. What about him?'

It was best to get straight to it, quick and clean. Keeping every emotion out of my voice, I repeated everything Dad said, including his 'option' for Charlie.

Lexi was silent when I was through, staring at me like she was trying hard to gather a response.

'Wow, your dad must really hate us,' she said at last. 'How is this an option? Just say he's trying to drive us up against the wall. Say he's going to bulldoze the inn if he has to. Say he's a damn bully and doesn't care.' Her voice rose with each interjection.

'Lexi....'

'I don't understand,' she said, raking a hand through her hair. 'I thought you were....'

'What? You thought I was going to help you talk my dad around?'

She said nothing.

'I did say that my attending your gatherings changes nothing.' My words, hard and crusty as they tumbled out of my mouth, sounded like they were coming from someone else.

'I thought....'

'You thought that a gathering was really going to change things? Make me convince my dad to abandon the plans he's been making for the past few years? Did you think that whatever we had between us might persuade me to help save your parents' inn?'

I hated how obnoxious, how abrasive, my words were. I would hate me then. It was like I was trying to show her the worst side of me so that she would be less disappointed when she discovered it on her own. As though the more she believed I didn't have a heart made of straw, the more I wanted to rip out a handful and prove her wrong.

And I hated how easily I could do that.

She stared at me like she didn't quite recognize me any more. 'I'm not with you because I'm trying to save my parents' inn. It's because I've seen who you really are, and I like that version of you.'

'You've only seen the version of me in our dreams, though. You don't really know me in real life. What we have—*had*—can't work here.'

Her brows pulled together. I resisted the urge to reach out and smooth out the crease between them. 'What are you saying?'

'That I'm Gerald Fang Junior from Kingdom Heights, and you're Lexi Lee from Long Street.'

'What are you *saying?*'

'I think we're only good together in the dream, when it was just us.'

She stared at me, deserted by my words.

I rose to my feet. 'Let your dad know about the offer. If he's not clear about it, we can put things in black and white.'

I hated saying *we,* as though I was part of my dad's plan, even though everything in me was resisting this. I didn't want to walk away just like that. It was cruel and low, I hated behaving that way with Lexi, who deserved none of this. But I forced myself to bring one foot in front of the other. Step by step, away from her. Retreating.

'That's not what you feel, Chris. I know it isn't,' she called after me.

My footsteps faltered.

She pounced on my hesitation, getting up from the bench and catching up with me. I resumed walking, keeping my gaze straight ahead, focusing on what Dad said. Family was my priority, and so was the business. It was my duty to protect those things.

'You know, I actually thought it would be a dream come true if you were Night,' Lexi said.

I stopped.

'But now that I see that you two aren't quite so different after all—hiding, eluding, running from yourselves—I'm glad you're not him. I don't want him to be this way.' There was more she didn't say that we both heard. *I don't want* you *to be this way.*

I turned around. Arguing was futile, but I didn't want her to get the last word. Not about me or Night. 'Good. I'm glad your fantasy boyfriend isn't a jerk like me. Now you can go back to dreaming about him.' I was sinking lower and lower by the second. Now I was just a petty, spiteful person who deserved none of her faith in me.

'I'm not dreaming any more, Chris. I'm wide awake now.'

I sighed, depleted. 'What do you want, Lexi? I can't change my dad's mind. I can't remove this thing between us. And I can't be the person you want me to be.'

She fixed her steely gaze on me. 'You don't have to do a thing. *I* want to speak with your dad.'

Chapter 17

Lexi

I had no idea what I planned to say to Gerald Fang. But the words had flown out of my mouth before my brain could catch up, and now all I could do was go along with it.

What would I even say to Gerald Fang? What did we have to offer that could make him leave us and our inn alone?

It wasn't until Chris's words came back to me—*I think we're only good together in the dream, when it was just us…. I can't remove this thing between us*—that I started questioning what I was really fighting for. Was it really the inn or was it Chris? Did I really just want us to go back to the way things were in the dream, where no one could come between us?

'Lexi!'

I stumbled off the bar stool, dropping my pen. Mum raised her brows at me when I straightened. 'Yell a little louder, Mum. I don't think anyone heard you.'

Mum chuckled and slid on to a stool next to me. It was a strange place to do the accounts, but it was the only place where I could focus. Aside from Danny behind the bar counter, there was only a handful of backpackers sharing a basket of fries over beer at the table in front of the TV. Not too noisy or too quiet.

'Your father saw you and Chris yesterday evening,' Mum said. 'He said you both looked upset, but he didn't want to get involved in case you got mad at him.'

'He followed me?'

She shrugged. 'Your father's worried.'

'He has nothing to worry about.'

'Uh oh. That sounds worrying.'

'Chris believes this multiplex thing is just the beginning of our problems. So I asked to meet Gerald Fang.'

Her brows shot up. 'What? What are you going to do? Have you told your father?'

I sent her a wry look. 'What do you think?'

'Lexi, you don't have to do this.'

'This inn means everything to you and Dad. I have to do whatever I can to keep it.'

She shook her head. 'I've been meaning to say this for a while … Do we really have to hang on so tightly to this inn?'

Was she really saying this?

'Mum, you and Dad started—'

'I know how we started this inn,' she said gently. 'I know why. We lost it to the fire the first time, and we managed to start again from scratch. We had a dream, we acted on it, we've preserved it until now.'

'And Dad's trying really hard to keep preserving it,' I said.

'I know why he's doing this.' She leaned against the counter and surveyed every inch of the bar-café. 'But why persist in making something work when it clearly isn't going to?'

'But if we relocate or give up the inn, won't you….' I gestured at her. 'I mean, this is the safest place for you, Mum.'

'I can't stay cooped up here forever. Someday, I'm going to have to step outside.'

'I will *not* give up this inn,' said another voice from my right. Dad stood with his arms folded, his mouth set in a grim line. 'It's all we have.'

'No, Charlie,' Mum said, her gaze just as resolute. 'It's all *you* have.'

* * *

That night, in the back alley of a bar near Long Street, I found another painting of Night's partially hidden between a pair of foldable tables with broken legs: a couple standing under two widely spaced streetlights on either ends of the canvas, separated by darkness and mist even though they were facing each other. Above them was a sky filled with a myriad of watchful eyes instead of stars.

Like always, Night had brought to the canvas what I couldn't articulate in words.

Unlike the previous paintings, this one wasn't very well hidden—half of it was in plain sight, illuminated by the streetlight. It was almost like Night meant for this one to be found.

A familiar thrill zinged through me when I spotted it. He might not know me, but finding a painting of his felt like receiving a letter from him, a pen pal from a faraway country. Somehow, I knew. He could hear me, read my thoughts, and understand every word I told him in confidence. Somehow, we were linked.

And someday, I would find him at last.

* * *

When Chris called me that afternoon, I thought it was to mock me. Because, 'my dad's agreed to have dinner with you,' sounded ridiculous when he said it.

I asked if he was serious. He assured me that he was.

'Why did he agree?'

'Because I said you're my girlfriend,' he said.

I paused. Did he just call me his girlfriend? 'So you didn't mean what you said yesterday?'

'I did.' His words were sharp, brittle things that pelted and hurt. 'But this is the only way he'll agree to seeing you.'

'You didn't have to do that.' *Especially if you don't mean it.*

His voice turned quiet. 'It's the only thing I can do. Have you thought of what you're going to say to him?'

'The truth. How my parents started the inn from scratch and how my dad believes it's the safest place for my mum, at least until her condition improves.'

'My dad's not going to give up on your inn—much less the entire street—just because of your parents' sentimentality.'

I almost slammed the phone down on him then. How could Chris be so completely different from the person I had met in my dreams?

'Are you really going to be like this?' I demanded. 'You've met the people there. How can you just let them lose their homes like that?'

'What's wrong with the new place we proposed? It's got better amenities, it's new, it's way better than what you have now. You said it yourself—a street is just a street without the people in it.'

I thought of what Mum said. Was I really being as unreasonably sentimental as Dad? The truth was, if Mum and Dad had to rely on the inn to sustain their marriage, then their marriage was as good as over.

Still, I had to try.

'You're relocating all of us to different places,' I argued.

'Not different countries.'

Finally, we agreed there was nothing more to be said until dinner that night.

Now, standing at the door to Chris's house, the nausea rising in me almost made me retreat. I wished my sister was here with me—Eliza never had a problem laying out the cards on the table. But if I told her what I was doing here she would tell Dad, and this would blow up into a bigger issue than necessary and Chris would be caught even deeper in this whole mess.

Chris arrived at the door shortly after I pressed the bell, dressed in a blue Nike T-shirt and dark grey sweatpants, his face flushed and slick with sweat. He broke into a smile when he saw me. My heart did a somersault in my chest upon seeing him, but I didn't know whether to go along with it.

'Your mood swings are giving me whiplash,' I said. 'Smiling at me now when you such a jerk yesterday.'

His grin faltered. 'I'm just … happy to see you,' he mumbled. He stepped aside and held the door open. 'Come in. Did you get here okay?'

'I'm here, aren't I?'

'It was a conversation filler,' he said.

'I know it was. Which is why I'm showing you how dumb it sounds.'

'You could've let me pick you up.'

'After our fight yesterday?'

'I was trying to make it up to you for being a … never mind.' Chris didn't bother explaining further, just led me into the living room wordlessly. The roomy penthouse had floor-to-ceiling windows that offered an unobstructed view of the city. I glanced at the web of lights below me, watching the sun withdraw its last rays as it slipped below the horizon.

'So this is the view from your window every night. Like the world is at your feet,' I said.

He snorted, joining me at the window. 'Hardly.'

'Chris?' Clare's voice came from the kitchen. 'Who was that at the door?'

'Lexi's here,' Chris called.

Clare and a stout, full-figured woman in a yellow apron came into view from behind the kitchen counter.

'Lexi! You're here!' Clare cried. 'This is Mandy, my nurse. We're—okay, *she's*—making dinner.'

'I'll help,' I said.

'No, no, it's fine. You're our guest. We're almost done, anyway.' She wiped her hands on her pants and emerged from the kitchen.

'Chris, you're dripping sweat everywhere. Go and shower. Lexi will have us for company,' she said, coming over to take my hand.

With a parting glance at me, Chris disappeared down the hallway.

Clare led me into the living room, then sat me down on the cream-coloured leather sofa. It looked too expensive to sit on, so I perched on the edge of it.

Clare chuckled. 'Just make yourself at home, Lexi.'

I shifted a little, but didn't get any more comfortable than before.

'So we haven't really had a chance to talk since that night at the rooftop,' Clare said, shooting me a wry smile. 'Keep a lady from a party for years and this is what happens.'

'Was Gerald—I mean, your husband—was he pissed when he found out?'

'Oh, you know.' She waved a dismissive hand, but I didn't miss the look she shared with Mandy. 'Chris said you wanted to negotiate with Gerald. You're either very brave or very stubborn,' she said, not unkindly.

'I don't know about being brave, but I inherited my stubbornness from my dad,' I said. 'I'd have to be, if I'm demanding a meeting with the CEO of Kingdom Heights when I don't have any bargaining chips.'

Clare stared at me, a tiny smile playing at the corners of her lips. 'I can see why Chris is so taken by you. You're very spirited. And goodness knows Chris needs some spirit in him.'

'I've been wondering for a while now—is he always so uptight?'

'Sometimes, I think he's obedient to a fault. And maybe it's my fault that he grew up like this. If not for my condition, Gerald wouldn't have sent me to Hopewood and Chris wouldn't have felt the need to take care of this family.'

This was something Mum said to me too. And I gave Clare the same reply I had given Mum. 'It's not your fault.'

She shrugged. 'I try to do right by him, but he's had to grow up too fast. Now he's a bit of a loner with his priorities all messed up. All he cares about is work, just like his father.'

'You said he draws, too?'

Her eyes lit up. 'That's right. Chris doesn't like to talk about it much, but you should see the stuff he paints. Wait here, I'll show you.' She left me where I was and headed down one of the five hallways that extended from the living room. This place felt like the central point of several rabbit holes. A rabbit common room.

While waiting, I called from the sofa, 'Need any help, Mandy?'

'It's all good, Lexi. Just keep Clare company and dinner will be ready in a bit.'

Chris emerged from his room, now dressed in a fresh white T-shirt and blue jeans. He dried his damp hair as he joined me on the sofa, sending flecks of water in my direction. I wiped the moisture from my arm.

Chris watched as I shifted in my seat again, a smile curling his lips. 'Who's the uptight one now?'

'You heard that? This room is bugged, isn't it?'

He laughed but didn't answer my question. This might be the first time he regarded a question as rhetorical. Before I could press the issue further, Clare returned to the living room, clutching a black sketchbook.

'Mum,' Chris said. It sounded like a warning, but Clare brushed it off.

'I'm just showing Lexi the portrait of her you drew.'

Chris closed his eyes, his face turning redder than it had after his workout. 'Please do not make your only son decide to dig a hole and bury himself alive.'

It felt strange to see myself on the page, a version of me from Chris's eyes. The girl in the portrait wasn't looking back out at me, but at something in the bottom left-hand corner of the page. Her gaze, sad but determined, was the first thing I noticed, even though it was half-obscured by a tuft of hair. I tucked the usual unruly one behind my ear as I flipped to the next page. It was another sketch of me considering the expanse of sky above as I ate bread on a rooftop.

There was something oddly familiar about the drawings, but I couldn't pinpoint what it was.

I peered up at Chris, who was watching me intently as I regarded the sketches.

'It's really…'—I couldn't say *pretty*, even though I wanted to, because that might sound like I was praising myself, so I settled for—'special'.

Chris snorted. 'Special is what people say when they think something is crap and they don't want to hurt someone's feelings.'

'Your sense of humour, then, must be special,' I said.

Before I could flip to the earlier pages, though his hand shot out and snatched away the sketchbook.

He cut off my protest. 'Every second you're looking at this is a second more of my suffering. Have some empathy.'

'You see, Lexi? You're his artistic muse,' Clare said, grinning. Chris winced and rubbed his temples like the corniness was an assault on his brain. Clare's grin grew even broader.

When Mandy called, 'Dinner's ready!' from the dining room, Chris sighed in relief, then stuffed the sketchbook under a stack of books on the coffee table.

'You said you *dabbled* in drawing,' I said to Chris as we made for the dining room. 'No one who just dabbles can draw this well.'

'He has a gift,' Clare said, settling into her chair at the dinner table. 'Chris, have you called your father?'

'He's on his way, told us to start without him.'

Dinner was a spread of shrimp salad, mushroom soup, grilled mackerel, and aglio olio.

'You'll have Mandy to thank for this meal,' Clare said to me as she sipped her soup. 'I'm not well-versed in the kitchen.

All I did was wash the vegetables because I'm not allowed near knives, pans, stoves, and other weapons.'

I was halfway through thanking Mandy when Gerald Fang entered the room. I turned around to greet him, but he came to a dead halt as soon as he saw me. Even when Chris got up to introduce us, Gerald Fang continued staring at me like I was a talking tree with claws.

'Dad,' Chris said. 'This is Lexi. Lexi, meet my dad.'

I stood up and extended a hand. 'Mr Fang.' I didn't add that it was nice to meet him, because it was never nice to meet the person trying to drive you out of your home.

He accepted my handshake, but his hand was limp. His face had turned significantly stonier. I didn't consider myself intimidating in anyway, so his reaction to me was more than puzzling.

I snuck a glance at Chris, who was regarding his father with a frown.

Clare cleared her throat. 'We were just getting started. Mandy's done wonders with this mackerel.' Her fish was untouched.

Gerald Fang joined us at the table, all the while keeping his eyes on me, though he didn't say a word. To say that he did not welcome me in his house might be a massive understatement. As I ate, I found my attention returning to him just as frequently. It became almost like a game, who was caught glancing at the other.

Clare kept up a constant stream of chatter about the process of grocery shopping with Mandy and preparing the meal, a chatter that I was more than thankful for, because the tension in the air felt close to snapping any moment.

At last, Gerald Fang spoke, cutting Clare off mid-sentence.

'I understand you met with a car accident about a few weeks ago?' he said, looking at me properly at last.

'Yes, I did,' I said.

'And you went into a coma?'

'Yes,' I said again. Where was this going?

'Do you remember what happened?'

I had gone over this with the police after I woke up from my coma, right before Chris arrived in my ward. This felt like a second round of questioning.

I picked my words. 'Not much.'

'Do you know who hit you?'

Finally, Chris spoke up. 'Dad, where's this going?'

'No, I don't,' I said in response to Gerald Fang. 'The police don't have any significant leads so far either.'

'But they have leads nonetheless?'

I set my fork down. 'I didn't come here to talk about this, Mr Fang.'

'I know what you came for, Alexandra.'

'Please call me Lexi. Alexandra is what my dad calls me when I'm in trouble. And I don't believe I'm in trouble now.'

'No. You're not. You're here to negotiate.' He said that last word like it amused him no end. 'Did you not find my offer reasonable?'

'What's reasonable about that? Are you mocking us?'

'Is that what your father thinks too?'

'He doesn't know about that. There was no reason to tell him anyway, because there's no way we can quote a higher price so that you'll leave us alone.'

'That's too bad, then. It's my final offer.' He paused. 'Is it safe to say, then, that your father does not know of this meeting either?' I didn't reply. 'Can't say I expected otherwise. After all, why would you tell him that you used this farce of a relationship you have with my son to help him keep his inn?'

'Dad,' Chris said.

'Seems like we're both using this relationship to fulfil our own agendas, then.' I shrugged. 'That's fair, I suppose.'

Chris started to protest but fell silent and stared at his untouched plate of spaghetti.

Gerald Fang flicked a glance at him before spearing a shrimp. 'I can understand why your father is so attached to that inn. After all, it's a sanctuary for your mother.'

'You know about my mother's condition?' I looked to Chris for an explanation, but Gerald Fang was the one who supplied it.

'You didn't think I would offer a contract to a bunch of people without doing a thorough background check on them, did you?' He raised his brows and crunched on his salad.

'Since you know about my mum, then you should know this inn is especially important to us. We *need* this inn,' I said.

'I'm a businessman, not a social worker.' He wiped his mouth with a napkin. 'Instead of letting your mother languish even further, I suggest you make her come to terms with reality. Yielding to her condition is only going to make it worse.'

If Manda weren't the one who had made the spaghetti, I would've emptied it on Gerald Fang's face right then and there. Where did he get off dispensing judgement and advice when he was doing to his own wife what he advised against, keeping her cooped up at home?

'I came here planning to appeal to your more humane instincts.' I couldn't help but laugh at that notion now. 'But I guess there's no room for that in your world.'

'It's never too late to realize that,' he replied.

Chapter 18

Chris

'You didn't have to do that,' I said to Dad as soon as I returned from seeing Lexi off.

He was on the phone, pacing up and down the length of his study. He hung up when I barged in. 'Knocking before entering is basic manners, Chris.'

'I think we're past that, given how you spoke to Lexi earlier.'

'You think I went overboard? You don't think what I said was right?'

'I think you didn't have to say it that way even *if* it was right.'

'Well, I'm sorry if her feelings were hurt,' Dad said as he settled into his chair. 'But you should have considered that before you arranged for us to have dinner.'

'And what was that about, questioning her about the accident?'

He glanced up from a folder he had flipped open. 'I was merely curious. You don't have to be so protective of her. She seems to understand that your relationship is a purely practical one, something *you* fail to grasp.' He returned to his folder. 'And here I thought she might be the sentimentalist.'

'What's your point?'

He set his folder aside and looked up at me. 'My point is, I don't want you to see her again. Neither do *I* want to see her again. This meeting will be the last.'

'You've never interfered with my personal life. Why are you starting now?'

'Because your personal life is interfering with your professionalism. How can getting a bunch of people to move out be so difficult for you? You've succeeded in handling far thornier issues than this.' He jabbed a finger at me. 'That girl is the problem.'

'You've met her all of once and you're convinced she's the problem. Is this even about Long Street, or is this just about her?'

'Even if it's not about Long Street,' he snapped, 'I don't want you seeing that girl ever again.'

'And I'm just supposed to obey that?'

He regarded me like he had just been slapped. 'What?'

'I'm supposed to just go along with what you say, do what you tell me to, without receiving an explanation?'

His eyes narrowed. 'Chris, where is this coming from?'

'It's coming from the fact that you keep forcing Mum and I to do whatever you want us to do—go to Hopewood, come back home, stay at home, stop seeing this girl. We're your family, Dad, not your employees. We don't exist to fit into your plans.'

He jabbed a finger at me. 'You were the one who wanted to get on board, after I sent your mother to recuperate at Hopewood. You said you wanted a hand in holding up this family. Now you're complaining that I'm pushing you around?'

I said nothing. He was right. How was it that he always managed to sound right in the end even though I had started out on solid ground? I had always obeyed him, just so I didn't have to be another problem for him to deal with—why was I going against him now?

'If it's not about Long Street, then what is it you have against Lexi?' I said.

He shook his head. 'That's not for you to worry about.'

'It is if you're forbidding me from seeing her. Dad.' I took a step towards him. 'Talk to me.'

He closed his eyes and pinched his nose bridge. At length, he let out a sigh and opened his eyes again. 'Remember that accident I had last month?'

'What about it?' The words crept out, hesitant, almost fearful.

'It wasn't just a scrape.'

Dread crawled all over me, embedding itself into my skin like millions of pins. 'What do you mean?'

'I hit someone. And I left.'

'You mean … a hit-and-run? You were in a *hit-and-run*?'

Maude's voice rang in my head. *The poor girl's been in a coma for almost two weeks. It was a hit-and-run.* Lexi had gone into a coma around the same time that Dad got in that accident. And those questions at dinner just now—

'*Lexi* is the girl you ran down?' I yelled.

'Keep your voice down,' he said, even though we were the only ones here. 'She doesn't know, apparently. And the police have no significant leads.'

I sank into the chair facing him. 'So you just fled? You didn't even try to help? Dad, she was in a *coma* because of you.'

'I know that. But I panicked, okay?'

I never thought Dad would know how to use the word 'panicked'. All my life I had only ever seen him ruffling feathers, not having his ruffled.

'That's not an excuse,' I said.

'The point is, it's over. She's alive and kicking now. But you can't tell anyone, Chris. I'm trusting you with this knowledge.'

Was it really over just because Lexi was okay now? What about everything her family had been through? What if the accident left some lasting damage?

'This is not over just because you say it is,' I said.

'Think of how this will affect us—affect our reputation—if word gets out,' Dad said, as though this were something he was working through logically, and *I* was the one who needed help in seeing reason.

'You should've thought of that before you fled the crime scene.'

Crime scene. That phrase sounded dirty, shameful.

'You will keep this between us, won't you?' he asked quietly.

I didn't promise him anything, and he let me leave without another word.

* * *

'He said *what?*'

I started to repeat myself, but Hayley cut me off with a hand. 'Wow, just when I thought he couldn't be more of a jerk.'

'Hayley,' Bobby warned. A part of me bristled in indignation, but another part was glad Hayley had no obligation to censor herself.

'I don't know why you keep defending him, Dad,' Hayley said. 'The guy has no redeemable points.'

'Watch it,' I said. 'He's still my dad—'

'Who humiliated your girlfriend at dinner. And while Lexi is my romantic rival and all, she and I are united by a common enemy.'

'Have you talked to Lexi?' Bobby asked.

'Not since that dinner,' I said.

'And you're here *painting*?' Hayley smacked her forehead. 'At least ask her how she's doing.'

'I would if she'd pick up my calls. So, the only thing I *can* do is paint.'

Hayley and Bobby left me alone after that, and I poured my aching self onto the canvas. I didn't really know what I was creating, but moving my hands around and watching the colours spill across the paper felt like a relief, like waking up my stiff muscles again.

Somewhere along the way, I must have fallen asleep, because when I opened my eyes, I was no longer in Bobby's studio. Instead, I stood in a pool of light in the middle of a clearing.

The smell of damp undergrowth wafted through the night air, but it wasn't trees I was surrounded by. Instead, all around me were stoplights. Overhead, the night sky was a blank canvas, the stars lost in the glare of the stoplights.

'Not again,' I muttered.

I recognized this piece—it was a man standing in the middle of a forest of stoplights, not sure which way to proceed. I had painted it a few months ago, after Dad and I had a disagreement on a spa resort project, and I started questioning if I wanted to keep helping him with the business.

And now *I* was the guy in the painting. Did that mean this was *my* dream?

'Oh, great. Just the person I want to see,' a familiar voice groaned.

Lexi emerged from the thick of stoplights, wearing the shift dress and white Converse sneakers I had last seen her in. She came to a halt before me. 'Of all the times to be stuck in a dream with you.'

'The pleasure is all mine,' I said, matching her tone.

She frowned, taking in the scene before her. She stared up at the stoplights, then at me. 'Huh. You're the boy in the painting.'

She recognized the painting too. Now would be a good time to tell her I painted it. But it felt like poor timing to pile this on her after that unpleasant dinner.

'I don't get one thing,' she muttered, glancing around. 'Where's that earthy smell coming from if there aren't trees?'

'When has any of this made any sense?'

'I wasn't talking to you.'

'Oh, is that what we're doing now? Ignoring each other, talking to the air?'

'Someone's talking.' She turned her head wildly. 'Can't figure out who.'

'Very mature.' I let out a sigh. 'Lexi, you knew that meeting wasn't going to achieve anything.'

'I know you could've chipped in. Put in a good word. But no, all you did was stare at your plate. Good job, Chris.' She turned to leave, but I held on to her hand, impeding her dramatic exit.

'I'm sorry for what he said to you,' I said. 'That was a little over the line.'

'A *little* over the line?' She flicked off my hand. 'I think he pretty much ran me over.'

I froze. *How did she know? She couldn't possibly—*

Then I realized the unintentional pun.

'Anything I said in your defence would have been regarded by my dad as a betrayal of him. I'm supposed to be working for him—*with* him,' I corrected myself.

Lexi shot me a baleful stare. Somewhere in the distance, a bird called. *Funny,* I thought absently, *I don't remember drawing any birds in this one.*

Finally, she turned to leave. I followed her, keeping a consistent distance behind her wide enough that even our shadows didn't touch. We wove our way through the many stoplights, picking our way through the muddy forest slick with decaying leaves despite the absence of trees.

This time, I understood why Lexi had touted tranquillity as one of the dream's finer qualities. It felt almost therapeutic just to walk in silence behind her, matching my footsteps with hers, listening to the gentle rise and fall of our breaths, until they were completely in sync. The dream felt either lonely or peaceful, much like how solitude felt like a nightmare or a relief, depending on how you looked at it.

I watched Lexi move soundlessly ahead of me, wondering when the best time would be to tell her, *if* there was even a right time.

We walked for what felt like forever before arriving at another clearing. Like the previous one, this one was also encircled by stoplights that drenched us crimson. We couldn't seem to leave the painting.

Lexi finally turned around. 'What happens from here?'

I wished I had an answer for that. 'We wait until one of us wakes up, I guess.'

She gave me a look. 'You know what I mean.'

'You and the Long Streeters start over at the new location, we build our multiplex.'

'And us?'

Was there still an *us* any more? What hope was there for us, now that I knew what Dad had done? An inexplicable fire flared up in me. Why did he have to tell me about the hit-and-run? What did he expect me to do with that knowledge—just stomach it quietly, pretend like it never happened, act like he wasn't a criminal?

Lexi was waiting for my response. When faced with my silence, she nodded. 'I get it. We'll go back to our own lives. Clean break and all.'

'With this dream thing, though, that might be hard.'

Stupid, stupid. Why did I say that?

Meeting Lexi was like flying, a sensation you couldn't forget. Like seeing a light you couldn't un-see. A collision you couldn't pick yourself out of and brush off as though it had never happened. It left you battered and shaken, but it also loosened your stiff joints and made you move more freely than you ever had. She had brought colour to my canvas. How could I ever go back to my old life again?

'Right,' Lexi said, turning away from me. 'So we figure out how this thing works and stop it from happening again.'

'Right,' I echoed stupidly.

'So we know the connection to all this is Night's paintings.' She leaned against a stoplight and folded her arms. 'Unless Night stops painting or we stop finding his paintings, it's unlikely we're going to stop meeting here.'

'Well, Night's probably not going to stop painting,' I said.

Although I suppose I could stop leaving my paintings around the city so she couldn't find them any more.

A thought occurred to me.

'Does that mean you root through back alleys and such in your spare time?' I could almost imagine her doing that, hell bent on getting closer to Night in whatever way she could.

'You obviously do that too, or you wouldn't know where he leaves his paintings.'

'I don't look for them on purpose, I come by them,' I said. 'World of difference.'

She snorted. 'His hiding spots get easier to figure out once you find the pattern.'

'Oh, yeah?'

She nodded. 'I think he secretly *wants* someone to find his paintings, but it has to be someone who really knows where to look. Because that's the person who knows him best.'

I wanted to tell her the truth right then. I wanted to tell her so badly that she was the one who knew me best—even better than Mum or Bobby or Hayley—because she was the only one who had seen me in my dreams, when I was simply, entirely, me.

'Do you still wish I were Night?' The question came out too loud in the stillness. A part of me wished she hadn't heard it, only because I wouldn't have to hear her answer, which was probably going to disappoint either way.

But she had heard it. And her response came in a voice equally subdued.

'Yes.'

Chapter 19

Lexi

'Try to see it from his point of view,' Eliza said at lunch the next day. 'It's not like jumping to your rescue would have changed anything. It'd probably just piss off his dad.' She squirted a mound of ketchup on the side of her plate and dunked a fry in.

'That's what he said, too,' I said.

'Right, see?' She waved a ketchup-drenched fry and sent it into her mouth. 'For all you know, he might have already argued with his dad for your sake. I know you and Dad are all for keeping the inn, but—I really hate to say this—maybe Gerald Fang's right. Is it really the best idea to keep Mum in the inn? If she's willing to try stepping out, why don't we support her?'

'But Dad—'

'Is just afraid,' she said, 'of what *might* happen if Mum loses it and we don't have the inn any more.'

I stared at her. 'I thought you were on Dad's side.'

'I'm Team Logic,' she declared. 'Whichever side that makes more sense.'

'Look at you, talking sense and sensibility now.'

'When your baby sister's in the hospital and you're the only one left to help Dad look after Mum and the business, sense and sensibility are the only two things you can rely on.' She picked up her burger and took a huge bite.

Digging into my stew, I told her about Gerald Fang's inquisition about my accident at dinner last night.

'Gerald Fang gives me the creeps,' Eliza said when I was through. She dipped another fry in ketchup and popped it into her mouth. 'I'm convinced he's actually a cyborg.'

A middle-aged man approached our table. Not Gerald Fang—or any other cyborg that we could tell—and he kept a polite distance, but Eliza and I jumped in our seats anyway.

'Lexi, am I right?' the man said. He had salt-and-pepper hair and smiling eyes. His white linen shirt, creased and rolled up to the sleeves, was splattered with paint, but he seemed well put together nonetheless.

'Yes,' I said warily. 'And you are?'

He extended a hand. 'I'm Bobby, a friend of Chris.'

'Oh, yes. He mentioned you. And Hayley.'

'That's my daughter. You look just like the girl in the portrait.'

'You mean the girl in the portrait looks just like me.'

He chuckled. 'Yes, that.'

'This is my sister, Eliza,' I said, gesturing at her.

'I was having lunch here with my daughter and Chris not too long ago. They serve pretty good sandwiches.' He raised his takeaway paper bag. 'Anyway, Chris told us what happened. He's kind of at a loss right now. He had an argument with his father because of this Long Street business. And you.'

Eliza shot me an I-told-you-so look—one I chose to ignore.

'Chris said you give art lessons in your home studio,' I said instead. 'Have you ever come across a student who painted these?' I pulled out my phone and showed him the pictures I'd taken of Night's paintings.

It was a long shot—Night didn't seem like someone who took formal art lessons—but it was worth a try. I showed him the pictures of the couple silhouetted by sunset, the girl and the white bird, and the man in the forest of stoplights. Bobby watched as I scrolled.

'These are good,' he remarked after I showed him the last photo.

'They are, aren't they?' I leaned forward, excitement rising in me. Eliza cleared her throat, and I sank back into my seat, collecting myself. 'So are these from any of your students?'

'These aren't by any student of mine.'

'What kind of art do you teach? What kind of students?'

'Lexi,' Eliza said. 'You're holding him up.'

Bobby shook his head, smiling. 'It's fine. If you'd like, you can come by my studio and look at some of their pieces. Hayley's at home, so you can meet her too.'

I turned to Eliza, who, judging by the look in her eyes, already knew what I was thinking.

'Just a quick trip,' I promised.

* * *

Less than half an hour later, we were at Bobby's house, an old-school walk-up apartment with a row of potted herbs out front.

'My wife had green fingers,' Bobby said when he saw me looking at the herbs—mint, pepper, rosemary, and basil. 'I'm just helping to keep her precious plants alive.'

Bobby had converted two rooms into a classroom, and an adjacent one as a private studio. He led me and Eliza into the classroom.

'Feel free to look around. I'll take these to Hayley,' he said, raising the paper bag of food.

The classroom had the dry coloured-pencil smell that lingered on your hands long after you were done, but it was also bright and airy with sky-blue walls covered with paintings—watercolour, acrylic, and oil—and drawings in charcoal, coloured pencil, and even ballpoint pen. The air was intoxicating with the scent of creation. Even Eliza, who never had the patience for art, stopped and observed each one.

I, however, was looking for *the* one.

A quick scan of the room revealed nothing that belonged to Night. I had pretty much expected it, but something inside me sank nonetheless.

'You know, I gave up on art after I failed it in secondary school,' Eliza said, staring at an acrylic painting of a street at night. She turned to me. 'I failed Art. Can you believe that? How do you even fail Art?'

'With the right amount of indifference and a skewed perspective,' I replied absently.

'More like a non-existent perspective,' she said, returning to the drawings on the wall.

There was nothing here that I was looking for.

Eliza was still preoccupied with the drawings. I left her considering them, navigated my way through the easels, and slipped out the door. With a furtive glance down the hallway, I slid into the adjacent room like a cartoon character, pressing myself close to the wall.

Unlike the classroom, the studio had bare white walls tinged golden by the afternoon sun. Against the wall at the back of the room was a long table; in the middle, three sets of easels and chairs were set up in a widely spaced circle.

On one of the canvases propped up on the easel was a charcoal drawing of a row of old shophouses. Another canvas was blank. And on another was a half-finished watercolour painting of a girl with a sun-dappled forest in her. The backdrop was a more treacherous-looking forest with its tangle of vines, thick canopy, and dense undergrowth. I lingered on every detail.

I didn't know much about art or painting, but the strokes and colours—the entire vibe—reminded me of Night. Half-finished or not, there was the unmistakable sense of space, filled with colours impossible to mix, and the fairy-tale magic woven in the painting.

Could these really be Night's paintings?

I headed to the cluttered table at the back, where rolls of canvas were piled next to stacks of books and papers. Right on the top of the stack was a black sketchbook with a scuffed corner on the top right—just like Chris's sketchbook.

I flipped through it, my heart racing faster with each turn of the page.

There was my portrait, and the one of me eating bread on the rooftop, the birds in the night, the flying girl with stars caught in her hair, the hand on the doorknob leading into the bakery, the couple walking in the sunset, and the man in the forest of stoplights.

It *was* Chris's sketchbook, no doubt about it. I stared at it, letting the realization sink in.

Chris. It had been him all along. Of course it had. Of course it *was*. How else did we keep finding our way into each other's dreams? How else did he seem to know Night better than I did?

Why didn't he tell me? Had he been laughing at me ever since I first mentioned Night? I tried to think back on all the things I'd said to him about Night, but that only made me want to crawl into one of these paintings and hide in there forever. How confidently I had described him, as though I knew him at all, when he had been standing before me all along.

'Lexi?'

The voice almost sent me rocketing out of my shoes. I closed the sketchbook and whipped around to find a girl slightly younger than me standing in the doorway, dressed in a grey T-shirt and denim shorts. She held a half-eaten sandwich in her hand.

'Hi!' I squeaked, like I hadn't just been caught riffling through someone else's stuff. 'You must be Hayley.'

'That's me.' Hayley's gaze dropped to the sketchbook on the table, then returned to me. 'What are you doing?'

'Just … looking around.' I gestured at the room, bringing my hand back to my side before she could notice it shaking.

She frowned. 'This is a private studio.'

'Right, sorry.'

I started to leave, even though I didn't want to leave the sketchbook behind. But Hayley was watching me and Chris's sketchbook, like I might bolt with it. But from the look on her face, I didn't have to bother pretending any more.

'It's him, isn't it? Chris is Night,' I said quietly.

Hayley paused, as though she was considering lying to me. At last, she nodded. 'You're the one who found his paintings?'

'How did you….'

'Chris told us.'

So now, not only was I the girl obsessed with a nocturnal painter, I was also a thief. Although 'steal' wasn't quite the right word, since those paintings were left out there for the taking.

'Hayley? Have you met—' Bobby came to a halt at the door as his gaze fell on the sketchbook, then travelled to me and Hayley. 'Ah,' was all he said at last.

'You said Night wasn't your student,' I said.

'I said those pictures you showed me aren't done by any student of mine,' he corrected. 'And they aren't. Chris isn't my student. I just offered him a place to work on his art. I *would* make him a student if he weren't so busy, but his life is already hectic enough so I don't want his art to face restrictions too—'

'Dad,' Hayley said, cutting him off. 'Someone's at the door.'

The doorbell was indeed ringing.

'Go easy on each other,' Bobby warned before heading down the stairs. Eliza found us in the studio not long after Bobby left. She introduced herself to Hayley, oblivious to the situation.

'He could've told me,' I said. It was hard to keep the accusation out of my voice.

'Who could've told you what?' Eliza asked.

'He wanted to,' Hayley replied.

Eliza's eyes volleyed between me and Hayley. 'Who wanted to do what?'

'He just didn't know how to tell you.' Hayley made to say more, but Bobby called for her from downstairs.

The three of us headed out to the hallway to find Bobby standing before a couple of policemen at the door.

'What's going on?' Hayley said.

'Take care of our guests for a while. I'm making a trip to the police station.'

'Again?' Hayley said, which struck me as weird. How often did he visit the police station? 'What for?'

'We have a new lead on your accident,' one of the police officers said, looking at me. 'We just need to verify a few details with Mr Goh, see if they tally with his earlier statement.'

I shared a brief look with Eliza. 'What new lead?'

'We're not able to divulge any details yet,' the officer said.

'If I'm not back by two-thirty, cancel my three o'clock class,' Bobby told Hayley.

After Bobby left with the officers, Eliza rounded in on Hayley. 'Why's your dad involved in my sister's accident?'

'He was one of the witnesses. Didn't catch who knocked her down, though.'

'I wonder what new lead they might have,' I murmured.

'Good,' Eliza said fiercely. 'Maybe we can find some justice for you at last.'

Hayley looked at us curiously. 'What happened exactly?'

While Eliza filled Hayley in on the accident, I pulled out my phone and thought of all the ways to convey that I knew the truth. *I know who you are. You lied. I have your sketchbook as hostage. Tonight will be the darkest Night of your soul.*

Finally, I settled for *9 p.m. tonight where you hid your painting in Long St.*

His reply gave nothing away: *OK.*

Dear Night,

Sometimes the more you find out, the less you know. I don't even know why I'm writing this to you, now that I know who you really are, but it's hard to quit a habit after all these months, ever since I first chanced upon your painting.

I understand why it's sometimes easier to lie than to tell the truth. Lies protect us from the moment where everything unravels, thread by painful thread. And you're diplomatic at best, conflict-avoidant at worst. Of course you would choose to lie.

I'm supposed to be mad that you lied, but I'm not. In fact, a part of me is dancing, screaming, 'I've met Night, I've finally met Night!' Who would have thought that the wildly talented phantom I had long desired to meet was the boy in my dreams all this time?

Bet you didn't expect that, did you? You thought I'd be disappointed when I learnt that you're Night, because uptight little Gerald Fang Junior couldn't possibly have anything in common with Night, much less be *him.*

But you see, that's what I'm happy—ecstatic—about. That you're not Gerald Fang Junior, despite what everyone says, despite what you *say. That underneath the crisp white shirt and tailored jeans is a nocturnal artist bursting at the seams with impossible colours and fantastical dreams. What I'm mad about, though, is you stringing me along when you knew the truth this whole time.*

Still, I know this changes nothing. Night or not, you are still Gerald Fang Junior helming the multiplex project. And I'm that girl from Long Street fighting for her home.

Can you find a colour for every emotion I'm feeling right now? You've always been able to find the right hue for everything I feel but can't put into words.

I'm not like you—I can't spill myself on to a piece of canvas. It all stays inside. It always had, until I met you.

Still yours,
Lexi

Chapter 20

Chris

So, there it was. That moment when it all exploded in my face.

The first and only painting I had ever hidden in Long Street was the one in Maude's shop. It was an uncanny coincidence that Lexi should find the painting of the flying girl with stars in the pockets, because now that I had seen her in the dream, it seemed like she was the one I had been painting all along.

What did I have left to say tonight? She knew that I had lied, that I had kept this from her all this time when I had so many opportunities to tell her.

'I screwed up, didn't I?' I groaned.

Bobby nodded, slow and thoughtful. 'Should've come clean right from the start. Would've saved you all this trouble and heartache.'

Should've, would've. Regret wasn't a word I came across often, but if it had a hue, I might have been able to pinpoint the exact colour right then.

I sank into my folded arms on the table. 'Guess this is really the end then.'

'You know how the story goes with faint hearts,' Bobby said.

'I don't get it. Hadn't she hoped I was Night? Why would she be upset?'

Hayley rolled her eyes. 'You *still* don't get it? It's not about who you are, Chris. It's about being honest about who you are. It's the same thing as not telling us you're the heir to Kingdom Heights.'

'You found out soon after we met, though,' I pointed out.

'No thanks to you,' Hayley countered. 'I'm just saying, a lie of omission is as bad as a bald-faced lie.'

'But I didn't think it'd do anyone good to know.'

'That's not for you to decide, though,' Bobby said. 'She was honest with you, and you chose to hide.'

I thought about what Lexi had said before, about me running and hiding. All this while I thought she was the one hiding in her dreams, but turns out I was the bigger coward hiding even when I was awake. Hiding behind the order in my life and pushing away the only person who had ever threatened to disrupt that order.

Even now, when I took my seat before my half-finished canvas, disappearing into my art felt like another form of escape. I needed to pour out a piece of myself. Maybe if I poured out the bad stuff, all that's left in me would just be Night.

At eight o'clock sharp, I made my way to Long Street. There, I spent ten minutes pacing in front of Maude's shop until Maude came over.

'Chris? What are you doing here at this hour?'

'I'm meeting Lexi here.'

'Ah.' She gave me a knowing smile.

I didn't want to tell her the actual purpose of our meeting. What *was* the purpose of our meeting? This was just one more reason for Lexi not to see me anymore.

'There she is,' Maude announced, nodding at Lexi walking down the sidewalk.

Storming down was more like it. She was clutching my sketchbook like it was a stone tablet she intended to crack my skull with.

'You two have a good time, now,' Maude said, completely missing the look on Lexi's face. She patted my arm, then gave Lexi a less-than-subtle wink before returning to her shop.

Lexi thrust the sketchbook at me, keeping her gaze wedged on it. 'I believe this is yours,' she said flatly.

I took the sketchbook from her. I might have imagined it, but for a split second I almost felt Lexi cling on to it before letting go. 'I wanted to tell you.'

She looked at me at last. Her stare was unnerving, like she was mentally merging my face with her image of Night. 'When? After I found out?'

Maude was watching us from inside her shop. When I glanced at her, she turned back to the fabric she was rolling. A moment later, she raised her head and gave us a sheepish wave. Lexi waved back.

I grabbed Lexi's hand and led her down the pavement. She didn't pull out of my grasp, which was a mildly positive sign. We came to a bench next to a streetlight, and I sat her down on it.

'I wanted to tell you,' I said again. 'I just didn't know how.'

'Like this. "Lexi, I'm Night." What part of that is so difficult to say?'

'Would you have believed me?'

She stuck out her chin. 'I would. Maybe not at first, but I would've come around. It's not that much of a stretch. And didn't I tell you I wish you were Night?'

Wish. Present tense. Another positive sign, but I didn't want to get my hopes up.

'I wish you'd told me,' she said. 'Why didn't you tell me?'

'I just didn't want you to be disappointed. You had big hopes for Night.'

'Even when I told you I wished you were Night, you thought I might be disappointed?' She shook her head. 'You know what, it doesn't matter. It actually makes things a lot easier now.'

'How so?'

'If you don't want to be Night—*my* Night—then I won't think of you as him. He'll remain as a fantasy, and we'll go back to our own lives. You can stop leaving those paintings around for me to find and we'll stop meeting in our dreams.'

Every word she said cut deeper into me. 'And when we're awake?'

She stared at her sneakers. 'Awake, we don't have any reason to see each other again. That's all I came to tell you.'

I reached for her hand again. 'Is that really all you came to tell me?' For some reason, it felt easier when I was the one breaking things off with her. Hearing those words from her felt more final.

'You were right,' she said with a shrug. 'We're only good together in the dream, when it was just us, no one and nothing else. You're Gerald Fang Junior and I'm the girl from Long Street, two different worlds.'

'I'm Night.' *Not Gerald Fang Junior.* My voice carried a tinge of desperation.

Lexi shook her head and smiled, a slow sad one that didn't reach her eyes. My confession was too late. She reached out a hand and laid it on my face. I pressed my cheek close against her palm. There was nothing else to say that would change anything.

'I'm sorry,' was all I could manage. The two words sounded trite, insignificant.

'Me too,' Lexi said softly.

I couldn't bear to see the finality in her eyes. This couldn't be the end of us. But wasn't I the one who had thrown in the towel first?

I reached for her hand and pulled her towards me. We fell into each other, and it felt so familiar and right. Here, in the flesh, in my arms, was the girl I had in mind when I brought my colours to canvas. She didn't mind my tainted world, my character deficiency—she was the canvas I had poured all my dreams onto.

I saw now that her faith in Night wasn't a flimsy fantasy, foolish or laughable. On the contrary, it was strong enough to make me believe in Night too, in *her* version of Night, one that was many times better than the actual one who hid behind his art.

I wanted to be her Night.

I didn't realize I had said that last bit out loud until she raised her head from my chest.

'I want to be your Night in real life,' I said again. 'But I can't guarantee that I can.'

'Maybe we could start small. Start at the beginning, retrace our steps until we reach where we left off in the dream.'

'I'd like that,' I said softly.

A smile broke out on her face.

'You feel like going for a swim?'

At my suggestion, her grin grew even broader.

We didn't get to swim in the end, since the all the pools were closed for the day. Instead, we arranged to meet at the Wild Ride amusement park the next evening. The thought of stepping into an amusement park again should have made me cringe, but I found myself now looking forward to the view from the top of the Ferris wheel.

* * *

I was reluctant to leave Mum to have dinner alone with Manda again, since Dad was working in the office till late tonight, but she was adamant that I should ditch our dinner plans to meet Lexi.

'Don't do the whole flowers and chocolate thing. It's corny,' she said over the phone. 'And whatever you do, don't get antsy. Girls hate it when guys go in for the kill before they're ready. You might as well push her off the Ferris wheel.'

'Mum!'

'What? It's your first date. I want to make sure everything goes well.' A sigh.

Of course, I blamed her for the anticipation that made me arrive at the Wild Ride amusement park half an hour early.

But Wild Ride was nothing like I remembered. I thought I must have gotten the wrong address, but the Wild Ride sign stood unmistakable against the orange sky. From the rusted metal gates to the chipped paint on the walls, though, the amusement park had obviously seen better days. Even the brown bear mascot had faded into a stained dishcloth colour, incongruous with the bright grin plastered on its face.

It was no surprise that there was hardly a soul around, save for a group or two of hot and sweaty tourists. Granted, it was a weekday, but this looked dire. Dad could transform this place in a snap if he wanted to.

Someone poked me in the shoulder, breaking my reverie. Lexi appeared next to me in a red tank top and jeans, smelling like a garden in bloom. I remembered what Mum told me about not 'jumping in for the kill' and settled for, 'You look great,' which Lexi seemed to appreciate.

'So this is the Wild Ride,' I said, gesturing at the magnificent sight before us. '*This*.'

She stared at it, doubt settling in her eyes as she took it all in.

'Oh yeah, it's wild. I can feel my toes tingling in anticipation already,' I said.

She stuck out her chin. 'Don't knock it until you've tried it. I think there's a certain charm about it, don't you?'

I gave her an are-you-kidding-me look that she ignored.

'Let's just get the tickets,' she said.

We were served by a sulky-looking woman with a beehive and cat-eye glasses.

'I feel like I'm in a time warp,' I muttered to Lexi.

The ticket lady gave me multiple once-overs while waiting for the tickets to be spat out by a machine. She slapped the pair of tickets on the counter and drawled, 'Be prepared for the ride of your life.'

'I look forward to it,' I said. Lexi giggled.

I was all for giving Wild Ride a chance, but it just wasn't cooperating. First, practically everything at the snack booths was sold out. Then, half the rides were under maintenance, save for the kiddie rides.

And that included the Ferris wheel.

Lexi's face fell when she saw the sign before the wheel that read *Ride Under Maintenance. We apologize for the inconvenience caused.*

'And the disappointment,' Lexi said, jabbing a finger at the sign. 'They forgot to apologize for that. What's the price of dashed hopes?'

'They could've mentioned that nothing works here. Would've saved us the time,' I said.

Lexi let out a sigh. 'This wasn't supposed to turn out like this. We were supposed to go on the Ferris wheel and see the lights from above.'

'This isn't the only place we can see the lights,' I said. 'There's somewhere I go when I needed some peace and quiet.'

Lexi's phone rang then. She held up a finger and told me to hold that thought before answering the call. 'E, what's wrong?' I watched as her brows pulled closer and closer towards each other. 'I'm on my way.'

'What's wrong?' I asked when she hung up.

'My mum,' she said by way of explaining. 'I need to get home. I'm so sorry about this, I—'

I took her hand and led her back to my car. 'I'll give you a ride.'

We spent the first half of the ride in silence. At a stoplight, I ventured a glance at her. 'What was that call about?'

'Mum and Dad are arguing about the inn.' She launched into an apology again, but I waved it away. The evening hadn't turned out the way we had planned, but we knew things weren't going to be the same as the dream anyway.

When we arrived at the scene, Charlie and his wife were standing at the end of Long Street, a distance away from the Welcome Inn. Mrs Lee had her arms thrown out like she was embracing the wind as she argued with Charlie. Eliza was there by the side with a few Long Streeters, watching them helplessly.

'Mum,' Lexi breathed, heading towards her.

'I thought your mum can't step out of the inn without having an anxiety attack,' I said.

'She can't,' Lexi said, breaking into a jog. I followed suit.

As we got closer, I noticed that Lexi's mother was trembling, like it was taking everything in her to hold herself together.

'Honey, get inside,' Charlie was saying. 'You're making a scene.'

'I don't have to stay in the inn forever, Charlie, I won't.' Mrs Lee gestured at herself. 'Look, I'm completely fine!'

She was a lot of things right then, and *fine* was not one of them.

'Mum, what's going on?' Lexi said, but it was Eliza she turned to for answers.

Eliza shook her head. 'She's trying to prove that we don't need the inn. She wants Dad to start packing, but you know Dad….'

'All right, Sara, you've made your point,' Charlie said. 'Now will you please calm down and get inside?'

Rule number one, according to Dr York, was to never tell a patient to calm down. It only served to rile them up more.

'You can't keep me in there forever,' Mrs Lee went on. 'If you'd let me buy my own medicine that night, Lexi wouldn't have met with that accident.'

Next to me, Lexi stiffened.

Charlie's eyes widened. 'Are you seriously blaming this on me?'

'If you hadn't insisted on keeping me in, things might have turned out differently.'

He gestured at her. 'Look at yourself! You're out for barely five minutes and you're already hyperventilating. How are you going to be okay with moving someplace else?'

'But I can't keep relying on everyone.' Her voice was shaky, but she struggled to keep it under control. 'I need to live my life.'

'Ever considered that while you're trying to live your life, the rest of us are planning ours around yours?' Charlie reached for her hand. 'Please let's just go inside.'.

Perspiration shone on Mrs Lee's face. 'I'm okay. I'm completely okay. I am not afraid.' She repeated this mantra over and over, not realizing that she was slowly crumbling to the ground as her breathing grew shallow.

Lexi and Eliza stepped forward to pick her up. More and more people had gathered to look. The proximity made the air baking hot, even though the sun had long set. Or maybe it was the dread that was creeping under my skin, hot and prickly like a dry spell.

These people needed their inn. To them, it wasn't just an inn; it was so much more than that. This was what Lexi had been trying to tell me all along. But I hadn't quite grasped what she meant until *this*.

'I tried, Lexi. I really tried,' Mrs Lee said, clutching on to Lexi's arm as her tears finally broke free.

'I know you did, Mum,' Lexi murmured. 'Let's get inside, okay?'

Lexi stepped into the inn with her family without a backward glance. She seemed to have forgotten I was there. My uselessness was a brick wall that I couldn't break through; all I could do was watch them head into the inn. A few Long Streeters followed them in, but I turned and headed down the street where I came from.

* * *

'That,' Hayley said, letting me into her house later that evening, 'must be the shortest date in history.'

'Something cropped up,' was all I said.

But of course Hayley wasn't satisfied with that response. She hounded me all the way up to the studio, where I settled into my usual seat behind the easel.

Bobby took one look at me and said, 'Don't worry, Chris. First dates aren't always the best. But it gets better, really. I remember *my* first date—'

'Why would you assume it sucked?' I said irritably.

Bobby raised his brows. 'Because if it went well, you wouldn't be this crabby.'

'Sorry,' I muttered. Bobby shook his head. 'Guess it's true what they say about the best-laid plans.'

'That bad, huh?'

In three sentences, I summed up the evening's events.

'Are you seriously moping because of a few broken rides and a missed chance to eat cotton candy?' Hayley demanded.

I shot her a look. 'First of all, I'm not moping. Second of all, it's not the botched date I'm bothered about.' Hayley raised a brow. 'Fine, not *just* that. I just—I wish there was something I could do.'

'Like what, leave their inn out of the multiplex project?' She snorted. 'The Kingdom will have to collapse before your dad allows that to happen.'

I told them what Mrs Lee said about Lexi's accident. 'Lexi must be beating herself up for that.' All I had seen in Lexi's eyes when she looked at her mum was guilt. First for the fire, and now the accident that triggered her mother's episode.

I dialled her number again but only got transferred to her mailbox once more.

'You think they brought up the accident because they heard from the police?' Hayley asked Bobby. 'I mean, you did verify their lead.'

I looked up at Bobby. 'The police? What did they want with you? What lead?'

'Remember that accident I witnessed a couple of weeks ago?'

I nodded.

'Alexandra Lee. I didn't realize that was Lexi until today.'

'Lexi? Lexi was the one you saw? I thought you didn't see her face.'

'I didn't,' Bobby said. 'They'd taken her to the hospital by the time I returned to the scene.'

'But you didn't see who ran her down, did you?'

'No.' His brows tipped towards each other. 'It's like I told you. I only saw a black Audi hightailing down the street. It was gone before I could do anything.' He sighed. 'Maybe if I'd been quicker, arrived at the scene a little sooner, that bastard would've been caught.'

'Dad,' Hayley warned. 'We've been through this. You did the best you could. If anyone's to blame, it's the driver who knocked down Lexi.'

Bobby nodded. 'Now that the police have a new lead, maybe they'll finally find out who ran Lexi down.'

My heart gave a lurch and my paintbrush clattered to the ground. Hayley and Bobby turned to stare as I scrambled to pick it up.

Straightening, I said as coolly as I could manage, 'So what's the new lead?'

'Someone took a photo,' Bobby said, taking a sip of his hot chocolate. 'Grainy, but they were able to make out part of the license plate.'

'And you verified it?'

'I just renewed my statement, confirmed some details about the car.'

Hayley shook her head, her lips curling in disgust. 'Who would do such a thing? Run someone over and then go about your life like nothing happened?'

I kept my brush to the page and kept painting.

The problem with secrets and half-truths was that they ultimately came to the surface. The harder you tried to conceal the truth, the longer you tried to fool everyone, the uglier the truth became, until one day it eclipsed everything.

* * *

Something was wrong when I got home. The house seemed to be waiting with bated breath. I waded through the tension that thickened as I approached Dad's study.

The door was ajar. I pushed it open wider and came to a stop at the sight.

'Mum?' I said.

She stood before Dad's desk, propped up on her arms. Her face was flushed, her eyes shining with tears, and her shoulders shook with each shallow breath she took. Dad, however, had on his usual poker face as he returned Mum's stare. Upon my entrance, he broke his gaze and turned to me.

'What's going on?' I asked, inching into the room.

Mum wiped her eyes before turning around, pushing the corners of her lips up in an awful mimicry of a smile. 'Chris, how did your date go?'

Dad's gaze sharpened. 'Date? That's why you left earlier today?'

'I left at six,' I said.

'Earlier than usual,' he said.

I shook my head and asked again, 'What's going on?'

'We'll talk later,' Dad said, a dismissal. But instead of leaving the room, I went over to Mum and laid a hand on her shoulder.

'Mum, why are you crying?'

'Chris, listen to your father,' she said. Go to your room. We'll talk later.'

'Really?' I said flatly. 'Go to my room? So you can come up with a story to feed me later?'

'No, I mean we'll talk later, *Clare*,' Dad said.

Mum turned back to him, looking like she had been slapped. Dad leaned back in his chair and waited until Mum brushed past me and left the room, slamming the door on her way out.

'Chris, you stay.'

'You want to issue orders, Dad, go get a dog,' I said, turning to go after Mum.

'*Chris*.' Something in his tone made me stop. 'We need to talk.'

I mimicked his pose and leaned against the door frame. He gestured at the chair opposite him. I hesitated for a moment before taking a seat.

'What did you say to Mum? Why was she crying?' I demanded.

His gaze fell to the documents on the desk before him; his body was completely still. When he spoke at last, his voice was quiet, almost subdued. 'I asked for a divorce.'

'What?' I leapt up from the chair, almost knocking it over. 'Why?'

'She reneged on our agreement. She was not to let anyone know about her *condition*. But now….' He spun his computer screen around and jabbed a finger at the headline on the webpage: 'Property Development Tycoon Gerald Fang Kept Wife's Mental Illness Under Wraps For Years.'

Everything from Mum's three-year stay in Hopewood to her recent episode was splashed out on the online news forum. Years of our hard work and effort in building up Kingdom Heights upstaged by one article. Before, a Google search of 'Gerald Fang Kingdom Heights' would give you articles about his numerous conquests and illustrious career. But with this little revelation, his career already counted for much less than his personal life.

'You think I was being over-protective?' Dad said as I read. 'This is exactly the sort of thing I was trying to prevent.'

I looked up from the screen. 'How is this Mum's fault?'

'If she hadn't gone to that Long Street gathering, she wouldn't have revealed her illness to a bunch of strangers. But no, she wants her freedom, she wants her space. I'm the villain for keeping her in Hopewood.'

'And you're convinced it's one of the Long Streeters who told?'

'Who else witnessed her little drunken episode?' He shook his head. 'Anyway, it doesn't matter who told. What matters is that now the whole world knows about her condition. Do you have any idea how this will affect the business?'

'Why would it? Our personal lives have nothing to do with our professional lives,' I argued. 'Besides, it'll blow over.'

He sent me a withering look. 'Don't be naïve, Chris. Whatever goes on at home affects what happens in the office. You think anyone would associate themselves with me now that I'm branded as this sort of husband? You should know that a positive image is half the work done.'

'You can't do this,' I said, but my words only hit a wall. His mind was already made up.

How could things here be so drastically different from the dream?

'I have to,' he said quietly, almost in resignation.

That was when I understood this wasn't as simple as it appeared.

'Is that really why you're divorcing her?'

He raised his gaze from the desk. 'What do you mean? You heard me.'

I repeated my question. His silence was answer enough. 'You heard about the new lead, didn't you? Did the police look for you?'

'Not yet. I know you think this measure is a bit extreme—'

'Understatement.'

'But I'd rather not get her involved. If she finds out, the blow might trigger an episode. I really don't want to deal with that.'

'So that's it? That's your solution? What makes you think *this* blow you're dealing her hasn't already triggered an episode?'

He turned to stare out the window, keeping his back to me. 'It's the only way I know how to … protect her.'

I sank back into the chair. Of all the ways to do so, this was what he decided on?

'Can you think of something better?' His voice sounded smaller when he had his back to me.

'What will happen to her? To us?'

He turned back around to face me. 'If anything happens to me, take care of your mother. Take care of the business.' The weight of his gaze was unbearable. 'I'm counting on you, Chris.'

'Dad, I can't—'

'Now's not the time to doubt your abilities.' He picked up his phone from the desk. 'Now if you'll excuse me, I need to call my lawyer.'

Dear Night,

Have you ever heard that fairy tale about the prince who met a girl in his dreams?

The girl was a spy sent by a neighbouring kingdom to infiltrate the prince's mind. But the prince and the girl fell in love in the dream, and when the prince woke up, he searched the entire kingdom for her. His friends told him he was out of his mind, but the prince ignored them and continued his relentless search for the girl. When he found out that she was a spy, he was heartbroken but still wanted to be with her. The girl did, too. So they both went into a deep sleep and met each other in the dream again. There, they lived out their happily ever after, together forever in a paradise for two.

I used to find the story sad, getting to live together only in their dreams. But I guess if there's any place to live forever, it's got to be in a dream with the person you love most. The thing about fairy tales, though, is that they end at happily ever after. But life doesn't end at that final image of bliss; it's not just a perfect picture frozen in time forever. What happens after the happily ever after? Do the prince and the girl live in their lonely little world? Do they lead their half-lives and then die in the dream? And what about the prince's kingdom that he left behind, his friends and family?

That's probably what you were trying to tell me the other day. That we can't live in our dreams forever, because life is waiting for us. But now that we've returned to the real world, does it mean that nothing in the dream counts for anything anymore? Can we only live out one life when we're awake and another when we're asleep? Is that why you're Chris in the day and Night after hours?

We know it's not possible to stay in that picture-perfect moment forever, but couldn't we at least try to prolong it? Some people persist for much less than what we have.

We can make our dream work. Can't we?

Dually yours,
Lexi

Chapter 21

Lexi

We didn't bring up Mum's little meltdown the next day. In fact, we didn't talk about it at all for the rest of the week.

Instead, we quietly signed the paperwork with Kingdom Heights, updated our website about the temporary closure, then went about the solemn, unspoken task of packing and cleaning. I could see the tiredness in everyone's eyes, especially Dad's, knowing that his partner and co-founder was no longer fighting for the dream they once shared.

The movers were coming in a few weeks' time, and Dad was adamant about keeping the place as pristine as possible until the very end. He would probably stay put until Gerald Fang hauled him off the property, but we all knew there was nothing he could do. Everything was changing, and even if we tried to remain where we were, nothing would be the same again. Sometimes, it was easier going with the flow than fighting against the current.

Most of our guests had left, save for a backpacker couple who were spending their last night here tonight. We didn't even have time for a final gathering at the rooftop, since everyone was busy packing and moving. Some had already moved.

I had seen the new place, and like Chris said, there really wasn't anything to complain about. The location was more convenient and had better amenities around, and everything was shiny and new.

But there was something innately wrong about it. It was too sterile and cold. It reminded me of the night I had briefly regained consciousness in the hospital bed, alien and foreboding. How was Mum going to get used to the new place?

Whatever Maude had said about change not being a bad thing, I was having difficulty comprehending. Because even the only good change in my life had turned out to be a let-down. After our dismal date, Chris had left me a bunch of messages and missed calls. But when I tried to call him back, he was the one not picking up. Nor did he reply to my messages. Maybe he had decided this wasn't worth his time and effort anymore and had thrown in the towel.

'Lexi,' Eliza said, snapping her fingers in my face. 'Don't pine.'

I blinked. 'I'm not.'

'Yeah? Is that why you've done nothing but stare forlornly at your phone since this morning?'

'I have not.'

'You're right. You've only been cleaning like a maniac.' Eyeing the washcloth in my hand and the spot on the coffee table I'd been cleaning, she called out, 'We might have to throw this table, Dad. Lexi's worn a hole in it.'

'Very funny,' I said.

Eliza patted my hand. 'He'll call, don't worry. Maybe he figured you're busy, you know, with Mum and the moving and all, so he decided to give you some space.'

'But I've called him back. Left him messages.'

'Maybe *he's* busy. Who cares? We have packing to do.'

'What's going on between you and that boy now?' Dad asked from the reception desk.

'Nothing,' I said.

'Nothing as in, it's over?'

'Nothing as in nothing.'

'They're in a stalemate,' Eliza supplied.

Dad frowned. 'I don't understand.'

So Eliza launched into a detailed explanation of the situation—or *non*-situation—to Dad. Sometimes, I was convinced she had started living vicariously through me ever since Ryan left her at the altar. Since I didn't want to listen to a play-by-play, I grabbed my phone on the way out and headed into the storeroom to get two fresh sets of towels.

The couple in Room 4 had left a few hours ago in search of breakfast, but I knocked twice on the door before letting myself in. There was something about a lived-in room—unmade beds and strewn clothing—that felt comforting. Sometimes, I almost didn't want to do housekeeping, just so the room would preserve a piece of its last occupant.

I plugged in my earphones and got to work tidying and cleaning up the room. Mindless physical work was just the cure. It made me stop thinking of everything that had happened since I woke up from the coma. It took my mind off how much I missed Chris; how much I wanted to say to him despite the letters to Night. It made me stop ruminating on all the little disappointments, the complications, and expectations that hadn't been present in the dream but we now had to contend with.

I pushed those thoughts aside and focused on my anger, a self-contained, self-sustaining flame inside me. There was always, always so little I could do.

Halfway through cleaning the dressing table, I heard voices coming from downstairs, probably Long Streeters coming for a final visit.

But a moment later, footsteps clomped up the stairs and someone yanked out my earbuds. I straightened and turned around to find Eliza standing before me.

'Thought you might want to know,' she said, 'Chris's mum is downstairs. With her carer.'

'What? Why?'

Eliza shrugged.

I hurried out to the landing. Mum had just emerged from the patio. She slid the door close behind her and went over to the reception desk, where Clare and Mandy stood. I watched them from the top of the stairs, washcloth and disinfectant spray in hand. Eliza joined me, resting her chin on my shoulder.

'Clare?' Mum said, glancing from her to Mandy. 'What….'

'Sara,' Clare said, grasping her hands. 'I'm so sorry about this.'

'Yes, it's a shame to leave this place,' Mum said. 'But, you know, it's probably time for a change anyway.' Dad let out a grunt of disagreement, which Mum ignored. 'Would you like something to drink?'

'I really am sorry about this,' Clare said again.

'If you folks were really sorry, you'd leave us alone,' Dad quipped.

Mum shushed him before showing Clare and Mandy the way out to the patio. But Clare stayed where she was. Her bottom lip started trembling, and she bit down on it. Mandy rubbed her arm in support.

'She just needs someone to talk to. Someone other than me,' Mandy told Mum. 'I figured you're the closest friend she's got, so….'

Clare's words were almost inaudible from where I stood. 'I'm here to apologize.'

'Why don't we sit down and talk,' Mum said.

Clare spotted me at the top of the stairs. 'Lexi,' she breathed. 'I'm so sorry.'

Eliza and I exchanged a look.

'Until you tell us what exactly you're sorry for, your apology has absolutely no meaning,' Dad said.

'Charlie, please,' Mum snapped.

It was only until Eliza and I headed downstairs and got closer to her that I realized Clare's eyes were red and shining with tears.

'It's Gerald,' she said, looking at me. 'It's Gerald. I'm so sorry.'

'What's Gerald?' Eliza asked.

Clare shook her head, choking on her sobs.

'The one who ran you down, sent you into a coma,' Mandy added, her voice low and grave. 'It's Gerald Fang.'

The air closed in on me. Clare's voice rang repeatedly in my head, blocking out all other noise.

It's Gerald. The one who ran you down. It's Gerald Fang.

Chapter 22

Chris

The police came knocking soon enough.

I was sitting in my office after lunch, wondering if I should call Lexi and what I would say if I did, when I noticed the staff in the open office space outside my room peering in the direction of Dad's office. I dropped my pencil, abandoning my sketch, and stuck my head out of the door.

'What's going on?' I asked them.

One of them pointed furtively to his left and mouthed, 'Police.'

I elbowed my way through the crowd that had gathered around Dad's office. Two police officers stood just outside, waiting for Dad to let them in.

'What's this about?' I asked, even though I knew very well what it was about. 'I'm his son,' I clarified. 'Chris.'

'Come in,' Dad called from inside. His voice sounded smaller than I had ever heard it. He had obviously been notified by security.

'We'll talk inside,' one of the officers said.

We stepped inside. Everyone else peered in through the glass windows, not bothering with subtlety. I drew the blinds completely and shut the door behind me.

Dad rose from his seat, stiff-backed. 'Gentlemen. What can I do for you today?'

The police wasted neither time nor words, informing us of their warrant for Dad's arrest. 'Suspected involvement' were the words they used, but it sounded to me as though Dad's culpability was already confirmed. I could scarcely breathe from the tension in the office, but Dad's poker face never wavered.

'I'll need to call my lawyer,' was all he said.

The entire exchange took less than ten minutes. Funny how someone's life could change in so little time.

Dad turned to me on the way out, his gaze as heavy as his hand on my shoulder. 'Take care of Kingdom Heights. Take care of your mother.'

I followed them downstairs, where they led Dad into the police car, then watched as the car pulled off. Only then did I realize how shallow my breathing was, how tightly my fists were curled next to me.

Everyone shut up when I returned to the common office, but their hushed whispers tailed me all the way to my office. I sat at my desk, rocked by the force and speed at which everything had happened. Everything was unravelling so quickly that I was left holding on to a frayed thread. But I had to survive, I had to protect Mum and Kingdom Heights. Dad trusted me to.

Deep breath. First things first.

I reached for my phone and made the necessary calls. It took all morning to update the board of directors and stakeholders, discuss a plan of action with the legal team, and field questions from clients, contractors, and partners. I threw myself wholly into work because it was the only thing that came with a clear checklist. For everything else, I didn't know where to begin.

Once that was done, I grabbed my car keys and headed out of the office.

Half a day was all it took for the media to get wind of Dad's arrest. By the time I set out for Long Street, there were at least ten reporters, seven camera people, and five news vans parked outside the building. Everyone surged forward when they spotted me in my car, pressing close with their questions and cameras as I inched down the lane.

I drove for a quarter of an hour to shake off the media, but the quiet of my car was a reprieve. My thoughts spun like a dog chasing its tail until I arrived at Long Street.

Lexi couldn't avoid me forever. I was done with unanswered calls and text messages. We had both done our fair share of running, and all it ever did was drive us in opposite directions, taking with us our unspoken words. There was no more order, only chaos. But there was only one person I wanted to find in the midst of it all.

And for that, I had to tell her the truth before it was too late again.

Dear Night,

There are some things you wish so hard to be real that they become real. A fairy tale. The ability to fly. The weight of a hand in yours. An invisible nocturnal painter.

One by one, all these have come true. My dreams were a fairy tale where I could fly and feel the weight of your hand in mine, where the phantom I believed in came to life.

But maybe they have never been real all along. Maybe they're just snowflakes that turn to water in your fist. Because I woke up and found that I am no longer in the fairy tale; I can no longer fly, and your hand is no longer in mine.

And the phantom I believed in? He turned out to be nothing like I imagined. Night was supposed to be wild and passionate and free and genuine. You are anything but. Night was supposed to be everything I wasn't, but you're not.

I used to wonder what it is you're afraid of. But lately, I'm beginning to understand. You cling on to everything you know, rejecting everything else just so you wouldn't have to face the unfamiliar. Deep down, you're a big mess. That's why you rely on your dad so much—for instructions to lead your tidy, ordered life—because without him you would be lost. You would rather keep his secret than do what you know is right, just so you wouldn't be left behind to clean up the mess that is yourself.

I wish I never found out you were Night. I'd rather continue believing in the version of Night in my head than find out he was you. You who led me out of the dream, but then left me at that place between dreaming and waking.

Maybe it's true, then, that some things are better in a dream.

Nevertheless,
Lexi

Chapter 23

Lexi

'Lexi. Say something.'

Eliza, like Clare and Manda, was watching me. Close by, Dad was going off on a rant—all I heard was his rough voice muffled by the air that had closed in on me—while Mum tried to shut him up.

'Chris,' I murmured. My voice sounded like I was underwater. 'Why did he…?'

'Chris was just trying to protect his father,' Clare said quietly.

'So he *knew* about it all along?' Eliza blurted.

Clare shook her head. 'Only up until a few days ago.' She peered at me, and I tried to focus my gaze on her. 'I'm here to apologize on behalf of my husband.'

Dad let out a snort. 'What, Gerald Fang couldn't have owned up on his own? He has to send his wife down?'

'Charlie!' Mum chided. 'Stop yelling at Clare.'

'I'm not yelling at her. I'm yelling at Gerald Fang. I hope he hears me from whatever cell he's in right now. He sent my daughter into a coma, triggered the worst episode my wife's ever had, and now he wants to take away my home *and* my business?'

Dad's tirade soon became a rush of white noise.

For some reason, all I could think of was how, at the end, we were all just fighting who we were and trying to reconcile with who we wanted to be. Like me, Chris had considered staying in the dream just so he wouldn't have to fight who he really was. Gerald Fang Junior versus Night.

Now, it seemed he had lost. Gerald Fang Junior: one, Night: zero.

'Lexi,' a voice broke through my thoughts, clear as a bell.

And there in the middle of the clamour was Chris, breathless and flushed as though he had run all the way here. A part of me still saw Night in him, but Clare's presence reminded me of who he was now, and maybe who he had always been. Gerald Fang Junior.

'Mum,' he said, spotting her. 'What are you doing here?'

'Apologizing,' Clare responded, 'on your father's behalf.'

'You—you know?' Chris said to Clare, ignoring Dad.

'I heard your conversation that night.'

Chris didn't seem to know what to do with that information. Like always, he seemed to have a lot to say, but didn't know where to start. Finally, his gaze settled on me. 'I just need five minutes of your time.'

'You will have five seconds to get out of my daughter's life, starting from now,' Dad said.

'Dad, please,' I said, not taking my eyes off Chris. 'Just five minutes,' I told him, then led him out of the inn. Behind us, I could hear Eliza and Mum trying to calm Dad down.

Long Street was the emptiest it had ever been. Most of the tenants had moved out, especially those who had signed the agreement early on with Kingdom Heights. Some had decided to close for good than relocate. Even Jeffrey was holding a moving out sale, slashing the prices of his precious antique furniture in preparation for his shop's imminent closure.

Chris and I walked in silence. When we neared the end of the street, he came to a stop and spoke at last. 'I wanted to tell you.'

'The way you wanted to tell me you're Night? There's a difference between wanting to do something and actually doing it, you know. There seems to be a lot of things you wanted to tell me.'

'I do.'

'Then just *say* it.'

'I….' He stared at me helplessly. And I finally saw what I'd missed this whole time—a boy made to grow up too fast, a boy afraid of being left behind, who had no one he trusted wholeheartedly.

'The hearing's the day after tomorrow,' he said. 'Dad's left me in charge of the company while he's gone.'

I waited for more, but he offered nothing else. 'Is that all you have to say?'

'I wish things had turned out differently. I really do. But we should have left it at the dream.'

What was he trying to say? 'So you're running away again?' I demanded.

'No, Lexi.' He reached for my hand and grasped it in both of his. 'Can't you see? I'm letting you move on. We were from different worlds right from the start.'

'If you're letting me move on, why are you holding on to me so tightly?'

He dropped my hand. 'We tried, didn't we? We tried to make it work.'

We *had* tried. But some things only worked in dreams. Maybe this was one of them. In our dream, we were an island of our own, away from everyone else and their problems. There, we just *were*. Here, there were too many inextricable threads that held us apart.

A sigh escaped me. 'Maybe it's a good thing it hadn't worked. One of us would probably get tired from all this trying in the end.'

He shook his head. 'After this whole thing with Dad blows over—'

'Then what? I pretend that you hadn't tried to cover for him? I pretend that he didn't drive us out of our home? We act like everything's fine and live happily ever after?'

Before I met Chris—met *Night*—I had believed in that ending. But somewhere along the way, I had stopped believing in fairy tales.

'You're right,' I said. 'Night's just someone I'd fantasized about. It was my *version* of him I'd fallen in love with, not him. Now I wished I'd never met Night at all.' I turned to leave, already regretting what I said.

By the time I returned to the inn, it was clear he wasn't coming after me any more. It felt unceremonious, the way we said goodbye, but maybe it was better this way.

Clare was still in the inn when I returned, sitting in the patio with Mum and Manda.

'Chaos in the Kingdom,' Eliza reported when I stepped through the front door. She told me everything she and Dad had learnt from eavesdropping on Mum and Clare's conversation, from the divorce to the media camping out at their house and finally, Gerald's sentence if found guilty.

'What if we don't press charges?' I said.

Dad's eyes bugged. 'Not press charges? Lexi, why are you helping him? Because of Chris?'

'No,' I blurted. Eliza and Dad did their eyebrow thing. 'But … what if Chris gets implicated?'

'So it *is* about Chris,' Dad said.

'Chris and I are done. Let's just move on from this. Things are already messy enough with the move and all.'

Dad crossed his arms. 'And whose fault is it that we have to move? At the very least, we need to seek some kind of compensation.'

'It's over, Dad,' I said, a bone-deep weariness settling inside me as I headed up the stairs. 'Just let it go.'

* * *

That night, I gathered the stack of paintings, folded up every one of my letters and slid them into individual envelopes. Chris might never find them, but I held on to the hope that he would pick them up the way I picked up the paintings he had left all over the city. This time, I would wait for him to find my words, if he ever did.

Chapter 24

Chris

This time, I let her go.

There was nothing else I could say that would turn this around. I had always been mistrustful of words—they could so easily be twisted, and they often didn't amount to anything much anyway. Here was proof of that. My actions had given her my answer, shown her my choice—my family over her—and that was the decision we were both going to live with.

'That's it?' Mum said when I explained everything to her. 'And you just let her walk away?'

I had expected Mum to have an episode after Dad brought up the divorce. I watched for the signs—a hollowness in her gaze, atypical behaviour, loss of appetite, and general malaise—but there was none, only a strange calmness that seemed to have settled upon her like a cloud. This time, it felt like I was the one strewn all over the place while she gathered up the pieces of me.

'Is this really what you're concerned about right now? What about the divorce?' I asked.

'Not happening,' she said with a shrug. 'Your father was one step too late. The police got him before he could get the divorce under way.'

'He did that to protect you.' I still couldn't believe that Dad would do something this drastic so that Mum wouldn't be implicated.

'I know.' She peered at me. 'You seem surprised.'

'I just didn't think he'd….'

'You didn't think he cared?' She leaned back on the sofa. 'You know what he's like. Heaven forbid he shows concern for anything other than the company.'

'I didn't mean….'

She gave me a knowing smile but didn't say anything more.

I glanced out the window. Three days after Dad's arrest, the media vans and reporters were still parked outside the gates of our apartment. It was a quarter past eight in the evening, but the reporters weren't budging.

'And since I can't do anything about my husband going to jail,' Mum said, 'I'm going to make sure my son doesn't let go of the one thing that makes him happy. Lexi is worth it, Chris.'

'I want to believe that too, but how are you so certain she is?'

She rested a hand on my cheek. 'Anything that makes you happy is worth chasing to the end.'

'This *is* the end. Our worlds were different right from the start.'

She smiled. 'But you ended up in the same place, didn't you?'

* * *

At close to 10 p.m., the news vans started leaving one by one and I managed to sneak off to Long Street. Though what was I planning to do when I got there? Listen to Lexi tell me again how she wished she had never met me?

Yet, I found myself parking my car in the usual spot and making my way towards the Welcome Inn. The street was half empty now, the shutters to the shops permanently down, notices stuck on them.

I came to a stop outside the textiles shop. Maude had hung the *Closed* sign on her door, but the lights were still on. Something twisted in my gut as I watched her carefully pack the rolls of fabric into cardboard boxes. It felt as though the curtains were being drawn before I had even gotten a chance to watch the performance.

Maude looked up and spotted me before I could duck out of sight. I gave a half-wave, not sure whether to head in. But she smiled and waved back far less hesitantly, beckoning me in, so I did.

'Not to sound corny,' I said, 'but it feels like yesterday when I stepped in here.'

Her smile was wistful. 'Ah, yes. We're all getting a little nostalgic lately.'

'I wish things didn't have to end like this.'

She gave a shrug, but her stare clung to the bare textile racks, now sticking out from the walls like empty arms. 'Endings and beginnings, who can tell one from the other?'

'So what are your plans now?' I asked, since she hadn't signed the contract for relocation.

'I was thinking of moving in with my sister and being a freelance seamstress.' Her gaze lingered over every inch of her shop.

I nodded at the rolls of fabric. 'Need my help?'

She waved away my offer. 'I don't suppose you came to help me pack. Go on and talk to her.'

Before I left the shop, I wandered over to the corner where I had hidden my painting. The sheets of floral and striped textiles were still hung there, in the portion of the shop Maude hadn't gotten to clearing yet.

My painting was still there, the canvas peeking out from between the sheets of fabric. It was the flying girl with stars in her pockets. She was exactly the way I remembered Lexi in her dream, feet trailing in the air, gaze pinned on the sky as the wind threaded through her hair.

But why was it back here? Someone had taken it weeks ago. Lexi.

Something landed on my feet. An envelope. *For Night,* it read in a loopy script.

'Chris?' Maude called from the entrance of the shop. 'Are you okay?'

'I'm good,' I said, rolling up the painting and backing out of the shop. 'I'll see you around, Maude.'

Letter in one hand and painting in the other, I raced back to my car. Then, with clumsy, eager fingers, I tore the letter out of the envelope and began to read.

Chapter 25

Lexi

In dreams, time was an irrelevant concept, a meaningless measure. Moments added up to become memories, and that was all that mattered.

Here, however, time was present and cruel. Minutes and hours and days had passed since I left Chris in the middle of the street with my words. Since then, I had read and watched every news update on Gerald Fang's court hearing and, finally, his sentence.

Chris became a character I heard and read about through social media, online forums, and the TV. Christopher Fang, not Chris, not my Night. Christopher Fang looked tired these days, and his face was so stony it might chip if you tried to carve a smile on him. I often thought back to our time in the dream, when he shot me that bemused smirk, like he was secretly laughing at me. Same face, different boy.

I knew he had found the letters. A few days after I had left one in Maude's shop, I went back to find it gone, along with the painting. Maude said Chris had left with a rolled-up canvas and an envelope. The painting of the birds I had left in the back alley was gone too, when I returned to look for it, and so was my next letter.

And while I wasn't expecting a reply, I couldn't stop thinking about the different ways he might respond to my letters. Throwing them away seemed most likely.

Nonetheless, I kept leaving them around, attached to his paintings. In the meantime, the resettlement kept me busy enough so that I didn't have to think about Chris or miss him. Because it was true what the Cheshire cat said to Alice, 'if you don't know where you want to go, then it doesn't matter where you go, as long as you do.'

Dear Lexi,

I've never been good with words. They just don't spill from me the way colours do on a canvas. Still, I'm going to try and do this.

You said before that there seems to be a lot of things I mean to say to you but don't. And maybe you're right. Maybe you're the one that I needed to crack me open all along.

The truth is, I can never find a way to say those things because I've never had someone I could talk to about them. About how the colours at the corners of the world seem impossible to mix, or how I sometimes dream of faces peeling off like chipped paint.

I'm not like you; I don't have an entire street full of people concerned about my business, nor do I attend weekly rooftop barbeques. After sending Mum to live in Hopewood, Dad threw himself into the business, often working late nights at the office.

You once said that where I live, I've got the world at my feet. But after years of living alone in a huge empty apartment, silence becomes your only companion and solitude becomes your safe haven.

Yet, while this solitude is supposed to free me from expectations, it has only made my dad's expectations of me more important. My world has shrunk to the size of my family, so I would do anything to protect it.

I'm not saying what I did was right. I shouldn't have kept the truth from you, especially when you're the victim.

Words, like art, can only do so much; so much of it is left up to interpretation. I can't be sure if what I'm trying to say will get across entirely. I can only empty myself and hope for the best.

Until I see you again,
Chris

Chapter 26

Chris

In my dreams, I chased her. My pounding feet shook my entire body, and my pulse throbbed with the rhythm of her name. *Lexi, Lexi, Lexi.* She became the only thing that kept me going forward.

But she remained out of reach, appearing as just a voice, a peal of laughter, a quirked brow, a whiff of her hair. It was defeating, knowing that I had come so close to seeing her and not being able to.

Didn't she say that some things became real the longer and harder you wished for them? Was this how she felt when she chased Night in her dreams, wished for his appearance? Did she taste the bitter tang of denied triumph, regret, and longing every time she found my paintings?

Even when I was awake, I was chasing her. With nothing to go on but the paintings and letters she had scattered all around the city—in the exact places where I had left them—all I could do was try to anticipate the next place she would show up.

'It would be a lot easier to just look her up, you know,' Hayley said when she saw me flipping through my sketchbook to check the dates I had left each painting. Lexi had left them in chronological order, but I didn't know which paintings she had found and which she hadn't, or when she would appear at the next place. 'For goodness' sake, just go look for her and stop pining.'

'I have no reason to look for her.'

'Then why are you chasing her?'

Because, stupid as it was, I just wanted to see her face when she left the paintings and letters, to see how she felt about undoing everything that tied us together. I just wanted to know that this wasn't the end of us.

Chapter 27

Lexi

There were days that felt like fairy tales, and days that felt like dissolved dreams. There were fools who waited, and fools who ran away. Chris and I have done our share of both. Was it safe to say, then, that we were both fools?

This was the last painting I was about to return. I wouldn't have to chase any more from now on, and neither did he.

I unfurled the painting of the girl with the galaxy in her and stared at it for the last time. Part of me wanted to turn back, keep the final and only painting of Night that I had left. This painting was my favourite, one of the many that made me believe Night was someone worth looking for, because he had painted someone I wanted to be. A girl with the universe held inside her.

Chris and I both had a version of each other we desperately wanted to believe in, a version of ourselves we longed to be, but that neither of us could attain.

I forced myself to leave the alley without looking back.

* * *

We tried to make moving day much less ceremonious than it was. Eliza and I figured if we pretended like it wasn't happening, then it wouldn't feel like it was. We packed our stuff into whatever boxes we could find and sat them by the entrance, waiting for the movers to arrive.

But they never did.

When we called them up, they only directed us to the chief operations officer at Kingdom Heights, who introduced himself as 'Samuel, Chris's colleague'.

'Didn't you receive the email?' he asked.

Dad frowned, exchanging a look with the rest of us crowded around the phone. 'What notice?'

'Kingdom Heights bought over Long Street, yes, but they won't be redeveloping it.'

'Wait a minute,' Eliza said. 'You're saying Kingdom Heights … is cancelling its plans for Long Street? So you're not chasing us out?'

'We won't be considering Long Street as part of the multiplex development.'

'Why would Kingdom Heights do that? Doesn't seem like a Gerald Fang thing to do,' Dad said.

'Besides,' I piped up. 'Gerald Fang is in….'

There was a brief pause over the phone.

'Mr Fang may be preoccupied for the time being, but his son is acting on his behalf in the interim. He's the one who issued the last email to you.'

Eliza scrambled for her work laptop and opened her inbox. At the top was the email from Kingdom Heights. The four of us leaned forward to read the email.

'Proposed upgrading of Long Street,' Eliza read. 'That's it? No overhaul, just an upgrading?'

'Since the initial proposal for Long Street met with a lot of resistance, we've decided to change our plans and focus on the amphitheatre and shopping complex,' Samuel said. 'But we will continue to invest in the development of Long Street. Revitalize it, if you will.'

Eliza turned to me. 'I can't believe Chris did this. He gave back Long Street. He gave up his kingdom for you.' She flashed a moony smile at me.

I rolled my eyes. 'For one thing, it's not a kingdom. And he didn't give it up for me.'

'Says you. But right now, Mum and Dad are already unpacking because Chris just returned the inn to us.' She widened her eyes meaningfully. 'For you.'

And he was. I hadn't seen Dad this chipper in months. Even Mum, despite everything she'd said, seemed relieved. Neither of them had given up on their dream, the one they had rebuilt after the fire. There were too many memories here. Eliza and I had grown up here; our family had been through so much here. Leaving it would be to leave a piece of us behind.

'I don't even know what you two are fighting about, really,' Eliza said, watching as Dad took over a box Mum had picked up. 'You obviously care about each other, want to be with each other. What's the problem?'

I couldn't find an answer that would make sense. So I settled for 'it's complicated'.

'It usually isn't if you listen to this,' Eliza said, poking my chest. She went over to Mum and Dad before I could respond to that.

It wasn't for me. That's what I kept telling myself as I helped unpack. It wasn't for me. Chris probably saw little or no point in taking over Long Street, or he had found a better deal. Or maybe he was so busy with his dad's scandal that he decided to scale down the multiplex project.

Either way, he hadn't done this for me.

And even *if* he had, it was probably just to assuage his guilt. He had done this on behalf of his dad, just so we would drop the charges.

But Chris hadn't just returned the inn to us; he had returned all of Long Street to its original occupants.

By evening, most of the Long Streeters had gotten wind of the notice and those who had already moved out had returned to find out if it was true. Because the notice came at the last minute, most of them didn't believe it. We gathered at the rooftop garden of the inn, debating the veracity of the letter.

'It seems official enough,' Anitha said.

'With a notice so abrupt, who can tell if they're not just screwing us over?' Jeffrey countered.

'And what,' Maude responded, 'would Chris get out of that?'

'Who knows? Maybe they're playing at something.'

I was about to slink away when Jeffrey said, 'Well, Lexi could call Chris and he could verify it himself. Saves us from the confusion.'

'I say,' Ben added, 'let's not look a gift horse in the mouth. We've seen the email.'

'Still, it wouldn't hurt to be sure,' another shop-owner added.

Everyone turned to me, expecting me to leap at the chance to make the call. But Mum threw an arm around me. 'I'm sure we'll hear from Chris about this soon,' she said. 'In the meantime, since it's Friday, who's up for a celebratory party?'

Chapter 28

Chris

In all the twenty years I had seen my father, he had never seemed so unsure of himself. It had been a week of serving his sentence, but already there was none of that steely conviction in his eyes or the set of his jaw, his drumming fingers as he waited for your response, which was sure to disappoint one way or another.

Now, he only sat motionless before us in that bleak, bare room, looking like he had a million words to say but couldn't quite string them all together.

I was facing the same problem. Words, like I had said in my letter to Lexi, were tricky things. They always fell short when you needed them the most and surged forward when you least wanted them. All I could do was stare at my father sitting before me and pick out all the things that seemed different in him—the shadow beneath his cheekbones, his ill-fitting clothes, the days-old scruff.

'The Watts-Cooper people will be following through with the final phase of the project,' I began.

Dad didn't reply, just stared at a spot on the table, in deep thought.

'I've also made some changes to the plans for Long Street....'

That got his attention. His gaze snapped up from the table and found mine. Out of habit, I braced myself for the rebuke in his eyes, the imminent tirade or frosty disapproval at my defiance.

I launched into my argument. 'I've mentioned before that we don't really need to give Long Street a complete overhaul, and I still believe that. All we need is to spruce it up a little, bring in a good mix of tenants but retain its original ones. I think a lot of people will appreciate its charm.'

'Chris.'

'Besides, I think the least we can do for Lexi and her family is to leave them and their home alone.'

'Chris.'

'I know you're mad at me, Dad, but—'

'*Chris.*'

My words faltered to a stop. Next to me, Mum flinched.

'Do whatever you deem fit,' was all he said.

'What?'

Then there was the usual annoyance he displayed whenever someone asked him to repeat himself. 'I said,' he began.

'I heard you,' I assured him hastily. 'But … I mean….'

'You've been working alongside me for long enough. You know the way I run things. For everything else, Richard and the other team leads can guide you along the way.'

Everything I had done ever since Mum got sick, everything I had worked for since I was seventeen, had been for this moment, when he would look at me and realize I wasn't too young, too weak, to be of any value or help to him.

'Thank you, Dad,' was all I could say.

He nodded. If we were like any other father and son, we might have hugged. But we only remained in our respective seats, listening to the things we were each not saying. Sometimes words weren't enough. And sometimes, words weren't necessary.

Finally, Dad turned to Mum.

'I did what I thought was right. I had to tell,' she said, before he could say anything. She didn't try to redeem herself like I expected her to. Suddenly, she seemed far stronger than Dad and

I had ever given her credit for. And maybe she had always been stronger than both of us.

'I know you did,' Dad said.

'And I'll understand if you still want to follow through with the divorce,' she went on. 'But I don't think what I did was wrong. Maybe I should've discussed it with you before going to them, but I would've told them anyway.'

Dad waited until she was done before saying quietly, 'Clare. I don't want a divorce.'

Mum sat back in her seat. 'Oh.'

'I never wanted it. What I want,' he said, 'is time. It's ironically something I have plenty of in here. But I want time with both of you. I want the last three years back.'

* * *

There was only one painting left.

That painting, even if I hadn't known it when I first painted it, was for her. She was that girl with the galaxy inside her. She had an entire universe contained in her, one I hadn't allowed myself to step into because I was afraid it would swallow me whole.

how many people went about their lives without exploring other worlds, other possibilities? How many of us were content to remain in the one we had known all along? Lexi was dreams and stories and chaos and everything counter to what Dad had given me. She didn't know it, but she had brought a part of her world into mine and changed it—changed *me*—forever.

I found the painting sitting under the benches at the pavilion. If you didn't know where to look, you probably would never find it, especially under the dim light of the pavilion at this hour.

I reached for the letter before pulling out the painting.

Like always, I made a thorough search of the vicinity, in case I had just missed her and she was still lingering around.

Hopewood Hill was a popular spot for lovebirds and stargazers, but clouds hung thick and low tonight, obscuring the moon, and there was hardly anyone here. The darkness buzzed and hummed, making its own music.

When it became clear that she wasn't going to appear, I rolled up the painting and tucked the letter into my pocket, then made my way down the hill and back to my car.

Chapter 29

Lexi

He was a figure tearing down the hill. I watched his silhouette slice through the pitch-black night. It was just past midnight, and clouds obscured the only light that came from the moon, providing me with some cover.

Chris had appeared just as I'd changed my mind about leaving the last and only painting I had left of Night. I was about to head back to the top of the hill to retrieve it but when I heard the crunch of gravel under tires and the footsteps that followed, I dropped everything and fled. As much as I wanted to see Chris, I wasn't quite sure what I would say if I ran into him. After writing so many letters to him, my words had run dry, as though I had bled them all onto paper.

Now, I pressed close to the shadows, watching for his reaction as he read in the lonely light of his car. I was too far away from him to make out his expression, but after reading my letter he threw the car into motion and pulled out of the parking lot.

I hopped on my bike and manoeuvred my way out of the grounds with the help of my headlight and the street lamps. He knew the grounds better than I did, so he navigated his way out to the main road with more ease. I kept a close eye on his tail lights and eventually caught up with him.

A shadow—large enough to be a wild boar—emerged from the darkness and scuttled across Chris's car. The Volvo screeched and swerved, veering off the path and crashing into a copse of trees.

Glass shattered. The asphalt hissed like it was cringing. Then everything fell still.

Dread snaked down to my toes. My phone had clattered to the ground sometime during the crash. My shaking fingers scrambled to pick it up and called for an ambulance as I sprinted towards the Volvo. His name pounded in my head with every step I took, making it hard to see or think straight. Chris. Chris. Chris.

He was slumped in his seat with his head lolled to the side, his eyes closed.

'Chris,' I called, afraid to touch him in case I aggravated his injuries. 'Chris, wake up.'

His eyelids fluttered open, and something unclenched in me.

'Chris. Can you hear me? It's me, Lexi.'

'Lexi…' he croaked.

'You're going to be okay. The ambulance is on the way. Stay with me.'

My palms were clammy against his when I reached through the window for his hand. My vision grew blurry, my face wet, as I tried to unlock the door with my free hand.

'Stay with me, Chris,' I begged, squeezing his hand hard enough for it to hurt. He only managed to send me a tiny smile before giving in and letting his eyes close. His hand went completely slack in mine.

The night wind skated across my skin and slipped down my back. No matter how I tapped him, shook him, called his name, or begged for him to wake up, there was no response.

'No, no, no.' My voice came out as a whimper before my sobs took over.

That was when I spotted the vibrant colours of Night's paintings in the passenger seat. There, the paintings, as well as my letters, were unfurled and gathered in a haphazard pile.

I grabbed them all and dumped them into my bike basket just as the wail of sirens began to loom. Why had I returned them to him? Why had I said all those things to him? I wanted all the paintings back, and I wanted to take my words back. But now it was too late.

Chris was still out of it when the police and ambulance arrived at the scene. Everything was a blur after that. But even all that—the ride to the hospital, the paperwork, and the arrival of Clare, Bobby and Hayley, and my family—did nothing to shorten the wait outside the emergency room. I couldn't stop replaying the image of Chris falling unconscious, the faint smile he sent me before his eyes closed.

Now, we were gathered at the plastic benches outside, but I was alone in my fear. We couldn't end this way. I couldn't lose him this way. I refused to.

'You mean to say,' Dad said, 'that you've been sneaking out at night looking for Chris's paintings?'

It took me a while to realize Dad was addressing me, and that his question wasn't rhetorical. I shot Eliza a look, one that she returned with an innocent shrug of her shoulders.

'And you've been rooting through back alleys and deserted pavilions all this while?' Dad went on, his voice rising.

'Charlie,' Mum said. 'Now's not the time, okay?' She handed me a cup of tea she had gotten from the vending machine.

I wrapped my hands around the cup, borrowing its warmth but not drinking from it.

Mum rubbed my arms. 'He'll be okay, don't worry.'

It occurred to me that this was the farthest she had ventured from the inn in years, that she was now in a hospital, a place that caused her extreme anxiety, for me. I clutched on to her, grateful that she was here with me.

Clare was kept busy with the paperwork and making calls. I had never seen her this together before. It seemed like she was the only one who had managed to hold herself together ever since the truth came out about Gerald Fang.

Now, I watched her speak to the nurse, wondering if I should go up to her and apologize. One way or another, I had left her family in a shambles by landing her husband in jail and her son in the hospital. But now seemed like the wrong moment to remind her of that.

Mum seemed to know what I was thinking. She wrapped an arm around me and squeezed. 'She's busy now.'

'I just want to—'

'I know,' she said gently. 'But now's not the time, okay? Let her catch her breath. You should, too. Drink your tea.'

I took an absent sip. 'I don't want to catch a breath. I've been doing that ever since we came here.'

'I mean from all that heavy lifting you've been doing.'

'What?'

She tucked the usual unruly tuft of hair behind my ear. 'You can't blame yourself for everything bad that happens to everyone, Lexi.'

'I don't....'

'You're still blaming yourself for the fire—for my condition—even after all these years. And now you're blaming yourself for what happened to Chris.'

'If I hadn't left those paintings around, he wouldn't have followed me to the last one. He wouldn't have gone up that hill. He wouldn't have gotten in that accident.'

I was aware of everyone else—Dad, Eliza, Bobby, and Hayley—listening to what I was saying, but I couldn't stop.

Eliza came to a halt in front of us. Like Dad, she was a pacer, unable to sit still while waiting. Now, she sank into the seat next to me and gripped my arm, glaring at me.

'You're kidding me, right?' she said. 'How is it your fault that Chris is in here? Did you make him swerve?'

'No, but—'

'Did you make him crash into that tree?'

'No,' I said again. 'But—'

'Then quit behaving like a martyr.'

'Eliza,' Mum warned.

'No, she needs to hear this, Mum.' To me, she said, 'You told me you don't want to be like Mum, that you don't want to be afraid to live. But that is exactly what you are right now. You are so busy taking the rap for everything and everyone that you've become afraid to live.'

'Eliza,' Mum said again.

But Eliza ignored her. 'You think blaming yourself now is going to help Chris? You think blaming yourself for the fire will help Mum? It just makes you miserable and afraid, and you'll always remain on the ground.'

I wanted to tell her then that I *had* flown before. That I hadn't always remained on the ground, staring up at the sky and wondering what it was like to fly.

But I knew she was right. I might have experienced flight before, but it was only in my dream, a place where I knew nothing bad would really happen if I took a chance. Awake, I was hardly brave. Awake, I feared falling as much as the next person.

Still, I ran. Like a coward, as always. Away from everyone gathered outside the ER, away from Eliza's words, away from the truth. I ran until the futility of it caught up with me. But it wasn't so much to escape than it was to arrive. To arrive at this point where I finally saw that I was just a prisoner of myself, that I had trapped myself in my fear and guilt for so long that I hadn't allowed myself to live.

It had been a long while since I let myself cry like that. I had even forgotten how it felt. Strangely, though, the harder the sobs ripped out of me the less it hurt. Breathing became easier the longer I cried.

At the sound of footsteps, I pressed my face into my hands. The footsteps slowed to a stop. I felt Eliza's arms around me as she rested her head against mine. Eliza had a way of entirely enveloping you when she hugged.

'I don't want to be sorry. I'm tired of being sorry,' I blubbered.

She shushed me gently, smoothing my hair the way she used to. 'I know.'

We remained like that for a long time, until I was properly drained and Eliza let go of me. We leaned back in our seats, not saying a word as we stared at the picture of a vase of sunflowers hung on the wall.

Eliza nudged me and nodded at the envelopes in my lap. 'What's all that? You've been holding on to them since we got here.'

I stared down at them. 'These are my letters to Night. To Chris.'

Eliza picked up an envelope from the pile. 'To Lexi,' she read, then glanced up at me. 'From Chris?'

I grabbed it from her hand and stared at my name written in Chris's tidy script. 'From Night,' I said softly.

'What's it say?'

'I don't know.'

'Aren't you going to read them?'

I couldn't bear to. Words were dangerous things—they could tear you apart and fix you back whole, they could steal a part of you and leave you undone forever. I didn't want to be stolen by Chris's words, because I was afraid that part of me would never be returned.

But my fingers expressed a different intent. They pulled the letters out of the envelopes and unfolded them.

Dear Lexi …

And so I began to read.

Dear Lexi,

Someone once said that death is far kinder than separation. So maybe this separation is punishment for my cruelty towards you—by staying silent and only saying what I ought to, not what I really want to. It's like all my unspoken words have piled up into deadweight that holds me back from you now.

There is nothing else I can do for you, and therefore no reason for me to see you. But you are an impossible shade that I never thought could be mixed, one that brought this ashen painting to its full vibrancy. And now that I've seen that fabled light at the corner of the world, the one with the soft colours that revealed themselves in that hour before dawn, I turn back to realize how monochromatic my life used to be before I met you.

When it came to my dad, right or wrong didn't matter. Family was something I had to protect at all costs. My dad was the one who held us up, and to help him I had to listen to him, trust him, rely on him. What mattered was holding ourselves above the floodwaters. It never occurred to me that maybe the problem lay in us all along, and it was a matter of time before we crashed into the waters below.

Before, I had said that we were too different right from the beginning. But maybe we are alike and it's our lives that are different. That was what scared me off the edge of that cliff, away from the person who would take me from the life I knew. You.

But now I want to fall off that cliff, if only to catch a glimpse of that corner of the world, a glimpse of the world through your eyes.

Until I see you again,
Chris

Chapter 30

Chris

If this was what being dead felt like, then I had to say I was a little disappointed.

The silence was awfully familiar. It had the soft hum of night, but not the distant sounds that accompanied it. The air was bated, anticipatory. If anything, I felt more alive than I ever had. There was space and vastness here, the sense of something just around the corner.

And footsteps. The sound of footsteps, for some reason, brought a smile to my face.

'Chris?'

When I turned around, Lexi was already running towards me. She threw her arms around my neck, and I pulled her close to me. She had on a red sweater, one that brought out the flush in her cheeks. Her body was warm against mine, solid and all too real. We held on to each other for exactly ten heartbeats before pulling away. My shirt was wet where her cheeks had rested on my shoulders.

'I thought you were dead,' she said. Tears continued streaming down her face and I brushed them away gently.

'Aren't I?'

'Your condition has stabilized. You're just asleep.'

'So … I'm not dead?' I asked again, just to be sure.

She rolled her eyes. 'No, you're not dead. You got in an accident.'

'Oh.' The wild boar that appeared from the shadows. The deafening collision. Lexi begging me to stay with her before darkness claimed me. 'That accident.'

She smiled and glanced around. 'I think we're back to where we first started.'

'So we're both dreaming? Or are you in my dream now? How does this even work? I knew we should have tried to figure it out the first time round.'

She laughed. 'Chris. Will you please stop trying to rationalize this? We're never going to make sense of this.'

I was still heady from being in such proximity with her after the past few weeks of separation. To hear her laugh again felt like, well, a dream. I didn't mind staying here longer.

She gestured around us. 'Doesn't this scene look familiar?'

It took me a while, but I saw it at last. The street, the two-storey shophouses, and the two of us silhouetted in the scant light in the distance. Our hands, linked.

The painting of the couple walking down the street towards the sunset. Except—

'It's dusk in the painting,' I pointed out.

'Same difference,' was all she said.

'So, what? You're saying we get to live in my paintings for as long as I make them?'

She glanced down at my hand in hers. 'So don't you dare stop painting.'

I gave her hand a squeeze. 'Does that mean you're not mad at me any more?'

She looked up at me and said quietly, 'I read your letters.'

'You weren't really supposed to read them.'

'Why not?'

'Because I meant to tell you everything when I finally found you. I mean, what's the meaning of this? Leaving my paintings back where you found them? We were supposed to collide, Lexi. Why are we running from each other?'

'I thought it was Night I was in love with all along. And when you turned out to be….'

'Not what you expected,' I filled in.

She tilted her head in concession. 'But it was you all along. You. Not Night. Not the wildly talented phantom I fantasized about, but an actual person, who stopped being afraid, who tried to protect the people he loved in whatever way he could, who—'

I pulled her close to me and kissed her hard. We didn't need words any more; we had wrung ourselves dry in our letters to each other to arrive at this moment. And this moment made the ones that came before it worth it.

After we pulled apart, Lexi laid her head against my chest. 'About Long Street … you didn't have to do that. We were all packed and ready to move.'

'That place meant everything to you and your family. I couldn't take it away.'

'Are you going back?' Her voice was small, almost inaudible.

I knew right away what she meant. Now that I was the one in the dream, I could understand why Lexi hadn't wanted to wake up. It was much easier to stay here, where we were insulated from reality.

But what we had here wasn't really a life. It was a beautiful and bizarre world constructed from my paintings, but it wasn't life. Life was made up of the beautiful, the strange, *and* the ugly. And it was up to us to find the things worth waking up for.

I pulled her close to me. 'Of course I am. I want to find out how this story plays out.'

Lexi seemed to understand this time that we couldn't stay. We belonged out there in the wild, waking world. She lifted her head from my chest and nodded.

Later, we made our way down the street, waiting for morning to come. Our footsteps echoed in the balmy night, but it didn't feel like goodbye to this place.

'I think your art was meant to save us,' she said suddenly. 'Somehow.'

'Somehow,' I echoed. 'How?'

'For one, we found each other in our dreams. And now we know where we want to go.'

'From now on, you don't have to root through secret places at night to find my paintings. I'll paint for you whenever you like.'

She grinned, then came to a sudden halt. 'Do you feel that?'

'Feel what?'

She shushed me. And then, in a reverent whisper: 'The light. The air.'

She was right. Something felt different now. The stirring of a dream as it shook off the traces of night. It was that hour where the world seemed completely malleable in our grasp, where things collided, merged and fizzed, and the world was painted in the softest colours of morning.

'Do you think we'll be able to make it back before dawn?' Lexi said, staring into the distance, where the rustle of waves grew louder by the second. Already, I could taste the tang of sea salt in the air.

'Race you there,' I said.

She grinned. 'No cheating this time.'

'Only if you don't let go. Otherwise, no promises.'

'Deal,' she said, giving my hand a squeeze. 'See you on the other side.'

And then, as morning began to chase away the night, we raced down the street, trying to catch first light.

Acknowledgements

This is a story I never thought would see the light of day. I was a starry-eyed 23-year-old when I first wrote this book in 2013, but after years of querying to no avail, I thought there was no space in the market for my little whimsical book. It was only when I finally pivoted into writing fantasy that I got signed by Penguin Random House SEA, after a decade of querying.

So when the acquisitions editor Nora asked me if I had any other projects under my belt—particularly romance—I pitched this one (and *No Room in Neverland*) tentatively, wondering if it would once again get rejected. Not only was it not rejected, but it also received a lot of love from the Penguin team, and I realised that, truly, all rejection is redirection.

My point is, thank you to the PRH SEA team for making this book come to fruition. It carries so many memories, along with a piece of that hopeful 23-year-old Joyce who was struggling to realise her dreams. Thank you for giving *Until Morning* a home, and for championing stories set in this part of the world.

Thank you also to the usual suspects: scribe sisters Leslie W., Catherine Dellosa, Eva Wong Nava, Meredith Crosbie, Nicole Evans, Vivian Teo, and all the authors in our wonderful group chat and many more I've met along the way. You all make this writing journey less lonely, and I'm so thankful to have met you all. I am constantly inspired by your creativity, kindness, dedication, grit and resourcefulness.

Thank you to Mr Martin Chan, as always, for igniting that spark way back in 2001. Without your encouragement, I would never have dared to believe I could ever become a writer, much less an author.

Thank you to the readers—too many to list—who have supported, shouted about, read, reviewed and recommended my work to other readers. Authors in this part of the world don't get as much exposure, but having you all provide some visibility is a much greater help than you may know. I am truly thankful for every one of you who reached out in whatever way. To see you connecting with my words and my stories is literally one of the mains reasons I write.

Lastly, thank you to my 23-year-old self who persisted with her dreams and never gave up, despite all the rejections and hurdles. We will never stop dreaming.